Five Raging Hearts

****

Wile E. Young

Judith Sonnet

Mathew L. Reyes

Roxane Llanque

Craig Brownlie

Introduction by

Bitter Karella

MANIFESTOS

SIGNATURES

DECLARATIONS

SIGNATURES

IDEAS

SIGNATURES

And I will war, at least in words (and -- should
My chance so happen -- deeds), with all who war
With Thought; -- and of Thought's foes by far most rude,
Tyrants and sycophants have been and are.
I know not who may conquer: if I could
Have such a prescience, it should be no bar
To this my plain, sworn, downright detestation
Of every despotism in every nation.

Don Juan, Canto the Ninth, **XXIV**
by George Gordon, Lord Byron

CONTENTS

Introduction

by Bitter Karella

Lately, for somewhat obvious reasons, I've been thinking a lot about my grandmother, who grew up in Nazi Germany. The stories she told about her childhood were always tightly curated, mostly amusing anecdotes about family gatherings or visits to her own grandfather's farm, but occasionally something would slip out about the true darkness of the time – like when the pastor of a local church, an outspoken critic of the Nazi regime, mysteriously disappeared in the middle of the night or when government inspectors demanded that her father, a Potsdam bank manager, provide a full family genealogy to prove that the family's suspiciously Jewish surname wasn't actually Jewish. It's hard not to see parallels to today when ICE agents disappear our neighbors and shoot protestors and the State Department confiscates passports from trans people and the President sends the military to forcibly occupy Los Angeles. The uniforms might be different from Hitler's original goons, but the spirit remains the same.

So! Things are bad in America right now. Trump's cadre of criminals is a corrupt, Christo-fascist, explicitly white supremacist regime unbeholden to the rule of law, building a yet more oppressive police state, and flexing its muscles to destroy the lives of anyone it deems a threat while obliterating any shred of our constitutional protections and raiding the public coffers for its own gain.

What can we do in times like these? Any answer seems inadequate, but even in these dark times, I try to remember that resistance to tyranny comes in many forms. Sometimes, even the most seemingly insignificant actions can still have meaning. It's flattering to think that we can defeat tyranny with the power of art, but obviously that's not the case. Kurt Vonnegut's famous quote about the combined power of every artist in the country to shift the needle of public opinion on the Vietnam War being comparable to a "custard pie dropped from a stepladder six feet high" unfortunately comes to mind.

But in times such as these, art isn't just for changing the discourse. It's for expressing truths, corny as that is, that powerful forces would prefer we forget. Our fascist overlords can never be satisfied with their grip on control because they can force us at gunpoint to profess our love for the regime though they know those professions are meaningless and they have no way of controlling what we truly feel in our minds and hearts. Creating the art of resistance is one way to show that despite their best efforts, the tyrants cannot dominate our minds, our hearts, our souls. Hopefully reminding us that we can be one small part of a greater resistance.

I'm honored to be asked to pen the introduction to this collection, five stories that speak truth against tyranny. In this collection, you'll find a coven of witches taking very direct action to make the world a better place, Nazis trying to bend the ghost of Charles Darwin to their perverted will, queer psychics revealing the true monstrous face of a nation, a suburban conspiracy of men, and a Thanksgiving gone very, very wrong. I hope they light a candle for you in these dark times. The best art always does.

6/12/25

Bitter Karella is a genderfluid transvestite goblin, best known as the creator of the three time Hugo-nominated microfiction comedy account @MidnightPals which asks what if all your favorite horror writers were to gather around the campfire and tell scary stories like in the classic Nickelodeon series "Are You Afraid of the Dark?" His novella "The Ballad of Horse Girl" is available from Tenebrous Press as part of Split Scream Volume 5, and her first novel, "Moonflow," debuts from Orbit's new horror imprint Run For It in September 2025.

A Shift of Lightning

by Roxane Llanque

Valeria had screamed with joy when the Atmospheric Research Institute of New Mexico had finally deemed her worthy of a solo shift at the Tower, as aspiring meteorologists affectionately called their ramshackle weather station up in the Magdalena Mountains. But now, with heavy rain splitting the night sky under her headlights as she drove her father's old Jeep up the steep path to South Baldy Peak, she wondered if the boys' talk about the night shifts were more than braggadocio.

"The girl will freak," Lincoln and Dean had whispered among themselves before they turned to her with condescending grins. "Wait 'til you're up there, in the mountain night all by yourself. The winds sound like screams – I swear, Val, they do - and when the lightning strikes right next to you? Yeah, you'll run after ten minutes."

Valeria rolled her eyes at the memory-- definitely braggadocio, but she felt determined to prove them wrong along with their sexist department head, Professor Brooks. For so long, he had rejected her requests for a solo shift with "A young woman, alone in that tower in the mountains? No, sweetheart, believe me: it's for your own good that we don't let you go there solo."

Brooks had a storm's temper and the boys often complained that he treated the female students more calmly. Like so many things, they didn't get that Valeria and her fellow female students would take his temper a million times over his slimy looks and his paw lingering on their shoulders. Valeria shuddered with the memories until her car suddenly bumped over the end of the climb. Herer headlights finally revealed Langmuir Laboratory, one of the last manually operated weather stations in the country, and its adjacent student station.

All her anger forgotten, joy flashed in Valeria's eyes at the sight of the lopsided tower sticking out of the unassuming shack of corrugated sheets. She parked in a dryish looking portion of mud, put up the hood of her raincoat, and jumped out of the car.

Rain poured down like needles thrown by the forceful mountain winds. As she looked into the dark cloudscape, she breathed in the fresh petrichor in the air. A white lightning bolt shot down in the distance, illuminating the valleys for a flash. Left in darkness again, thunder shook the mountains and sent a happy tremor through Valeria. She ran the last bit towards the Tower, lifted her massive ring of keys to the beaten door, and stumbled inside with a relieved laugh.

Harsh lights flickered alive, revealing the inside of the weather station. A ragtag collection of disused university tables held three computer stations all connected to their array of sensors outside. Valeria particularly loved the antique instruments scattered around for decoration. While hanging up her dripping raincoat, she lovingly traced her fingers over the old Stokes sphere, an archaic sunshine recorder which looked a bit like a crystal ball wrapped in a sextant. Whoever had used it last had left a band of parchment, burn marks showing the strength of the sun on a day long gone.

Opening her programs, she noticed the electrical hum of the ceiling lights and the sensors' irregular beeping. Raindrops hammered down on the roof with unfaltering might, and Lincoln had been right on one account: the peak wind howled in a voice that sounded much like a human wail. Valeria looked up at the darkness outside the windows rattling in disharmony with the fierce winds pressing on the panes.

It *was* a little eerie being alone up here, but if the boys thought that the sounds of weather – you know, the thing they all signed up to study for life – would scare her, they were in for a surprise. She resolutely tore up a bag of hot Cheetos, put her abuela's favorite Chavela Vargas *rancheras* on, and began her work.

It turned out working a storm night was very much not a one-person-job. The winds and discharges changed so much that she had a challenging time noting everything down. Still, she had to occasionally close her eyes against the unusually short intervals between the lightning strikes. Curious... but when she checked the voltage, they were all within the normal range of two hundred to three hundred million volts. She shrugged it off and went back to scribbling down data like a madwoman until her hand cramped for half an hour straight. She conceded she needed a break. Massaging her wrist, she walked to the window and stared into the pitch-black darkness. She frowned as it suddenly illuminated. A strange row of blue lights, too small and too quiet to be helicopters, steadily approached Baldy Peak.

As Valeria reached for the binoculars on the sill, a familiar static climbed up her neck and into her black braided hair as a green lightning bolt split the sky and struck the rod on Langmuir's roof. The whole station trembled, and Valeria had to shield her eyes from the bright light. She gasped against the roar tearing at her eardrums. When it died off, she took a shaking breath as sparks danced before her eyes.

"What the...?" A green super bolt! To her knowledge, green lightning had only been recorded once – certainly never in New Mexico. She rushed to her computer and checked the lighting stats. The graph showed a sharp spike, towering over the marks of the last bolts with a staggering three hundred sixteen billion volts. Valeria stared at the outrageous number, willing it to disappear. Even for a super bolt, it had no right to exist within the known parameters of the atmosphere.

But it refused to depart. As the seconds passed by, Valeria bit her lip and gazed to the old landline. It was to be used strictly in emergencies, but then she remembered the outright brawl between Professor Brooks and the gentle Professor Janner. The latter had failed to inform the former of a particularly beautiful occurrence of Sangre de Christo Glow last week. Valeria suspected the temperamental Brooks might consider this an emergency, too. Hesitantly, she walked to the phone and picked up the receiver.

A loud knock on the door made her shriek, whirl around, and wind the phone's cord around herself in the process. It came again, this time much more insistently. Who on earth was that?

The next knock was more of a bang.

"Open up, boy, it's raining devils out here!"

It was a female voice and Valeria took a relieved breath. At least it wasn't a man. She hurried over and ripped the door open to stare into the faces of three strange women cramped into the narrow doorway. The foremost was a lady of maybe fifty years, skin of a similar bronze as Valeria's. She looked at her with pleasant surprise, her elegant features slowly forming a smile. "Well, La Llorona strike me – they finally sent a girl up here!"

Her companions beamed with delight, eyeing her with unveiled curiosity. Valeria swallowed. "Um, I'm sorry... I wasn't expecting anyone. Are you... from the institute?"

The women cackled as though she had made the most fabulous joke. Confused, Valeria scanned their odd attire. They wore dark capes over robes made from strangely shimmering fabrics and tied with huge leather belts.

When the other Latina noticed her confusion, she smiled and laid a tattooed hand on Valeria's shoulder. "Ah, dear girl, don't be scared. Look what you've done to the child, Mave!" That was reproachfully directed to the woman on her left, a paler lady with birdlike features and curly red hair peeking out from under her shimmering hood. "I *told* you not to warm up before we even reach the Tower. You know how it frightens the young ones!"

Mave gasped and pressed a finicky hand to her chest. "She's a scientist of the skies – she was probably delighted! Weren't you, dear?"

Valeria blinked. "I-I'm sorry, I'm not sure what you're-"

The lady with the hand on her shoulder gently squeezed it. "We'll explain in a moment, querida; may we come in? You wouldn't leave three ladies in the rain, would you?"

"Um, of course not, please..." Valeria quickly stepped aside, letting the ladies enter in a neat duck row. They pulled down their capes in unison and hung them on the hooks, displaying an odd familiarity with the space. Their leader with the tattooed hands – vibrant swirls of watercolor, Valeria noticed – then turned and walked up to her, studying her face with attentive eyes. Finally, her gaze fell on the jewelry around Valeria's neck, her mother's cross and the little thunderbird pendant her cousin had given her for her birthday.

Her smile softened. "You're a true child of this land, are you not, niña?"

Valeria nodded slowly.

"What's your name?"

"Um. They call me Val."

The older woman tsked, waving her hand. "None of that. Your real name."

Unconsciously, Valeria stood a little straighter. "Valeria Montero."

"Encantada, Valeria. I am Tayanna. You already met my friend Mave... and that gloomy one is Bayou." She pointed to the third woman who carried herself with much more reserve than the other two. She was clad in a black robe embroidered with turquoise lines, and two startlingly dark eyes stared intensely from a round brown face. She nodded at Valeria, who nodded back with hesitation, a strange unease building in her chest.

Tayanna sighed and put a hand on her cheek. "Ah, we do hate to impose like this on young sky scholars; I know the warnings your male colleagues have given you must have been hopelessly inadequate. But see, if they informed you properly, no new students would sign up for this lovely operation anymore, and we can't have that."

Valeria's unease quickly transformed into full blown alarm. "I don't- what are you saying? Do you know Lincoln and Dean? Did they know you would come here tonight? To do what?"

"Nothing for you to worry about, darling," Mave cooed. "We merely get together for a little contest at your Tower every other month. And while we hate to barge in on you like this, we need your scholarly expertise to operate it."

"A contest? What contest?"

"The Thunderbolt Challenge." Bayou spoke for the first time. Her voice sounded velvety and quiet, but the intensity in her eyes started to freak Valeria out.

"You... you want to look at the lighting sensors?"

Tayanna smiled. "Ah, not quite." She slung her arm around Valeria's shoulder – she smelled so strongly of ozone that Valeria coughed. "We need your lovely instruments to measure our lightning. See, we are witches of science."

Witches?

Mave stepped forward and raised her hand. Static filled the room as Valeria felt the familiar presence of electricity building up... until a band of lightning sparked from the red-haired woman's fingertips. Valeria's eyes widened as the small bolts danced around the woman's hand and dipped the room in green light – green like the bolt of unearthly power from before. She stared at it for about ten seconds; then she ran for the door. She wrung it open, fully intent on escaping into the mountains without so much as a flashlight. She slithered to a stop when she found herself face to face with two other women, flanking three gagged prisoners, their hands shackled with crackling bonds of lightning.

***

They put her on a folding chair on the Tower's roof. Tayanna and Mave had whispered something, and, for a moment, Valeria dimly thought that the rain had stopped, but when she looked up, only the small piece of sky above the Tower was protected from the raging storm by an invisible shield. She gulped against the fear rising in her.

Blissfully ignoring Valeria, Bayou and the other two witches, who had introduced themselves politely as Vivienne and Ceto, prepared whatever unholy thing they came here to do. Stunning Vivienne, looking like Snow-White-gone-punk, drew a pentagram onto the roof with glowing fingers; next to Valeria, Ceto and Bayou connected a laptop to the station computers. Valeria stared helplessly at their other prisoners, two silver-haired men in drenched suits, a pale one in blue and a Latino in beige, the latter strangely familiar. The last prisoner was a slightly younger woman with platinum-colored locks clinging to a lifted face. The trio stood encircled by a corral of lightning erected by Tayanna. They mumbled incessantly against their gags and looked at her pleadingly. With her heart clenched, Valeria turned to Vivienne as the witch finished the nearby peak of a pentagram.

"What will you do to them?"

Vivienne smiled with a dangerous glint in her green eyes. "Nothing they don't deserve, ma belle. You shall see soon." Without warning, the witch invaded Valeria's space, blood-red painted fingernails making her flinch as they danced over her skin.

As she felt a sensation like warm water running over her face, Valeria could not make out the words Vivienne spoke. Her vision flashed red and she gasped.

"There. This will protect you from our lightning."

Valeria blinked rapidly against the pulsing in her gaze, until the otherworldly glow gave way to Vivienne's coruscant eyes. She swallowed against her hammering heart. "The super bolt from before – that was you."

Vivienne nodded lazily to Mave, who held up her hand excitingly.

"Ooh, me, that was me! Too bad I wasted it on warm-up. I just always get so excited for the contest, you know." She laughed, apparently oblivious to the horror on Valeria's face.

Tayanna stepped from behind the prisoners, dragging her finger down one of the men's arms, who whimpered behind his gag. "Do not worry, niña," she said sympathetically. "They are no innocents; they are getting what they deserve."

The three poor souls mumbled loudly again, and Valeria couldn't take it anymore. She jumped off her chair. "Listen, *please-*"

But Vivienne pressed her down with considerable strength. "Shhh, don't make us bind you, too." She stopped short when her green eyes fell on Valeria's décolleté. Valeria followed her gaze and saw that her necklace had ridden up from under her shirt – both cross and thunderbird now visible again.

Vivienne's grin grew equally beguiling and terrifying. "You love them... the storms," she deduced with sparking eyes. "Same as us."

Valeria shook her head vehemently. "Natural ones! Not the destruction that they cause or this... vengeance you want to take on these poor people."

Vivienne's grin died, and she raised her chin. "Lighting is the balancing of penned up energies in the atmosphere, is it not, sky scholar? Alors, the atrocities these mortals here wreck on human lives upset that balance. Since the so-called justice system of your insipid country has no interest in restoring it, we have to do the job."

"A-fucking-men," Bayou agreed as she stood up from her work, stretching languidly. "Set-up is done, Tay."

Tayanna produced a parchment roll from her robe, her dark eyes meeting Valeria's. "You will hear their crimes in a moment, Valeria Montero," she said beseechingly. "Then judge our judgment for yourself." She cleared her throat, and, when all her companions had gathered in a half-circle, she spoke: "Welcome sisters, to the sixteenth Thunderbolt Challenge of New Mexico! It is my immense pleasure to be your host and judge today. Please welcome my co-judge, Ceto Terranes, who joins us all the way from Aeaea, Greece!"

Bayou, Mave, and Vivienne cheered and applauded their fellow witches, who bowed with much flair. Tayanna's eyes flashed to Valeria. "And we welcome our gracious Tower host and guest judge: the young sky scholar Valeeeeria... MONTERO!"

All the witches clapped; Mave wolf whistled. Valeria shrunk back in her chair. "What do you mean, guest judge?"

Ceto tilted her head, hand smoothing over the band that held back her short brown locks. "Why, as gratitude for your compliance, you weather apprentices always get to be guest judge! Isn't it great?" Her voice was melodious in her Greek accent, but the words still wreaked havoc on Valeria's heart.

"What? I won't-"

"We'll each make a generous donation to your Tower, too," Vivienne interrupted with a purr, trailing her fingers over Valeria's forehead. She threw back her luscious black curls, a sweet scent breaking through the petrichor. "Did you never wonder who all these anonymous donors to Langmuir and your Tower were, chérie?"

"I-"

"I'm afraid it's not optional, Valeria," Tayanna added regretfully. "It won't be a fair judgment without a deciding voice, and we will have to obliterate you if you refuse to cooperate. If you don't, you're not scared enough of the consequences, and you might not be scared enough to keep your silence on our little gatherings and we can't have that. But it would be a shame. The sciences need more upstanding young women such as yourself."

"A real shame," Vivienne agreed with a flirtatious wink in her direction, but Valeria had no room to process that right now. "Are you saying... are you saying you had Dean and Lincoln help...*judge* you murdering people?"

Mave made a face. "I do not care for the Lincoln fellow. Once or twice, I thought about burning him too, but 'nooo, you can't take a judge prisoner, Mave.'" She imitated with a bad Spanish accent and a dirty glare in Tayanna's direction, who fondly shook her head.

To Valeria she said: "Judging justice, querida. And the flair we do it with; no reason it should be boring, no?"

Anger filled Valeria's chest at the women's blasé attitude. Through her fear, she sat up. "I won't participate in your slaughter. It's not right, whatever they have done-"

"Shhh, beautiful," Vivienne cooed. She snaked a pale arm around Valeria's neck, her dark locks falling into the younger woman's face.

Their heavy sweetness filled Valeria's lungs and she swayed, a sudden lazy warmth cloying her mind.

Vivienne put a hushing finger against her lips, her eyes pensive. "So brave... for them? Humans who despise you for the color of your skin and the thunder in your blood. Why? You think if you save them that will earn you their respect?"

Valeria couldn't answer. Her mind clouded. Vivienne's feline eyes churned her insides like a vortex.

"Vivienne! No magic-charming the guest judge!" Ceto's sharp voice snapped Valeria out of it and she blinked heavily as Vivienne drew back with a roguish laugh.

"I don't need magic for that," she declared confidently, and Ceto rolled her eyes.

"French witches, I swear to Circe! Ahem, so. An applause for our host and the founder of this noble institution, a keeper of this land: Tayanna Ácoma!"

Still dazed, Valeria dimly noticed the witches applauding with noticeable respect for the eldest witch.

"And now for the contestants: the winner of last month's challenge, Bayou of the Jena Band of Choctaw!" A blank stare from the native woman. "Mave of the Amherst Coven!" Mave curtsied, raising the hem of her robe. "And last but not least, our hatchling from France: Vivienne de Rhône!" The Greek witch rolled her eyes at Vivienne's flamboyant twirl. "As ever, each offender will be presented to the contestants and their crimes read. You will be assigned to one of them – one offender *only*, no matter how much they enrage you. Looking at you, Bayou!"

Bayou grumbled something about animal abusers deserving a whole hurricane of wrath, and Valeria watched with a fist pressed to her mouth, hoping against hope that this was some fucked-up fever dream.

Ceto held out her arms. "Each contestant then shall bring their assigned offender to thunderous justice. You will be judged by three criteria: power, aesthetics, and panache! The judges will give out marks from one to ten, one meaning boring sparkler and ten meaning lightning par excellence! Mave, please give Valeria her ranking cards."

Mave produced shiny messing plates with embossed numbers on both sides and gave them to Valeria.

"Alright! Contestants, spark hands."

Mave, Vivienne, and Bayou walked to the center of the pentagram and held their fists together: from each hand a tiny red bolt sprang forth and together they created an explosion.

Tayanna raised her own arm. "Let the Thunderbolt Challenge... BEGIN!"

Under the boisterous cheers of the witches, their leader unrolled her scroll with gravitas. "Charles McAllister, step forward."

A break appeared in the lightning corral, but the man in the drenched blue suit refused, fiercely shaking his head. Ceto raised her brows before she jerked her hand towards the pentagram, pulling the man by her force. Eyes wide with fear, he stumbled into the pentagram's center. There, Ceto's spell appeared to hold him within its confines. Tayanna gave him a sharp gaze over the rim of her scroll before she read: "Charles McAllister! You stand accused of sexual assault on two young women interning at your consulting firm in the springtime of this year."

Mave, Vivienne, and Bayou proceeded to loudly jeer at him in several languages, baring their teeth and cursing mightily. Valeria found herself appraising him with new emotion. He certainly looked the type: narcissism and cruelty left lines in a man's face recognizable to any woman on this earth. They were there now, brimming beneath the indignant anger emanating from him.

Tayanna proceeded in a cold voice. "When the women turned to Human Resources, you threatened and extorted them. When the parents of one of your victims pressed charges, you threatened them as well, and when the girl's father, a Mr. Matzeck, would not budge, you pulled strings, so the biggest client of his construction firm terminated their contract. Faced by financial ruin, the family finally signed your blood settlement."

No voice but the storm's was heard on the Tower. Charles McAllister stared to the floor, while the other witches fixed him with unabated fury.

Tayanna walked to the edge of the pentagram and stopped right in front of the businessman, their faces inches from each other. Valeria was surprised to see a sweet smile appear on the witch's face. "So, Charles? What do you have to say in your defense?" She removed the gag from his mouth.

The man sputtered angrily. "I paid them! Come on, I *paid* them! You don't have any right- *mhmmmmm*!"

Tayanna shoved the gag back into his mouth. Her smile morphed into lines of steel. "Your money may outbid your victims' rights in the human world. But these mountains are another realm - one you cannot buy with all the money in the world. Now... please enjoy the treatment you subjected those girls to. Face a power that leaves you at its absolute mercy." She turned on her spot and motioned to the waiting witches, all looking ready to extinguish the man. "Any woman present who wishes to speak in this pathetic man's defense?"

All of them turned to Valeria, who trembled with the weight of the desperate eyes of McAllister on her. He pleaded unintelligibly behind his gag and Valeria felt bile rise in her throat. "I... I do not doubt what you accuse him of is true. I mean, I know what the girls have been through, I-"

Vivienne swirled around to her with new urgency. "A scumbag like him touched you? Give me his name, bijou, I'll put him on the list."

Valeria decided to appeal to whatever sympathy the woman seemed to hold for her. "I am grateful you want to get justice for those girls, I am. I wish I could have had that. But... are you sure that all the legal channels have been exha-"

"The family of the girl who pressed charges signed the settlement, sweetie," Mave interrupted her. "The other girl's father won't speak to her. No one with any power wants to help them but us."

Valeria released a shaking breath. "But-" she started before she froze. McAllister threw himself against his invisible confines. The other two offenders watched with eyes as wide as hers. When he realized it was no use, he turned around and desperately craned his head to point to something in the back pocket of his tailored dress pants... his wallet.

Tayanna scoffed in disgust and gave Valeria a final questioning look. Valeria found her mouth too dry to speak.

"Mave," Tayanna called. "This one is yours."

Mave cackled and did a little celebratory dance.

Valeria's mouth dropped open when the redhead walked up to the man and pulled a smartphone from her belt. Holding it at arm's length for a selfie with the screaming McAllister, she made the devil sign with her other hand. "Say 'scumbag,'" she lilted and snapped the picture.

Bayou groaned. "Mave. Some dignity please?"

"Oh, let her have her trophies," Vivienne laughed, steel in her eyes. "I'm glad to see one Irish witch with a smartphone instead of a pointy hat."

Mave stepped back from the pentagram and raised her arms to the sky. She threw a wink over her shoulder at Valeria. "Told you, sweetie. Witches of science." With that she threw her head back and danced a swirling motion with her body. Her hand drew circles in the air above her.

Valeria blinked upwards when green light pierced the dark sky over the Tower.

Mave chanted deep, repeated staccato sounds in a language which Valeria did not recognize but knew instinctively to be ancient. As the witch's chanting grew louder, the green light increased. Wind picked up around them, cutting through McAllister's whimpers. The green reflected in the hungry eyes of Vivienne and Bayou.

Valeria felt electricity building as her hair rose before her face with static. Her heart beat heavy in her chest, she gasped for air against the pressure rising around them until Mave screamed her final incantation and threw her hands toward the pentagram.

A monstrous bolt of green split from the sky and struck the heart of McAllister with a force of innumerable volts.

Valeria closed her eyes when the lightning engulfed him in green fire, the air around her crackled and seethed until the smell of burned skin overpowered any other sensation. Valeria tore her head away from the gruesome scene and retched over the edge of the Tower.

Light turned to darkness, but she kept her eyes closed tightly. Her breath came in tight spurts. She only opened them when she felt warmth on her cold neck, blinking against smoke and gagging at the burning stench as Vivienne's slender hands massaged her shoulders in a calming motion.

"Breathe."

Valeria faintly registered Bayou complaining to Tayanna about seducing judges again. She swallowed her bile and made herself look past Vivienne's waist to the pentagram. Where Charles McAllister had stood just a moment ago, a pile of glimmering ash, liquid iron, and a half-melted skull remained. Her gaze glued to the dark holes where panicked eyes had been, their terror like phantoms imprinted on her own. Another faint voice... Tayanna's, asking her for the voltage reading. She pressed a hand to her convulsing stomach, and mechanically dragged her focus to the giant spike on the computer before her. Against a mouth like sand, she read out the highpoint: "T-two hundred... two hundred eighty million volts."

Mave jumped into the air. "Woo-hoo! Still got it, baby!"

Bayou, Tayanna, and Ceto responded with impressed applause.

As Mave frolicked to McAllister's ashes to take a second selfie, Valeria felt Vivienne's hot breath by her ear. "Now didn't that feel good, Valeria?" Her sultry voice infused her name with so much fire, it didn't sound like her own anymore. "Forget your compassion for those who give you none. Imagine the pig who did to you what this one did to those other girls in his place. Allow the *rage*... let it free you."

Valeria's skin prickled with either lingering electricity or what might well be a spell from those dark lips; she was in no state to determine which it was.

"Judges, prepare your marks!"

Vivienne lifted her hold and sauntered to her fellow competitors, while Tayanna and Ceto moved to flank Valeria.

"First category: power. Judges, choose your marks in five, four, three-"

Valeria shuffled the messing plates in her lap with unsure hands and helplessly looked once more toward the pile of ashes, trying hard to recall the arrogant lines they had once composed. She couldn't do this. She would not do-

"...two... ONE!"

Valeria closed her eyes... and suddenly saw *his* face. Saw his leer in the dim light of the public bathroom, felt his grubby hand holding her in a vice-like grip, pawing her with the other while she struggled... and with that old pain, helplessness, and anger flaring in her chest, she held up the number nine with a strength that surprised herself. To distract herself from the revulsion and guilt threatening to empty her stomach again, she looked to the other judges.

Tayanna had given an eight, Ceto held up a nine like her. Tiny bolts sprouted in Mave's red locks with her excitement.

"Two hundred eighty million volts..." Valeria repeated hoarsely to herself. She returned the nine to the other plates and pressed them against her stomach, still feeling sick. Her mind, overstrained with adrenaline and shock, sluggishly proceeded to process the *contest* in which she now participated.

For aesthetics, Mave's marks lowered considerably: with a seven from Valeria and only a five from both Ceto and Tayanna. Bickering ensued. Mave delivered a passionate laudation on "classical form" while Ceto and Tayanna deemed her bolt "unimaginative" and "boring." But apparently the judges' marks could not be contested.

Mave's panache marks varied with a four from Bayou, to a five from Tayanna, and finally a tentative six from Valeria. At her final score of 6.4 the bolts in Mave's hair became frighteningly busy as she blurted out dark sounding curses in the same language she had used in her chants. At Tayanna's behest Valeria recorded the score.

With no reprieve, Tayanna lowered the prisoner's barrier and led the second man into the pentagram. Unlike his antecessor, this man did not struggle. Visibly shaken, he entered on his own quivering legs, stepping into the ashes of Charles McAllister.

While still trembling herself, Valeria looked up at the next accused. Her apprehension joined by an unsettling anticipation, she forced down the painful flashes of her assailant's face.

Tayanna moved up to him with her scroll. "Michael Santos!"

As if on cue, a natural lightning bolt came down at a distant peak of the Magdalena Mountains in the still raging storm. When its thunder followed, Valeria wondered how much of the lighting she had observed in her life which might have been the wrath of witches.

"You stand accused of having orchestrated the discharge of more than one billion gallons of raw sewage into the Rio Grande in your role as COO of El Paso Water. You failed to report this to the environmental agencies. Even after being found out, your position remained unaffected. Is that correct?"

Now Valeria knew why he looked familiar. The pollution scandal had been heatedly discussed at New Mexico Tech, with local news source *Paydirt* running a profile on the C-suite of El Paso Water. But with all the daily scandals of their world, the discussion had eventually died down. Valeria realized with some shame that she hadn't thought about it for weeks. Did really none of them have to walk for such a scandal?

Tayanna ungagged the COO. His dark eyes turned ruefully to his judges, and he talked a mile a minute: "Ladies – what you accuse me of, is true... but it was not by design! There were breaks in one of the wastewater lines and the sewage entered private homes! We had to divert it to protect the people. We were planning on informing the authorities, but, you must understand, the protection of our reputation..." He droned on and on, as surely as if he had been prepared to defend himself all along.

Valeria realized then that he *had* been – his own skin his only objective, the health of the flora and fauna of New Mexico be damned. Slowly, his pleas drowned in the sound of her blood rushing hotly. "You actually think you're innocent. "

It was an incredulous yet outraged statement, and only when she felt everyone's eyes on her that Valeria realized it had come from her lips.

Michael blinked, then folded his hands as if in prayer. "You are young, Miss. I know it seems easy and straightforward when you talk about these things in a classroom, but in the real world-"

"You're called Santos," Valeria interrupted him. "Are you really Michael? Or Miguel?"

The man froze. His dark eyes jumped over her face, finding features not unlike his own. "I- yes, I was born Miguel."

Valeria shook her head in disgust. "Your own land, Miguel. Your own people?"

Tears sprung to his eyes. He dropped to his knees as he sobbed: "Please! By God, please spare my life! There must be other ways I can be punished. Take my money! Take my car, everything! I can- I can leave this state-"

"And do as you did again elsewhere?" Tayanna's voice sounded more sad than angry. When she met Valeria's gaze Valeria felt like she was given an actual choice for the first time. "Will you speak in Miguel's defense, Valeria?"

Feelings warring in her chest. Valeria looked at Miguel, who begged outright now. "Por el amor de Dios, por favor, ten piedad! Jovencita, no quieres hacer esto, no eres como ellas..."

All his invocation called for decency, and none of it applied to him. What else to expect from a man who sold the vaporization of others back to them as rain? Slowly, Valeria shook her head at Tayanna and the older woman smiled. "He's yours, Bayou."

The Choctaw's eyes brightened dangerously, and she moved in front of the still begging Miguel. Through his pleas she shed her dark robe and revealed white and turquoise painted arms, which she raised above her head.

In awe, Valeria watched how the rain next to the witch slowly solidified into two watery, transparent... drums? Bayou snapped her fingers, and two lines of raindrops froze into drumsticks made of ice. With each hit of her arms, the icy sticks beat down on the ghostly drums, sonorous bass notes making the Tower shake. Each hit reverberated through Valeria and soon it felt as though Bayou played the heartbeat in Valeria's chest.

Miguel blanched more with every hit, until he collapsed, a shaking bundle on the jolting ground. The compassion that stirred in Valeria's heart swiftly droned out in the quickening beats on Bayou's rain drums. Then suddenly, the right drum fell silent, while its sister aggressively picked up speed. Synchronous with its frantic beats, red electricity sparked in the stormy clouds above. It vellicated, until Bayou sharply bent her left hand with a scream and the charge turned to a curve of lighting descending on Miguel, only to stop an inch from his right temple. In the abrupt silence following, he stared at the violently sizzling energy frozen before him and whimpered with a flicker of hope.

Bayou's arms quaked with holding the lightning back. Sweat ran down her arms. With a mighty cry, she struck down her right arm. The correlated drum picked up as well as she forced a second thunderbolt to descend from her right side. Miguel's eyes reflected the red in a frightened grimace of understanding until Bayou connected her hands in a slap.

The twin thunderbolts skewered his head. Fiery red arrayed his body, building until Valeria had to close her eyes against the brightness. The icy drumsticks fell to the roof and shattered, leaving their beat to trail into the once again prominent sounds of the storm.

Mercifully, Bayou accomplished her burning without the haunting stench. All the witches clapped with exalted enthusiasm at her performance. To that small mercy Valeria ascribed her ability to gaze toward the pentagram without her stomach turning this time. What was the wonder she felt at the intricate ice crystals melting into the red ash? She put that to her love of her field.

What's wrong with you? A voice in her head chimed up. *They're killing people and you're complicit.*

Did these men not kill themselves? Did they not deserve justice when the world they ruled would never dispense it?

The judging of Bayou went by in a breeze: all three judges unanimously gave her a seven for power after Valeria noted her voltage, a nine for aesthetics, and a whopping ten for panache. Bayou merely had a pleased line around her lips in celebration.

All eyes turned to the lone woman in the prisoner's barrier. Tayanna's eyes increased tenfold as she circled her.

"Lorraine Abington. You stand accused of sponsoring the anti-abortion ordinance in the city of Hobbs, New Mexico. You-" Tayanna briefly closed her eyes, fighting for composure. "You are a woman who made it her goal to deny other women their right to self-determination. You are a woman who wants women to be as powerless as we were for centuries, enslaved to the yoke of hateful men. *You*... are a traitor of the highest order. What say you in your defense?"

When Tayanna removed her gag, Lorraine Abington shook with righteousness. Her surgical skin remained expression-less, only her eyes burned clearly with hate. "I have nothing to say to you demons. You may have the power of the devil, but I'm a child of our lord. You may burn my body, but my immortal soul will go to heaven... where none of you will ever walk!"

The white of Lorraine's eyes grew wide. "We used to *burn* creatures like you. But my work on this earth will not be in vain. Soon, we will have our rights back! The right to cast off your evil spells, you gay deviants-"

"Oh, thank you *so* much." Suddenly Vivienne stood behind Valeria again, sliding her hands onto her shoulders. Valeria blinked, once more enthralled by the perfumed locks falling around her. "But you might want to see what our friend here wears." And she moved aside Valeria's braid to reveal her necklace with the cross and thunderbird pendant.

Lorraine's eyes widened. Vivienne laughed charmingly, letting her fingers dance over the cross to Valeria's collarbone. "I don't know about you, but I don't see her bursting into flames. By the way, our Valeria here's a scientist. Unlike you, she works to advance our world. You have anything to say to that?"

Lorraine gulped before she pulled herself together and bared her whitened teeth. "Some wolfs walk in sheepskin! She will share the same fate as you. This is what your people want, right, wetback? To kill and replace our race in our own count-"

Valeria paled at the menacing words, even as Tayanna stuffed Lorraine's mouth with her gag. She opened her mouth, but Valerie beat her to it.

"This was my people's country long before your pathetic ancestors ever set foot on New Mexico ground. Vivienne, this cabrona is yours."

The French witch hummed, brushing her neck. "A l'ordre, beautiful." Vivienne trailed her hands off Valeria with a grin. She started to dance. Unlike Bayou, her movements were flowing, her hands orchestrating the raindrops round the Tower into echoing bells, small tremors sounding from the water. Soon, they sparked small flickers of electricity that jumped around Lorraine. The woman's eyes filled with more hatred with every drop that grazed her. Vivienne pivoted so rapidly that she made a blur of blue and black. The charged drops flew in spirals now.

Valeria watched with dark pleasure as the currents connected. Flickering bolts of all colors traveled between the charged drops, until they formed a mother bolt. It branched into rapidly growing flashes of violet, green, red, and white. When the lightning swirled around Lorraine, the woman lost her composure. She sank to her knees. Her crazed eyes looked toward the sky as if she expected God to do something about it.

Abruptly, Vivienne ended her dance on one knee before her, reaching through the pentagram and grasping the woman's chin. Her chest heaved with exertion. Lorraine's eyes turned wildly to the witch, who blew her dark hair out of her face with a sickly-sweet smile.

"If you see God...tell her 'Hi.'"

In one last pirouette, the web of lightning wrapped around Lorraine's body like an electric python. Lorraine's shrill scream echoed through the sizzling might. Her costly skin melted with dazzling speed until her head burst into flames of a hundred colors.

Valeria released a shaking breath when it was over. Her chest and eyes burned with unfamiliar energy. The air around the pile of ash and bones in the pentagram still zapped with wayward electric charges.

Vivienne lay on the floor, her chest heaving. As Mave and Ceto helped her up Vivienne caught Valeria's gaze. "Ah," she hummed, "There it is."

Valeria fisted a hand into her braid. "What?"

"In your eyes. Freedom."

***

Tayanna declared Bayou the winner. While no one could match Mave for strength and Vivienne's aesthetics score ranked supreme, the Choctaw witch boasted the best over-all performance.

Ceto pulled a bronze medal embossed with a crown of lightning from her robe and turned to Valeria, "You should do the honor, Valeria. You displayed great poise - more than any of your fellows."

Valeria felt completely drained. A headache pulsed behind her tired eyes and colorful shadows, remnants of the otherworldly lightning she had witnessed, danced before them. Something had ignited within her.

She threw Tayanna an unsure look. When the older woman nodded, she took the medal and stepped to the proud-looking Bayou. Valeria gave Bayou a tentative smile as she hung the medal around her neck and was surprised when the witch clasped her forearms.

For the first time, Bayou's dark eyes held genuine warmth as she regarded Valeria with a respectful nod, "You've done very well, sky scholar."

Valeria lowered her eyes, overwhelmed by the warring emotions within her. "I... thank you. You, um – you deserve this."

Bayou smiled, which was a terrifying sight. As soon as Valeria stepped back, the champion triumphantly raised both arms to the sky with two arrows of lightning exploding from her fingertips and like that their shield was broken.

Spanish, French, Greek, and English curses exploded as they were all drenched in rain.

Valeria threw back her head and closed her eyes gratefully. The drops cooled her aching skin and soothed her confused heart. She did not open them when Mave said her goodbyes.

The older woman mumbled about newfangled gimmickry, but commended Valeria for her strong stomach.

Ceto patted Valeria's cheek.

Bayou raised her chin, forcing her to look at the champion, "We'll see you again. Sister."

Tayanna palmed her face gently. "It's alright for you to be troubled now. But think it over after your rest, and I promise you that you will see things clearer than ever before. Vale?"

Valeria nodded, unable to hold back the tears filling her eyes. "I... I will, señora."

Tayanna smiled and reached into her robe: she pulled out a shimmering brooch adorned with three turquoise stones under an engraved cloud. She pinned it on Valeria's jacket with a satisfied look. "You've been such a darling, a weather witch in spirit. Take this as a token of our appreciation. It carries protective charms. Know that our month's donation will be more than generous."

Valeria traced a shaking finger over the brooch, trying to focus her mind on the good of the institute until Vivienne stood before her.

Still weak from her effort, her verdant eyes looked as roguish as ever. "Aw, chérie, do not cry." Her soft hands moved the wet strands from Valeria's face, stroking her skin. "I have a gift for you as well." She took a tiny notebook bound in blue leather from her robe, placing it in Valeria's hand and covering it with hers.

Valeria stared down at the rain running over their joined hands, but Vivienne ducked so she could meet her eyes. "If there is anyone giving you trouble... anyone who abuses their power at all – you can sign their names here. And nominate them for our next challenge if you wish."

Valeria hastily pushed the gift back into the witch's hands. "Thank you, but I won't be needing this."

Vivienne gave the most beguiling laugh. "Of course, beautiful. Whatever you say." Her hands pushed the book back into Valeria's chest while kissing her cheek, lingering lips hot on Valeria's ice-cold skin.

When Valeria came out of her daze, she saw that both the ashes and the pentagram had vanished, no trace of the terror that had occurred mere moments before.

The witches stood by the edge of the Tower, each holding staffs of gnarly wood, tip lights flickering alive. Vivienne gave her a final wink. Tayanna offered a dignified nod. "Until we meet again, Valeria Montero." They jumped off the edge and flew into the stormy dark.

***

The storm lasted through the night and Valeria, normally calmed by the wild sounds of the sky, could not find merciful sleep. In the morning the storm finally died. In place of lightning, violent memories flashed before her eyes: the screaming accused; Vivienne's vengeful, beautiful eyes; lightning more powerful and ethereal than she had ever seen before. Through these thoughts of unleashed nature, her present worry seemed laughably mundane: arriving on time for the Tower team meeting at the University in an hour. They would review her first solo shift which featured an undisclosed meteorologic execution.

Valeria went through the motions while she drove to the institute, unable to come up with anything she wanted to say to the men, unable to form any coherent thought at all.

The men greeted her with nervous smiles and fidgeting hands when she arrived, face pale and eyes shell-shocked. After apologies, desperate excuses, and countless pleas for Valeria to consider their impossible position, they raised the spectre of the scandalous shortage of science funding that was only to get worse after the recent election. Without a word from Valeria, they offered to share their limited budgets if she would remain mum should the university administration inquire into station activities.

Not participating in their groveling, Professor Brooks' became berserk the minute he spied the shimmering brooch on Valeria's jacket. He demanded an explanation.

After an intense look at him, Valeria explained quietly and in a matter of fact tone, the events of the night.

Under uncomfortable gazes from Lincoln, Dean, and Professor Janner, Brooks jumped straight into a tirade on the witches. His chest puffed out with indignation. "For three years I've stood by their carnage, kept their secrets, and *you* get a magic reward? You?! Why, because you're a *girl*? Why, I should–"

The only one not cowering before the senior professor's frightening temper, Valeria raised her brow, enraging him even more.

"... a goddamn insult! It's unbelievable! Feminist nepotism, that's what that is! Janner, she's in your research group. Can't you even teach your students some humility? Next time I see that wretched Tayanna's face I will-"

As he blustered on, Valeria silently reached into her pocket and took out the little blue notebook Vivienne had given her and carefully wrote two words in it.

Brooks saw and sputtered, shaking his fist in her direction, and finally grasping her arm tightly. "Are you listening to me, girl? What are you writing?"

Valeria folded the book and gave the professor an innocent smile. "Just taking notes, sir. I am listening."

***

To Selina The Weather Witch of Equations

*Roxane Llanque is a German Bolivian writer and multi-media artist. Her award-winning short film **Aberration** was selected for the Madrid Human Rights Festival and her story The Tell-Tale Present won the 2023 Outstanding Miniature of World Pride Australia. Her essays were published in magazines like Bright Wall|Dark Room, Broad Sound, and Latina media, while her fiction was featured in the anthologies **Not Your Papi's Utopia: Latinx Visions of Radical Hope**, **We Are All Thieves of Somebody's Future**, and **Demons & Death Drops**. She is currently working on her first novel. When she is not writing she can be found cheerfully playing wistful Spanish songs on her guitar, on her website **https://roxanellanque.com**, or on social media @roxanellanque.*

WE SING
OUR BODIES
MONSTROTIC

BY MATHEW L REYES

Preamble. You called us monsters, so monsters we shall be. Go ahead: Call us unnatural. We will show you the most natural thing in the world, life's ecstatic bookend to the womb's release. Call us angry. We will laugh because you do not know anger. We have tried it all. Appeasement, silence, discourse: you name the civilities and we have executed them with precision every time, and every time you ask for more and give us less. This ends now.

We understand that change can be frightening. Your bones will re-set, though in unrecognizable ways. Many of you will not complete the journey required toward realignment, but it is a sacrifice we are ecstatic to make. Let us begin.

• Excerpt from the *Monstrum Proclamation*

***

Adam scanned the food court from the second floor. He gripped the glass railing and leaned over the chasm of pink and teal tiles, columns, and neon lights. Not so far from the madding crowd today, they teemed below in the hundreds. He was certain nobody watched him, or almost certain.

Several times Adam caught others looking away as he turned his head. Did those eyes belong to the authorities? Were the eyes a product of paranoia? He'd stayed alive this long by assuming that the answer to both questions was yes.

Did people hear the incessant growling of his stomach, notice him staring at the food court's trash bins? Was someone reporting him to security even as he wandered? It wouldn't be the first time he'd been tossed out of a warm building for trying to eat.

But eating wasn't his goal, not today. Watching for the *watchers* took precedence.

Adam walked toward the downward escalators. Someone in a yellow overcoat jostled him but said nothing and continued on their way. To his left, outside of a women's clothing store, a man stood with a toddler. The sticky-faced child pecked away at a green, cottony substance.

A chime sounded. Adam looked up.

"Attention shoppers." The automated mall voice was sexless, toneless. "For today only, see renowned psychologist and popular author, Dr. Abraham Fisher, speak on his new book, *The Sinner from the Sin*, and purchase a signed copy. The event starts in ten minutes in the main plaza. Thank you and have a shopporific day."

Fisher. The name struck a chord, from the time of the gray walls, the needles, the straps on his arms. Anger embraced him unbidden.

He winced. Adam's temples throbbed.

The central plaza was close. He took the escalator down to the first floor.

I've got to find them. They must be watching for me.

As he stepped off the escalator and trotted down the mall's corridor, he fished in his pockets and withdrew the message he'd found in a restaurant dumpster last night. The grease-soaked paper had MALL OF AMERICA written in block letters followed by today's date and the words *Watch for us, as we watch for you. Be ready to rise.*

Whether it had been planted for Adam or left for any person to find, he didn't know. In the shelters around Minneapolis, rumors abounded of a group moving in the shadows, a group of people with special traits, perhaps even traits like Adam's.

His head continued to throb.

The plaza was more of an atrium. Five bright blue columns rose from the edges, coming together at the top of a glass dome three floors up. The candy pink walls and marble flooring reflected the dome's white light. Potted plants slithered upward, vivid green under the light. A stage was set up at the atrium's center.

Adam stayed near the columns at the crowd's edge. Fisher's name had sparked an anger in him that Adam couldn't ignore. Finding the watchers was crucial, but he'd find them after seeing the man he hated above all others.

The audience stood tightly packed. Any tighter and Adam would not be able to breathe. With the oncoming headache, which was already difficult enough. His stomach protested again—when had he last eaten?

Two chairs sat on the stage.

Adam waited.

Doctor Fisher. The Fisher King. Last of those greats who guarded the Holy Grail and its secrets. Wounded, cursed, until the day when one chosen by God came to heal him, relieve him of his sacred duty. Dr. Fisher. The Fisher King. King of Fishers.

"Follow me," Adam said at a whisper, "and I shall make you fishers of men."

"What you say to me?" A man wearing an old, tattered red hat looked at Adam. "You say somethin?"

"Sorry," Adam said, "Reciting a grocery list. Didn't mean to disturb you."

"Uh huh. You just watch it."

Adam moved away. Willing the aching at his temple to cease, he raked his hand through his brown curls and focused on the stage.

Two people walked toward the stage. The cheering crowd, a sea of flesh, bone, and blood, parted for this Moses and his follower.

Adam clenched his shaking hands into fists. The throbbing pulsed with a sharp edge, like a glass splinter piercing his forehead. "Go away," he whispered to the headache.

The two figures reached the stage. The first, a squat and sweaty man whose pink flesh shone under the lights, dabbed at his face and sat in one of the chairs. The second was taller.

Adam forgot his headache for a moment as he stared at the taller man.

Dr. Fisher was as well-built as Adam remembered. His hair was cropped close, as was his beard. His rosy cheeks stood out under the glow of the mall's lights. Wearing a black suit and a red tie, he smiled and waved at the sea of flesh, which rose in noisy waves of adulation. At first glance, Fisher's eyes looked too large, but Adam realized he wore eyeliner.

"A Fisher of Men," Adam repeated. "It's him."

The sweaty interviewer raised a hand as Dr. Fisher sat. The audience fell silent. Cameras flashed. A film crew held a thumbs-up to the interviewer.

"Hello, America!" the interviewer said. "My name is Uriah Murdstone. You all may know me from my work with the Midwestern State Media Association. I can't tell you all how pleased I am to be here today with Dr. Abraham Fisher!"

Murdstone, Adam thought. Uriah, urea. Urine in a stone, a murder stone. A fleshy stone excreting urine instead of sweat. Now that was his face to Adam, a great, fleshy rock with two black pits at its center, leaking urine from its pores and its pink mouth.

Adam's eyes twitched as the headache worsened.

"You may know today's esteemed guest," Murdstone continued, "from his work with the White House as well as his career as a psychiatrist. Dr. Fisher has also served as the chairman of President Jakof's Commission on American Morality for the last ten years."

The audience clapped and several cheered. A sea of hands waved. Dr. Fisher nodded.

Murdstone continued. "Today, the Doctor is here to talk about his book, *Sinner from the Sin: A More Compassionate Solution to the Problem of Gender and Sexual Minorities in the United States*. Dr. Fisher, thank you for joining us. Why don't you tell us a bit about your book?"

Dr. Fisher smiled. His muscles flexed under his suit. He clasped his hands in his lap before saying, "Thank you, Mr. Murdstone. I'd first like to thank you for doing such a bang-up job cleaning house here in the Midwest. The public has had to deal for far too long with unreliable news from bully pulpit anchors and fake journalists attacking President Jakof and the good work he's doing."

Applause.

Oh, yes. He knew that voice. Adam's hands trembled. He looked around.

The person in the yellow overcoat stood across the room from him. A pale woman, she glared at Dr. Fisher before meeting Adam's eyes. Did she belong to the watchers? Or were Fisher's people onto him?

"Only doing my part for my country," Murdstone said, waving a hand.

"An important part," Dr. Fisher said. "As for my book, this has been a long time coming. But the work for justice, for the fight against moral decay, is good work, hard work."

"Why don't you tell us a bit about your findings in *Sinner from the Sin?*"

"Certainly. It boils down to this: our findings from Project Spectrum largely confirmed the long-standing wisdom about sexual and gender minorities. These people deserve all the compassion and support we can give them."

Project Spectrum. Adam's neck muscles twitched. His eyes felt hot.

"Reparative therapy with a religious aspect alone," Dr. Fisher continued, "while crucial in reviving the spiritual and moral compass of these people, is not, in and of itself, enough to accomplish our compassionate goals."

"A genetic component is crucial as well, correct?"

"Just so." Fisher leaned forward, his hands clasped together. A wedding ring glinted under the atrium lights. "Through nearly a decade of research, we've isolated a genetic component for sexual and gender deviancy, which means we can finally, *finally* help these individuals with genetic reparative therapy."

The crowd hushed. The sea of flesh and blood and bone stilled.

Murdstone wiped his forehead with a white cloth. "So, you are saying—"

"Nobody need be prisoner to their flesh any longer. We can remove the sinner from the sin with technologies and therapies our forefathers could have only dreamt of."

"Simply remarkable." Murdstone again wiped his shining forehead with the white cloth.

The audience muttered. A woman raised her hands and praised God. A few others followed suit.

A pulsing needle dug into Adam's eyes, piercing the membrane and boiling the gelatinous fluid within. Adam lifted a trembling hand to his face and winced. His stomach roiled, though it held no food to eject. This was no typical pain but felt like a cluster of sharp glass expanding just behind his eye.

A voice came from above him: *Someone find the spoiler! Everything could go wrong—find them!* Not a far away spoken voice but floating within Adam's mind.

"Reparative therapy," Dr. Fisher said, "is still in its infancy. And I outline in *Sinner from the Sin* that the so-called homosexual and transgender rights movements never needed to happen. Our mistake was to approach the subject from a purely religious and moral standpoint when, in reality, if we had *begun* with something like Project Spectrum, the gender minority activist groups never would have needed to exist."

Adam forced his hand to steady as he lowered it. He glared at the two men on the stage.

Project Spectrum. He clenched his jaw as that facility flooded his mind:

White walls and men in coats. Syringes injecting. Scalpels slicing, needles sewing. Cold steel floors. Beds without mattresses. Bundles in the corner, little heaps of skin and bone, shriveled heads on slouched shoulders, dull eyes staring sightless. Calling mother, father—come get me please, please—oh no, my son, not until you've healed, and admit how lucky you are to be pioneering God's work. And so on and so forth and—

"...to implement these initiatives." The more Dr. Fisher talked, smiled, the more Adam's body trembled.

Murdstone said, "Can you comment on how the White House and Congress will implement this?"

"The President has already promised that, within a year, we can roll out what we call Enhanced Genetic Reparative Therapy, or E.G.R.T., for all gender and sexual minorities, free of charge of course, and..." Dr. Fisher winced and raised a hand to his face.

"Are you okay, Dr. Fisher?" Murdstone leaned forward and twitched. The two men sat still, staring at each other. Murdstone's fleshy rock of a head tilted on his neck. He shook his head and blinked.

Adam's headache reached fresh heights of agony. His face grew hotter, from anger or pain he didn't know. He stared at Dr. Fisher.

Find the spoiler! I can feel his power!

Adam's eyelids twitched. The pain in his head became too much, so he simply pushed it out through his eyes. A molten heat flowed from him, as though it were a tentacle writhing from his head. Dozens of angry tentacles, desperately squirming for something to latch onto, to squeeze into oblivion.

Dr. Fisher's forehead shone as sweat ran in fat drops to his beard. He fanned himself and then stood.

"Sexual minorities," he said, his voice booming now, "should never have been given the—the rights to organ—to..." He gasped, and the tendons in his neck stood out as he clawed at his neck. Murdstone stood, spilling his glass of water.

Someone in the audience screamed.

A bulge appeared at Dr. Fisher's crotch, stretching the fabric of his pants.

Still as stone, Adam stared at Dr. Fisher. He stabbed the tendrils of rage and pain into the Doctor's body, slipped them beneath Fisher's skin, and pumped him full of heat and pushed his blood downward. Adam could feel the separation of skin, fat, and cartilage, as though he were slipping his fingers under Fisher's skin. He flexed his fists. How far and deep could he go *this time*?

The audience edged away from the stage. Both men stood. Murdstone awkwardly patted Dr. Fisher on the shoulder as Fisher's erection continued to swell.

"Oh God! It burns!" Fisher tore at his belt and pants. Women in the audience screamed, and someone fell to the marble floor as Fisher released his fleshy, red burden from its prison. It darkened to purple as it continued to grow and tighten until—

Stop him!

—Fisher's exposed flesh ruptured, sending waves of blood splashing to the stage floor, all over Murdstone and onto the faces of those nearest the stage. His skin turned white as his body emptied of blood. Dr. Fisher stood still for a moment, then he fell into Murdstone. Murdstone squealed, a high, whining pitch that drove Adam's rage into renewed fury.

Uriah Murdstone clawed at his skull while the flesh swelled around his black-pit eyes. He shook his head and shrieked over the noise of the audience, who scrambled to get away from the stage. Murdstone's eyes bulged. His body inflated for a moment, and then, as he grabbed at his white handkerchief to wipe sweat from his face, his forehead cracked.

It was as though someone had pushed a shotgun to the back of Murdstone's head, tilted it upward, and fired. The head, there one second, became a cloud of red mist, bone, and hair.

The bodies of the doctor and the journalist collapsed onto each other.

Adam's breathing relaxed, and his hands stilled. The headache was gone.

Around him, the crowd scattered like frenzied ants. Some cried 'murder!' while someone shouted about terrorists. The man with the red hat vomited on the floor and flailed around, hitting a woman in the face and knocking her down. A mother holding a toddler ran, slipped in the vomit, and tumbled, sending the child screaming under trampling feet. Other children wailed into their parents' shoulders.

Adam tried to reach the trampled toddler, but the stampeding crowd knocked him back. He fell against a pillar and grabbed the vines to steady himself, but they tore away and he sprawled to the floor. Unable to stand, Adam instead crawled behind the pillar to get away from the thousands of stomping feet. Someone tripped over his ankle and fell. Adam managed to stand on the other side of the pillar just in time to see a yellow flash.

Something sharp pricked his arm.

"You're coming with us," a feminine voice said. "Bathsheba is going to kill you. She'd had a whole lovely demonstration planned, and then you went and fucked it up."

Another voice, now more distant: "Yes, Hagar, but don't hurt him."

"He'll be fine. C'mon, help me..." The voices danced together, and Adam felt as though he could dance, light as a feather and soft as butter, skipping through the blue skies of his childhood, before things had gone so poorly, back when he'd been happy, back when—

His vision dimmed.

***

First, the pounding gray. Rather, gray around him and pounding within his head. Then the gray lightened, and Adam became aware of a leather-dry tongue lolling out of his mouth—were those really his lips, swollen and cracked?—and of his fingers, stretching out. Soft something under his body. Dark figures emerged from the gloom above him. The blurs of light and shape sharpened. He lay in a bed.

"He's awake." A familiar voice.

"You really nailed him, didn't you." A new voice, soft.

The familiar: "Look, it was either drug him and take him or risk leaving him to the pigs."

A third voice: "You are certain that it was him?"

"Yes. I could feel the power boiling off him."

Adam blinked and looked around him. He lay in a small infirmary. Two other beds lay empty on the opposite side of the room, each with turned-down sheets. The cinderblock walls were bare. Fluorescent lights fixed into the ceiling cast a blueish glow.

"Hey there, sunshine," said the familiar voice.

Three people stood around him. The first was the woman who'd worn a yellow coat at the mall. She stood over him, now wearing a yellow blouse and loose pants. Her long, white hair atop a porcelain face made her look like a doll.

She said, "Sorry about the poke. You'll have a sore arm for a bit. But you really caused a lot of trouble for us."

"Peace, Hagar. Let the poor fella breathe." This voice belonged to a man who stood over Adam on the other side of the bed. He held a clipboard and peered down at Adam over thick, green-frame glasses. He smiled "Welcome back to the land of the living. That's more than I can say for Uriah Murdstone or Abraham Fisher."

Adam cleared his throat. "Who...you people?"

The man set the clipboard down and tilted his head. "Who are any of us, really? Under the flesh and flashy clothes and the hurt? What does it mean to be *us*, I wonder?"

"Uh. Okay."

"Sorry," the man said. His warm, green eyes met Adam's, and Adam's heart fluttered in turn. "You can call me Lazarus. Nice to meet ya."

Adam laughed, weakly. "Like from the Bible?"

Lazarus said, "I used to have another name. We all did. I was...oh, what was my name? Hernandez was my last name; I know that for sure. But you see, they took my name when they registered me for Spectrum, and they never gave it back. Lazarus is the only name I have."

The woman in the yellow blouse glared at Lazarus. "Christ, Lazarus. You'd tell a total stranger the building codes if we weren't around to stop you."

Lazarus nodded. "That's Hagar. She's a real sweetheart."

"Okay, you two." The third person, who'd been standing at a distance, joined them. She was tall, broadly built, and wore a grand, purple miter over a pile of red hair. She reminded Adam of old photos of drag performers, back when those were permitted. With amethyst robes and dark, flawless skin, she looked like an angel of salvation.

Her hands rested on the bed railing, fingernails tipped with swirling galaxies of color. "Ignore them. They bicker every day. Hagar does have a point, though."

Hagar sniffed and folded her arms.

The tall woman continued. "You're lucky that Lot's Wife was watching for respondents to the notes we left around the city. If she hadn't sensed you when you started to put on that little *show* of yours, our people wouldn't have been able to extract you. You'd be dog meat. So, thanks are in order. And an explanation of who you are and how you blew up a man's dick on national television. I'm Magdelena, by the way. You may call me Mother Magdelena or Mags."

Adam cleared his throat. "You're the people who left the notes." Hagar and Magdelena nodded. He tried to sit up, but the effort winded him, and his head fell back on the pillow.

"Hey, you need to rest," Lazarus said, putting a slender hand gently on Adam's chest. "We'll get you food, too."

"When we determine that you're not a threat," Hagar added.

"I'm not," Adam said.

Magdelena laughed and patted his knee. "Baby doll, you blew a man's dick up and then vaporized the head of another. Lot's Wife just checked in on the site, and they're *still* cleaning up the blood. The Mall of America hasn't seen this much blood since the Black Friday ritual of '32. You may be a lot of things—but harmless, you ain't."

"Lot's Wife? The pillar of salt?" asked Adam.

"Oh no, don't ever say that to her." Magdelena did a sign of the cross. "Woe unto the man who calls her that. She's our...how do you say it?"

"Spy," Lazarus said. He sat on the edge of the bed, at Adam's waist. A gentle warmth radiated from his body, and Adam's tension abated somewhat. Lazarus had a face sculpted from marble, hair woven from threads of night, and a smile that Adam felt he could drown in. "Or remote viewer."

"So she was the one watching for me?" Adam asked.

Lazarus nodded. "She doesn't like groundwork. She'll eat with us but try not to perceive her too much. She's rather introverted. Most us are. Comes with the trauma."

"You aren't soothing him, are you?" Magdelena said. "We agreed there'd be no—"

"Peace, Mags. I'm not. What can I say? I just have that sort of calming presence." He grinned, then stuck his tongue out at Magdelena.

Hagar said, "So, stranger. What's your name?"

"I've called myself Adam. I don't remember the rest. From before..."

Hagar said, "Spectrum?"

The word again. Spectrum. Rainbow. God's promise to not flood the world again, and a symbol of togetherness, inclusivity. Flags of spectrums of all colors had once flown in some places; he could remember that much. He'd seen the last one when he was about ten, and then something on the news about those flags being classified as hate speech against the followers of Christ and President Jakof, and then no more, nothing but the gray walls of that place, the weekly calls from his parents, and—

"Adam," Magdelena said. "As good a name as any."

"Project Spectrum," Adam said. "They took that name on purpose. Why do you know about that? Who told you?" He tried to sit up but fell back again.

Magdelena and Hagar looked at each other, but Lazarus merely put a hand over Adam's. "We know about it because we are its survivors."

Adam looked from Lazarus to Magdelena to Hagar. Magdelena was what Fisher had called a gender minority. And Hagar? He didn't know. But Lazarus. The gentleness of his eyes, the delicacy of his voice—the only men he'd known like this had been within those gray walls. Most of those voices had disappeared from the facility over time until Adam was left with a quietude that drove him mad.

Again Adam cleared his throat. "I thought I was the only survivor."

"We are the lost, the dispossessed," Lazarus said, his voice soft. "We were discarded by our family as children, when our *deviancy* became clear, when the government rolled out its not-so-secret project and told our families how patriotic it would be to send their children to participate in the study, as they called it."

"A study in nightmares," Magdelena said.

Hagar folded her arms over her chest again and said, "Are we going to tell him everything, then? Christ almighty. Look, *Adam*, you may not be dangerous, not to us, but you still haven't told us why you decided to kill two high-profile government employees."

"I...didn't mean to."

Hagar snorted. "Oddly, I believe it. So. What's your story?"

Adam cracked his neck. He started at the beginning, as much as he could calculate a beginning. At first, a life of easy days and carefree summers—that, the time of Before. And then the gray walls holding him and others, men made beasts, women made chattel, people made non-people, all for the greater good of society. When his usefulness had ended, they dumped him in a homeless encampment in Minneapolis, or so he thought. His memory was hazy. He'd wandered the streets, each day like the last. Until, one day, while digging in the dumpster for food he came across a note inviting him to the Mall of America.

Every so often he'd lose his temper when he heard talk about people like him, those who dared defy the dictates and constructs of society by following their natures. When that anger ticked up, it sometimes grew into a headache, which sometimes necessitated a *release*. Did that release have effects beyond his control? Sometimes.

"Definitely," Magdelena said. "You and your temper changed things for us. We intended a show for the country, but your raw power was not in the cards. Also, may I see your right arm?"

Adam lifted it, knowing what Magdelena wanted. She grasped his under-arm just below the triceps and looked.

"So you were 001481. I was 023887."

Hagar, looking at the ground: "000326."

"084419," said Lazarus. He stared in the distance.

Adam said, "You didn't check for the mark when I was out?"

Lazarus tilted his head and said, "After decades of having no autonomy, of having our bodies violated, day after day after day, why would we continue that cycle? And you're one of us."

"Just propose to him, Lazarus," said Hagar.

"That was almost a joke," Lazarus said, winking at her.

Adam's cheeks burned. He cleared his throat and said, "I still don't really understand who you people are, other than other Spectrum survivors, and what exactly it was that I 'ruined' for you."

"You'll get your answers," Magdelena said. "But first, you need food."

***

Dinner was spaghetti with canned sauce, barely tasting of tomatoes or noodles or cheese, and over-stewed green beans, and dry cake from a boxed mix. Filling but not food fit for consumption, according to Hagar at least. For Adam, every bite was divine because it came hot off the stove instead of from a dumpster. He sat with Hagar, Lazarus, and Lady Magdelena in a cramped kitchenette.

Magdelena explained that they were an underground—literally—group of castaways inhabiting an old survival bunker south of Rosemount. They were the broken and dispossessed, the discarded who had survived and escaped Project Spectrum. They also had certain abilities of the mind, side effects from the constant genetic experimentation.

"So," Adam said. "You're like me. Your dumpster message was pretty vague."

Magdelena said, "We are nameless, jobless, without hope or fear, with nothing to lose because we've lost everything. We are Monstrum."

"We left those messages," Hagar said between bites of spaghetti, "because we knew that Project Spectrum dumps its few survivors in the area when their sick 'conversion therapy' experiments end. Honestly, we weren't sure anybody would respond to our notes."

Adam scoffed. "Experimentation? Dr. Fisher called it God's therapy."

Hagar raised an eyebrow. "I take it you knew him, then. For us, he was a shadowy figure behind one-sided glass. The Mall of America was the first time I saw him in person."

Adam leaned back in his seat. "He visited me a few times. Every few months, after the side effects of their latest injections wore off, he'd ask me questions about how I felt. He'd ask about my home life. Ask me if I *chose* homosexuality and whether I wanted to get better."

Magdelena shook her head. "I heard he'd picked a few kids to do further testing on."

Adam cleared his throat and allowed the memories to come back. "He'd read from the Bible, passages from Leviticus, First Corinthians, Romans, as though he preferred the old-fashioned conversion therapy tactics. And we'd talk. Or I'd refuse to answer his questions, and he'd withhold my food until I'd answer. He told me I was doing God's work."

"No wonder you blew his dick off," Magdelena said, her voice a mix of awe and disgust.

Adam snorted. "The first time I started to get those headaches was when he questioned me after starving me. He told me an important donor was coming to visit, and that we needed better results. Fuck all what that had to do with me, but he pushed, asked if I was repentant, asked if I felt less...sinful due to whatever they injected into us. None of it made sense. It was autumn outside, and the facility heaters weren't on. I got so angry at him, and the room started to heat up. We both started to sweat, and he left. It was the last time I saw him."

Lazarus and Hagar put their hands over Adam's, which rested on the table.

"I remember," Magdelena said, sighing shakily, "that one of the first rounds of injections made me brutally ill. I was bedridden for days. But I was lucky. I had to miss a round of injections, while whatever they put into the other people in my ward caused a hemorrhagic fever. I was the only one in my hall left, so they moved me. They eventually dumped me in an alley in Minneapolis."

Adam shook his head. "God knows why they dump those of us who survive into the city. They need a large homeless population to keep the 'normal' people upset and distracted. And to drive the national narrative that we're unstable. Who'd believe a homeless person smelling like piss that the government experimented on them? Thank God I found your note."

"The question," Lazarus said between bites of cake near the end of the meal, "is whether you want to join us in the battles to come."

"We won't force you," Lady Magdelena said.

"I'd like it if you joined us," Lazarus said, smiling wide. A bit of chocolate icing clung to his upper lip. "After all, why else would you have responded to our note?"

Adam nodded. "Of course. I'll stay. Whatever you need from me."

"Then the next step," Lady Magdelena said, "is to make peace with Bathsheba."

"Peace?"

Lazarus nodded, then stared up at the ceiling. "You did kill her ex, after all. That was a pleasure she'd been saving for herself. Good luck, my friend. Bathsheba can be quite...well. You'll see. After that, go see Lot's Wife. She's eager to get a gander at you, too."

"At any rate," Lady Magdelena said, "may the nascent flesh be with you. You'll learn about *that* soon enough."

***

Adam knocked on the metal door. The sound echoed. He stood in a corridor with sheet-metal walls that rose up into a nebulous gloom. It felt as though he was in a cave.

"Who is it?" The voice was sleek, catlike.

"Adam."

"Enter!"

He slid the door open. Steam spilled from within, smelling of lavender and curling around his feet. Little tendrils of it snaked their way along the gritty concrete floor.

"Close the door! Do you want all the heat to escape? And shoes off. Don't track that grit in here."

He slid the door closed once inside and kicked his shoes off. The room was vast. The floor was white tile, small squares laid out in a diagonal pattern. Powder-blue walls glistened, collecting the perfumed steam drifting around the room. At the back, in the center, an enormous bathtub sat on four gilded legs. Its white ceramic was polished to a mirror shine.

The woman within the tub lay in mountainous clouds of soap suds. Pink and powder-green mixed with the white, as though she were bathing in some divine elixir. Her blond hair fell in curls around ivory-pink shoulders. As she turned to face Adam, he looked down to avoid her severe gaze.

Bathsheba.

She licked her lips. "There's our dicksplosion guy. A new specialty. Come closer. Let me have a good look at you."

Adam walked up to the tub. Bathsheba reached for a bar of chocolate resting on the tub's rim and lifted it to her mouth. She bit into it with pearlescent teeth. The melting chocolate covered her fingertips; brown drips dropped to her wrists and into the tub. A glass of milk rested on the floor below the tub. Several pieces of bacon were taped to the wall behind her, slanted this way and that.

Adam knelt at the tub to be at eye level with Bathsheba. He watched as she ate the chocolate bar, which had a gooey caramel center that drizzled down between her fingers and into the bath water. She stared at him as she ate. "Why do you have bacon taped to the wall?"

She shrugged. "Have you ever been going about your day and thought, *well now, I just have the most insatiable craving for bacon. I must have it now*. If you tell me you haven't, then you're lying. I have emergency bacon and emergency chocolate. Seeing you reminded me that I did not get to crush Uriah's face between my hands."

"I'm truly sorry."

"He had it coming," she said, licking chocolate off her fingers. She inhaled deeply, luxuriantly moaned, and settled into the suds. "I only saw the red mist that had been his head. I'll never get to feel his brains between my fingers, and I needed my emergency chocolate. A girl's got to have her little comforts, you know. As for the bacon on the wall, I suppose that depends on how this conversation goes."

"How it goes?"

She leaned forward. Water dripped from her shoulders, down her breasts. She stared at him, catlike. "Scrub my back. You'll find the loofa behind me. It's the least you can do."

Adam tentatively picked up the loofa, dipped it in suds, and scrubbed her. His hands trembled.

"I married Uriah Murdstone in the fall of '28. I needed an unwitting beard, and he was an old family friend, a very humble and meek man."

"My father was humble," Adam said. "And my mother always apologized for putting others out. Effective weapon, humility."

"Just so, Adam. A few years into our marriage, Uriah caught me in the bath with a friend of mine, Lamia Saint Francesca. He had her taken away, and then he had his way with me. Again and again. To set me straight, so to speak. That didn't work, so he sent me to Project Spectrum. I'd hoped to run into Lamia. I have to believe she's still out there, somewhere.."

"And you and Hagar were at the mall today to get him?"

"Mhm. Hagar is a telepath. I am the mistress of illusions. We'd planned on having a little practice run of a project of ours. I create for Uriah the illusion of hell, and Hagar fills his head with voices, destabilizing him and his friend Dr. Fisher on national television, making the public lose trust in them. But *you* went and lost your temper and altered their bodies on a molecular level. And revealed our existence."

Adam soaked the loofa in more suds and continued to scrub. "Again, I didn't mean—"

"Yes, yes. Enough of that. You're impressive. Mags is practiced in the art of psychokinesis, but *you* seem to be able to alter flesh itself. Perhaps you didn't see how Uriah's head almost morphed into something like that of a goat before it exploded. That goes beyond mere psychokinesis. You, Adam, are the first we've encountered with the power to truly bring about the nascent flesh."

There it was again, the phrase *nascent flesh*. New flesh. New skin; skin of what, exactly? Metaphorical? Literal? A mantra, a belief in something. What was so new about it? Their abilities, conferred accidentally after years of testing in the labs of Project Spectrum, testing that had killed or vegetated most of the patients?

Flesh coming apart at the seams, splitting from fat and muscle, melting, molding, reshaping into something—what? Was it only the power to destroy the flesh and the life it held?

"Adam? Are you there?"

"Yes. Sorry."

Bathsheba turned to him. She lifted a hand and cupped his face with wet fingers. Her nails sparkled like sapphire. A lapis lazuli ring shone on her middle finger. He put a hand against hers, then held both hands to his face. His mother's hand had once felt as comforting.

"My dear, you are one of us. I know your pain. I have *lived* it."

Adam said, "Mother caught me with Jacob Piercingwell in bed in the eighth grade. We were only playing around. Afterward, I saw him in the Spectrum labs. Only once."

She took his hand in hers, leaned forward, and kissed his hand.

"The world," Bathsheba said, "is not built for those like us. For a time, we thought perhaps we could carve out a space in it, but they took that space away, too. The old flesh, the old ways, will never make room for us. So, enter the nascent flesh."

He nodded and said, "The nascent flesh." Adam blinked.

The bathroom was no longer opulent; its walls were the same rusted sheet metal as those in the hallway. Adam's bare feet no longer perched on the edge of a white-tailed dais, but on a dirty floor. His hands rested on the edge of an old tin bathtub filled with warm water. Bathsheba's beauty alone remained. Sunlight shone through a dirty window near the ceiling. They were in a basement.

"The beauty. It's gone."

"For now," Bathsheba said. Her voice turned stone-like. "Only for now."

***

The White House. Its floors are spotless, its rooms quiet. The portraits of past inhabitants have been stowed in the basement, each replaced with the withering gaze of the man who has lived in the building these past ten years.

The Oval Office. Blood-red curtains are draped over the windows. A golden carpet is spread over the center of the room. Upon it rest scarlet couches.

President D.T. Jakof. He hovers over the desk, his head tilted to the side. His face is a canyon of crags, his skin tanned to a shade of paprika except for the pale flaps and folds not held back by tape. His hair is dyed burgundy, though the roots are white. His watery eyes regard each person sitting in supplication before him. Drool spills in little strands from the corners of his mouth.

An aide wipes the drool. Nobody acknowledges the gesture.

"Mr. President," a woman says as she approaches the desk with a syringe. "Just one moment, sir." She holds his hand, wrist up, rubs the skin with alcohol, and inserts the needle. Clear fluid flows through the tiny needle into his blood stream. A few seconds pass.

The President blinks. He has come back a little.

"Tell me what happened," he says. "Are people still eating the dogs in Minnesota?"

"No sir," an aide says. "That was a long time ago, in a different state. This was at the Mall of America. Doctor Fisher and some journalist."

"It's bad, Mr. President. A few days ago, unsavory elements—"

"No," the President says. "Less words."

"At approximately 3:00 p.m. Central Time," the aide continues.

"Shorter!"

The aide winces then bites his lips. "Bad wokes killed man. Loyal Americans dead. Wokes not found. Yet."

The Chief of Staff, a woman with blown-out hair and a leather jacket in a pale imitation of Loretta Lynn, leans forward. "As of now, we still don't know the method of assassination. Homeland Security and the Department of Patriotism haven't found ammunition casings."

The President pounds both fists on the table weakly. "Me! Talk to me!"

"Yes, Mr. President," dime-store Loretta says. "No kill method found yet. Homeland and Patriots looking."

He sits back in his chair. His wrinkled lips pucker and his watery eyes squint. "Good. Find them."

A knock from without. The door opens. In comes the billionaire who has purchased the President's previous three elections. He wrings his hands together, the fingers little writhing worms, and lowers his head. Greasy black hair is combed over his bulbous head, and his cheeks puff out as he smiles.

"Greetings," he says. "Vox Populi, Vox Dei."

Everyone in the room minus the President repeats the greeting.

D.T. Jakof looks up at Obediah Heep. His lips quiver again. "Vox is on?"

"No, Milord," Heep says, scuttling to the President's side. "Not yet. But your ratings are through the roof. Everyone loves you. They're saying you're the best President, that you've done more for America than any other President."

The President smiles and stares into space.

The Chief of Staff stands. "Mr. CEO, any news?"

Heep circles the room. Each person, including the President, watches him as he tilts his head this way and that before saying, "I believe, that is, I have been informed, that the attack on our patriotic colleagues was coordinated by a group of castaways. You will recall Project Spectrum. Do you, Madame Chief of Staff?"

"I do."

"Louder!" the President says, staring at Heep.

The billionaire nods. "Project Spectrum, a very good project that our President came up with, ostensibly used genetic manipulation to eradicate sexual and gender undesirables but was intended to formulate new biological weapons. While neither goal was fully accomplished, some interesting side effects did crop up."

Heep nods in the President's direction. "As you know, Spectrum formula 592 extends life. When I saw Dr. Fisher's...genitalia. How it exploded. How that journalist's head swelled, almost became that of an animal, and then became nothing but mist, I knew that the Spectrum castoffs must have had something to do with it."

"I knew it, too," the President says.

"Of course you did," Heep responds. "What happened at the Mall of America demonstrated some of the less...savory abilities expected from Spectrum. The subjects must have gained abilities post-release."

"Could they have been missed in the laboratory?" interrupts the Chief of Staff.

Heep pauses before continuing. "I posit that some element of their degeneracy has interacted with the genetic treatments to create...monsters. It is likely we are looking at a preternatural explanation for the tragedy in Minnesota."

The Chief of Staff eyes the President, who is playing with a crayon that someone left out for him. The adrenaline injection has worn off.

She says to Heep, "It'll need to be kept under wraps. And the fuckers will need to be found, rounded up, and exterminated. I'll have Homeland work on it."

Heep bows to her. "Vox Populi..."

"Vox Dei," she finishes.

The Oval Office. The White House. Pennsylvania Avenue. Washington, District of Columbia, The east coast of the American continent, a whirl of color and a blur of sound, over the mountains of Appalachia and the plains of the Midwest, and then—

***

Adam blinked.

Lot's Wife shuddered as she withdrew her hand from Adam's. Her skin was warm. "Please don't make me show you more. I get so sick when I go that far." She sat behind a thin silk screen that allowed Adam a view of her outline. He'd come here after visiting Bathsheba, and Lot's Wife had offered to show him their adversaries.

"I won't make you," Adam said quietly.

Lot's Wife sighed. "How I hate looking at those people. Everyone teases me about how I never leave my quarters. But tell me, if you could see all the world's misery when you closed your eyes, wouldn't you want to stay in the one place you felt safe?" Her hand rested on the table that sat between them.

Adam placed his hand over hers and squeezed. "I wouldn't want to leave here either."

Her room was little larger than a walk-in closet. Old volumes of Jane Austen, George Elliot, Sylvia Plath, Toni Morrison, Zora Neale Hurston, Simone de Beauvoir, and others lined a bookshelf. Red curtains laid over the back wall gave the impression of a large window temporarily shuttered, lending the room some artificial depth. A plush carpet kept the chill of Minnesota winter out.

She shifted behind the screen. "Through skin contact, I can give anyone visions of what I see from afar, but I can't read minds like Hagar can. So I can't know what those bastards are thinking."

"Does Magdelena know they're looking for us?"

"Oh yes. We just don't know how close they are to finding us. How long we have to prepare."

"Prepare?"

She nodded. "For whatever they have planned."

***

The Spectrum hideout, an abandoned bunker from the second World War, lay just outside of Rosemount, twenty or more miles south of Minneapolis. Lady Magdelena had found it, converted it into a safe house, and from there had gathered the others over the past year or so since Spectrum had shuttered. It was almost cozy, nearly warm, and just as safe.

Adam stood at the top of the steel trapdoor that led into the bunker. The remaining Minnesota prairie surrounded him. A bitter wind swept in from the west, carrying with it the scent of pine. Dry snow spun in the air, piled into drifts, and settled against trees at the edge of the rolling fields. Adam held his arms close to his chest and shivered.

Clanging below signaled someone ascending the ladder.

Lazarus pulled himself out of the bunker. He wore a deep green peacoat that came down to his knees with a chartreuse scarf around his neck. "Jesus wept, what's the temp right now?"

Adam laughed, still staring out. "Fifteen with the wind chill."

"And you're fine with just the sweater?"

Shrugging, Adam said, "I've slept under overpasses, in alleys, and other places best left forgotten. In much colder conditions."

Lazarus sidled up to him. His body radiated warmth. They stood pressed together, staring into the prairie. "Mags wants to have a meeting to discuss next steps," Lazarus said. "Now that you're recovered, we've got to figure out what we're going to do."

"What was the plan before I came?"

"To undermine the public's trust in the institutions. Use the same playbook they used to get into power. Though we *do* have something they don't."

Adam turned to Lazarus. "What is that?"

Lazarus looked at Adam and smiled. "Righteous rage. Though it's hard to feel anger when I'm standing next to you. It's hard to feel anything but your presence."

"Oh come on," Adam smirked, then rolled his eyes. "No need to charm your way into every conversation with me. You've won me over, Laz."

"Laz, huh? I like it."

Adam cursed himself. He'd sunk into familiarity with these people. Despite the fact that nothing ever lasted in this world, he'd not only allowed his guard down, but he'd accidentally given the man of his daydreams a nickname. He bit his lip and said, "Laz it is, then."

"I don't just mean to tell you that your presence is charming. Though, it's true." Lazarus shrugged, bumped Adam's shoulder with his as they stood in the newly fallen snow. "There's a power boiling under your skin. We can feel it."

Adam turned to Lazarus. "The nascent flesh."

"Yes. You let a whisper of that power out that day in the mall, according to Hagar. Yet you manage to hold it in. How? Why?"

"It erupts when I get pissed," Adam said, "or scared. First comes a headache which becomes a migraine. Then it becomes unbearable and I have to just...let go."

"I'm sorry," Lazarus said. "That must be terrifying. Also...it's not good to have so much raw anger built up. Surely there's a better way to channel it." He drew in closer.

The innocuous friction of their bodies sent little shivers up Adam's arms and through his belly.

"Hey," Lazarus said. "Can I try something?"

"If it's a kiss, you need to buy me dinner first."

"No." Lazarus snorted. "Not yet. I want to see if...oh, I don't know. Take your glove off." Adam obeyed, and Lazarus then said, "Now, hold my hand."

Hands warm despite the chill in the air. Fingers wrapped around fingers, eyes staring into eyes, flesh connected to flesh. Adam had only glimpsed this sensation in the brief halcyon days with Jacob. Before his parents' betrayal. Before the years at Spectrum. Here, now, he felt Lazarus's skin, and his every nerve tingled.

Lazarus grabbed Adam's other hand and the warmth continued to spread. Lazarus's emerald eyes widened. Adam imagined gems shimmering in shallow waters, white sands underfoot. Blue skies. A treasure island of their own making. Swimming together by day, alone together, deliciously isolated without everything and everyone who—

Adam jolted. Emotions that weren't his flooded through him. Joy, curiosity. Anger, fear, anxiety. Playfulness, empathy, hatred, jealousy, contentedness. Everything flowed from Lazarus to Adam, and in turn he felt as though he were losing a part of himself.

Touching completed a circuit between the two. Lazarus, his ability to affect emotions, became a part of Adam, as Adam became a part of Lazarus. Power cycled between them. Adam's vision swam with the sensation of the power coursing through them both, and he wobbled. Lazarus steadied him.

"Shit, are you okay?" They broke contact. Adam's vision stopped swimming.

"Yeah. Just got dizzy."

"Sometimes, when we touch each other, there's an exchange. It's like how Lot's Wife showed you what's happening in D.C. I wanted to see if we had that same connection. I had no idea it would be so strong. It was like, my power was flowing into you, and yours into me. I felt the atoms of our skin dancing. I..."

They stood in the cold, staring at one another, stilling their breathing and calming their emotions.

"I can't control it," Adam said. "My anger or my...this."

"You can."

"Teach me. I trust you."

Lazarus smiled. "I promise not to break that trust. I'll teach you what I can. But first, let's get out of this weather."

***

They sat at a round table made of Formica stained yellow by years of use. Knights all, each equal to the others. A family in a Camelot of their own making. But here there was no Arthur, no Percival, Lancelot, or Tristan.

No Mordred, Adam hoped.

Six figures of no renown, legend-less nobodies cast away by the world: a red-lace veil draped over her little face, Lot's Wife looked at her lap; glittering like the sun with a plastic daffodil in her hair, Hagar looked at Lazarus, sitting next to her like a smiling jade statue; silent Bathsheba swathed in sapphire silk gazed at her manicured nails; and in her violet robes and Papal miter, Lady Magdelena glanced at each of those around her and lastly at Adam, warmed by the pink sweater Lazarus had given him.

Magdelena began the meeting. "Hagar, do you have a final assessment of the Mall incident?"

Hagar nodded. "Bathsheba and I could have achieved our aims without the *radical* results that Adam gave us." Bathsheba snickered. "But we managed to get by mall security. Bathsheba made us inconspicuous."

"It was difficult," Bathsheba added, "to maintain the illusion in a high-density crowd."

Magdelena nodded and adjusted her robes. "And Hagar, you think we can replicate this?"

Hagar said, "Assuming Adam learns control, I think the three of us can do even more."

"Then the nascent flesh is ever closer." Magdelena glowed under the fluorescent lights. Within her twilight robes a thousand stars sparkled, as though they possessed an innermost light, an energy fueled by a spark of the divine.

Magdelena continued. "Adam, Lazarus gave you the gist of our goal—undermine Jakof's authority. But with the six of us sharing power, we can do so much more." She shifted in her chair. "If you can control your anger and your power, we can replicate the MOA on a national level."

"According to plan, you mean," Lot's Wife said. "We are not monsters. What happened then shouldn't happen again, Magdelena."

Hagar narrowed her eyes. "Don't tell me you're getting cold feet."

Lot's Wife inhaled slowly and leaned further over the table. "Hagar. I can't be party to a slaughter. I....it feels monstrous."

"Funny," Adam said, "don't we call ourselves Monstrum?"

Lot's Wife sighed behind her veil.

Magdelena continued. "Anyway. The nascent flesh, the total alteration of the body through genetic manipulation that was forced upon us, making us something new—this is what we will use to strike back against them. We know that the President's image is carefully crafted by his team of handlers, especially the shadow behind the throne, that godforsaken Heep."

"And the Supreme Court. All Jakof's appointees," Bathsheba said. "Plus a Congress unable and unwilling to reign him in. We cannot change anything without causing *massive* distrust in the entire government."

Magdelena looked at Adam. "You know we share our abilities when we touch. It's how Lot's Wife shows us her visions. It's how Hagar channels her telepathy, increases its power, and how she can push Bathsheba's illusions further. We're a mix-and-match fleshy monstrosity, my dear, and now you're one of us. And, with you, we're going to bring about the nascent flesh, our flesh, our truth, to the nation."

Hagar said, "The State of the Union Address for the First Financial Quarter is at the end of March. We could wait until Q2, but given that they know about us, the timetable is...rushed."

"It's one of the few times that the nation has compulsory viewing of the President," Magdelena said, "Our best bet to get close to Jakof and Heep, their cronies, and mind-fuck them into oblivion on national television. We've discussed more drastic methods, but we did not have a...consensus."

"I don't want us to become them," Lot's Wife said.

"My dear," Magdelena said, turning to Lot's Wife, "We understand. Do you have any idea of where they're at with finding us? I know it's difficult, but...we must see, if we can."

Lot's Wife tilted her head this way and then that. "I can do that." Finally, she nodded. "Everyone, join hands." Lot's Wife extended her hands.

Adam accepted her hand, smooth and cool like cream, smelling of vanilla. He joined his other hand with Lady Magdelena. As hands joined, a buzzing sensation pulled at Adam, squeezing his muscles gently. The feeling started in his groin, moving up his belly through his chest and arms, like connecting to a large battery.

Lot's Wife bowed her head. "Close your eyes."

Adam closed his eyes.

***

Heep paces the Oval Office. President Jakof sits in his chair, napping and drooling onto a set of crayons set on the storied, ancient desk. The Chief of Staff stands in front of the desk. Nobody else is present.

"How has Homeland Security not found their location? They've got to be near the Twin Cities."

The Chief of Staff sighs. "Sorry, Mr. CEO. We checked the Mayo Clinic—well, now the former Project Spectrum facilities in Rochester. Nothing."

"But they must be in Minnesota. Former locations where gender and sexual deviants gathered."

The Chief of Staff purses her lips. "It hasn't all been a waste. One of the old theaters in Minneapolis was a hiding place of sorts for the...undesirable elements. We rooted the roaches out, but nobody there had any clue about former Spectrum subjects. Security cameras at the Mall are still being sorted. We'll find them." Heep stops pacing.

The President stirs, blinks, and looks up. "They never believed what I could accomplish, you know, with the windmills and the fake dinosaurs. Nobody could have believed it."

Heep waves a hand. "Yes, yes."

The President continues. "I'm the best President, the only—"

"Shut the fuck up," Heep says. He leans over, putting a sausage-like finger in the old man's face. "You don't even know where you are. Your hundred and fifth birthday was last week, thanks to my research, and you didn't know it until we pumped you full of adrenaline. Just sit there and color in your goddamn coloring book and leave the adults to talk."

The President puckers his withered lips as though preparing to give one of his lauded, hour-long rants, but then the old bag of a face deflates and the man sinks into a nap.

"We will find them," Heep says to the Chief of Staff. "It's late February. We must destroy them by the end of Q1 so the President can deliver another win at our State of the Union."

The Chief of Staff nods. "My only concern is that..." She trails off and narrows her eyes. For a moment she stands perfectly still, pad in hand, staring out of the window.

"Jean? What is it?" Heep smiles.

She shakes her head. "A headache."

Heep inhales deeply. "Jean, perhaps you should go rest."

"Perhaps I should go rest." Her voice is distant, her gaze blank.

"Yes," Heep says, continuing to grin, his cheeks swelling out like those of a greedy chipmunk. "Go rest. You aren't using your skills to their fullest. You aren't using our resources to their fullest. Go."

The Chief of Staff nods, then bows slightly. "I'm going to go rest and think on how to better use our skills and resources to their fullest."

"Vox Populi," Heep says.

"Vox Dei," she answers.

Heep walks toward the President. His fingers trail over the papers and documents. A glint hits his eyes as he stares down at Jakof. And then he looks up and smiles. "Come visit me in Washington if you vermin dare. We'll have a fun time, and I'll have your power, too, like I had the others.'" He snaps his fingers.

***

Adam jerked back in his chair. A jolt of pain ripped through Adam's body, starting with his hands and traveling to his head.

The others around the table also leapt back, letting go of hands and breaking the circle. Her eyes bloodshot almost to the point of hemorrhage, Lot's Wife let out a chirping yelp and tore the veil from her head. A thin stream of blood trickled from her button nose. "Oh, *fuck*," she said.

Magdelena leaned over Lot's Wife. "Are you okay? What was that?"

Lot's Wife shook her head and closed her eyes.

Adam stood from his seat, walked over to the kitchen sink, and ran a paper towel under cold water. He returned the towel to Lot's Wife and offered it to her. She squeezed his hand in thanks and draped the towel over her forehead.

Bathsheba walked around the table and knelt beside Lot's Wife. She removed the veil, took another paper towel, and wiped the blood. Lazarus took Lot's Wife's temperature and felt her pulse.

"Is she going to be okay?" Hagar chewed her nails and paced.

Bathsheba stood. "I think so."

"Pulse is normal, temperature is a little high, but fine." Lazarus poured a glass of water for Lot's Wife. "Whatever that was, it hit all of us, but her the hardest."

Sipping the water, Lot's Wife opened her eyes. The redness had subsided to pink. The nosebleed had stopped.

Hagar said, "What happened? What did you feel?"

"I felt..." Lot's Wife trailed off. She stared down at her crumpled veil on the table. "One minute I was fine, and then I felt someone looking at me, watching me. Trying to get into my head. And then I lost my grip on the scene and snapped back here. Christ, that hurt. Adam, can you help me to my room?" She lifted a hand. Adam helped her out of her chair and then, at her behest, placed her veil back over her face.

As he walked back with her through the dusty corridors, Adam tried to recall the sensation he'd felt before they'd been evicted from the Oval Office. It was, he realized with cold fear, the sensation of somebody outside of their group trying to get *in*.

*****

The first dawn of March came slowly. Pale fingers of light bled into the sky's dark canvas and spread until the eastern evergreens were crowned with gold. Adam stood outside of the bunker, bundled up in several layers, watching the sun rise.

Heep had psychically evicted them from the Oval Office. Lot's Wife refused to risk another remote viewing. Clearly, Heep had taken some of Spectrum's more 'successful' serums for himself.

Wind whistled through the bare trees.

The hatch opened, protesting against the cold. Hagar stepped out and then held her arms to her chest. "How can you stand to be out here? I figured you'd be sleeping all morning, the way Lazarus has been working you on controlling your *emotions*."

He smiled. "When I was a kid, I hated early mornings. Mom and Dad would drag me up for school every day. Nowadays, I find a sort of peace in them."

"Hmm." The two stood shoulder-to-shoulder staring northward. After a pause, Hagar said, "You're all right, Adam. I like having you around."

Adam nudged her with his elbow. "You ain't the worst thing yourself."

"Fuck off." He felt the smile in her voice. "You've smiled more these past few days. Have you and Lazarus...you know?"

"He's mostly helping me control the anger."

She turned and gripped his upper arm. "Adam, you hold on tight to that man, and don't let him go. He's too good for this nasty world. If this is over, *when* this is over, and we make it to the other side, you take him somewhere nice. Somewhere you can find a...new way of living."

A motor of some sort whirred in the distance.

Adam nodded. "I'd like that. Hell, I'd like it if we could all find somewhere. Part of me wants to just...get away now."

She shifted, toeing a bit of snow with her boot. "With Heep knowing about us now, that's a big *if*."

"We can push a lot with our abilities when we link up." He brushed his nose. They had to do *something* about Heep.

Hagar tilted her head. "Adam, did I say something to anger you?" She stared into his eyes. "You don't *feel* angry. But...and I'm not trying to read your mind, but I feel so much...hate."

He laughed. "Hagar, I promise I'm not angry, no more or less than I am, given the general state of the world, but—"

"No." She pressed a cold hand against his cheek. "It isn't from you. You feel fine. But I feel hate coming from somewhere. Who on—"

Pop!

Hagar jerked back. Crimson erupted over the yellow of her thick overcoat. Her eyes widened as she lifted her hand to her neck. Blood cascaded between her fingers.

Shouting in the distance. The sound of thunder. Something whizzed past Adam's face.

He ducked, fell with Hagar as she collapsed into the snow. She opened her mouth to speak, but no words came out. Adam screamed and pushed out with his mind, trying to knit together the shredded flesh at her jugular. He pulled her up, pressed his hand against her neck. She'd lost too much blood, though.

Take, her voice said within his mind. *Don't know if it will work. Try! Take!*

She gasped and pressed her forehead to his. A flash of pain, and Hagar's life reeled through his mind like a movie on fast-forward. Dancing in a dim living room in a pink dress, hovering over a grave sobbing her eyes dry, kissing Delia Fox behind the bleachers at school and being caught and sent to *that* place, a flash of gray, of needles, of cold chills, and then Lady Magdelena's warm face caressing her cheeks, scenes of a lifetime of love and hate and fear and joy and—

Nothing. The wound had knit together too late.

Adam looked up. A wave of hatred came with the bullets flying over his head. A dozen men in black with the emblem of Homeland Security ran toward them. Adam lurched toward the hatch, lifted it, paused and looked back. Hagar deserved to be inside, out of the cold.

Adam shut himself in and locked the hatch.

Through the narrow halls, tripping over boxes, shouting. Calling them, raising his voice until his vocal cords strained.

"Adam! What happened?"

Blurred forms gathered in the hall. Adam found himself just outside of the kitchen area. Familiar voices clattered around him, forming dissonant words that clashed and confused him. He didn't remember turning the corner or going past the personal quarters. He pointed back to the entrance and screamed.

Lazarus put a hand on Adam's wrist. Adam's heartrate steadied, and his breathing slowed as the sensation of peace overcame him. "Hagar," Adam said, "dead. Homeland Security; they're here."

Lot's Wife and Bathsheba clasped each other's hands. Lazarus swallowed and stared past Adam toward the entrance.

"Oh Christ," Lady Magdelena steadied herself against the corrugated metal wall. "Oh Christ, oh fuck." A tangible sensation roiled off her, off all of them. If Adam reached out with his hand, he might feel the tendrils of their grief between his fingers.

"She gave me her powers," Adam said. "I don't know how. But I can *feel* your thoughts."

Above, an explosion. The floor trembled beneath their feet.

"We've got to get away," Lady Magdelena said. "There's another exit."

"Think," Lazarus said to her, to all of them, "We have minutes, maybe less—is there anything we have that *must* stay in our hands?"

"Just the clothes on our backs. Food, medical," Lady Magdelena said. She nodded to them. "To the kitchen! We have everything we need in there."

They scrambled to the kitchen. Someone banged against the hatch above, and the metallic clang echoed throughout the bunker.

A small explosion in the distance.

"We aren't going down like this," Lazarus said. "We have the means to fight back."

Smoke filled the halls beyond the kitchen.

"We have no choice," Bathsheba said. She threw her knapsack aside and nodded to Magdelena. The two stood near the doorway. Magdelena closed her eyes and lifted her palms. The three knives they used for cooking hovered over the counter and drifted to her.

Footsteps tromped closer.

"Lazarus, see if you can project panic at them," Magdelena said, "Adam, if Hagar really did give you her power, use it as best you can. Mind-fuck them. Don't let her gift die in vain."

Panic had been the wrong emotion, Adam later thought. In the moment, he only felt a vague nagging at the back of his mind as he prepared to enter the minds of the men who ran down the hall.

A flashbang grenade sailed into the room, but Magdelena raised a hand, and the cannister bounced, midair, back into the hallway. Magdelena fell back and swiped her hand at the door, which slammed shut as the grenade went off.

Even with the heavy door shut, the flash glowed between the joints, and the *bang* rattled Adam's bones. Outside in the hall, men screamed. The tenor of their panic oozed through the wall. Adam pushed out with his mind, but without direction or know-how on *mind-fucking*, it was like grasping at water. His ears rang, and everything sounded through heavy fog.

The door exploded inward. It knocked Magdelena to the floor, where she collapsed in a heap of hair and robes. Her miter rolled across the concrete and echoed like a bell as it hit the wall opposite. The knives clattered to the floor.

The Homeland Security thugs had pushed through whatever Bathsheba had shown them. Three men in black entered the doorframe, weapons raised but shaking.

The panic Lazarus had induced and the terror Bathsheba had shown them weren't enough. One of the men, a burly figure, said in a deep voice, "Open fire!"

Adam dove to the floor, rolling under a table.

Rat-tat-a-tat.

Red mist. A body hit the floor. *No.* Not him.

Lazarus. Staring, staring at Adam as blood spilled from his beautiful green coat. Those eyes so bright, now haunted by encroaching death. Lips moving to whisper untold secrets. Hands grasping. Fingers scrambling over blood-soaked concrete to find other hands.

Adam reached out.

The thugs continued to scream.

Lazarus closed his eyes but continued to breathe heavily.

They couldn't do this. Not after everything he'd survived to this point. Not after finally finding a place where he belonged.

Another body dove to the ground. Lot's Wife. She bled as she scrambled under the table.

The whistling of bullets stopped, and the men began to scream.

"Adam!"

He peeked out from under the table

Bathsheba stood, staring down the soldiers, sending them God knew what heinous imagery which terrified them into dropping their weapons.

The anger roiled beneath Adam's skin, rising again like it had that day at the Mall of America. He stood, slipping in blood as he did. Bathsheba maintained her stare at the soldiers, but he felt her anger, coming off her in cold, blue waves. Icy anger, deep as the ocean latched onto his anger and mingled with it. He placed a hand on Bathsheba's shoulder.

Adam saw what Bathsheba showed the soldiers: visions of damnation, monstrosities from a primordial depth, things without shape or form, nightmares of hell. Adam funneled those visions into himself, pulled them in along with Bathsheba's power.

Hairs rose on the back of his neck. His skin prickled. The lights in the room dimmed.

Adam focused on the soldiers. The angry pain in his head reached a peak, and it poured out of his skull in waves. With a thousand fingers, it felt its way under the soldiers' clothing and into their skin.

"How dare you," Bathsheba said. "How dare you come in here."

"You will not leave," Adam said, his voice a whisper.

The soldiers screamed. Their hands contorted. They clawed at their helmets.

Adam felt it. The vision Bathsheba had shown him, now a guide. He wove her hatred with his anger at seeing Lazarus dying on the floor, of Hagar dying in his arms. Adam funneled their rising power toward the soldiers.

He stretched their skin and split it, elongated bones and fused flesh to fabric, cracked cartilage and pulverized brain matter. Protruding veins spilled blood. Helmets fell away as faces twisted. Eyes bulged, exploded to reveal writhing brain matter squirming like the tentacles of some abyssal creature. Mouths opened to vomit, and in doing so released chunks of stomach tissue. Bodies fused together. New limbs jutted from Kevlar vests, creating multi-jointed abominations with claws soaked in blood. A nearby soldier's head fell from his body. Tentacles spilled from his eyes and the head scurried over the concrete to a dark corner to die.

One by one their bodies fell, and the mess of new limbs and merged torsos and fatty tissue spilled over onto the floor, and all was quiet. By their will, the soldiers had shifted from the old into the new, the nascent flesh — a rebirth in the most abominable sense.

"All dead," Lot's Wife said. Her whispering voice shook. "A helicopter and two jeeps outside. Nobody in them."

Adam fell to his knees. The exertion left him feeling like a husk. He wanted to roll under the table and sleep. But...

Adam pushed himself up, slipping in blood, and fell next to Lazarus, assessing the wounds. One bullet wound in the side, on the ribcage. Another bullet in the leg, but not the femoral artery, as the wound was near the knee. Lazarus breathed. Unconscious, and with a faint pulse.

"I can save him. Hagar died too fast. But *I can save him*!"

"Not here," Magdelena said. "We've got a safe house a few miles down the road. If we leave now, we can—"

A dead soldier's walkie talkie crackled, then a distant voice said, "Anderson...copy? Report, report!" Adam scrambled over to the deep-voiced soldier's body. His was the only walkie functioning.

Thinking on the fly, Adam cleared his throat, deepened his voice, and said, "Anderson here. Site secured. Target eliminated."

The walkie crackled. The voice said, "Reception's...come again...you say eliminated?"

"Affirmative," Adam said, his hands shaking. "All targets eliminated."

A pause. The walkie crackled again. "10-4. Secure bodies...report...half an hour."

"10-4," Adam said. He set the walkie back on the soldier's body and looked at the others. "Thirty minutes till they'll expect to hear back. I need ten. The rest are yours, Mags."

***

In Lazarus's bedroom, Adam knelt over Lazarus on the blood-soaked bed. From the distant kitchen, the sound of crying. Anger, fear, resolve wrapped together, coming out in waves from those left alive.

Focused only on the man he wanted to save, Adam barely registered the sounds of grief. Destruction was easy. For healing, he needed precision and focus, skin-on-skin intimacy to find every broken part of Lazarus to heal.

Adam stripped off Lazarus's shirt and ran his hands over the cool, firm skin.

Lazarus's training echoed in Adam's mind: *Imagine that your power is an invisible extension of your body. Stretch out your hand, extend your fingers beyond the physical; let them feel the flesh you want to alter. Focus your anger to a laser point, hone its edge and you'll be able to reshape the body, to destroy or to heal.*

Adam pressed his hand against the bullet wound in Lazarus's ribcage. Lazarus moaned weakly. Adam pushed his finger into the bullet wound. He found tears on the smallest level, in veins and fat and muscle. He made every wound in Lazarus's body his own.

They must become one flesh. He pressed further and deeper into Lazarus. Lazarus moaned, weak. Adam lowered his face to Lazarus's. He lay his lips upon Lazarus's forehead, pressed his waist against Lazarus's, entangled their bloody legs, and allowed himself, his anger and his fear and his love, to flow freely with the power now coursing through both of their bodies.

One flesh, one blood. Lazarus moaned again, in pain, but stronger.

Their clothes dissolved. The warm, bloody bedsheets became a womb around them. Sweating, caressing, they embraced within its folds. Fingers pressed against chests. Lips fought to devour. Two hearts beat as one. Flesh knit together.

Their ecstasy rose. Lazarus moaned again, stronger.

When it was done, Lazarus, though unconscious and covered in his exquisite blood, was alive. He'd briefly become lucid when they became one flesh. And now his pulse was weak but steady. Lazarus would survive.

***

The five gathered in the kitchen. Only Adam and Bathsheba were uninjured. Hagar's body lay on the table.

Bathsheba caressed Hagar's hair. Lot's Wife stood over them both. Gunfire had pulverized one of her hands, and it would need surgery.

"Adam, do you think Lazarus can be moved?" Magdelena pressed an ice pack against her temple. "We can't stay here. We'll get what we can into the pickup." An old, blue Chevy was currently stashed in the woods near the safe house.

Adam nodded, "I can carry him. But he can't go too far, not without medical care. And Lot's Wife…"

She moaned. "I'll live. And we have got to leave."

Magdelena set the ice pack on the table and stood. "There's a church in Edina, Amherst Memorial Baptist. Not one of *those* Baptist churches. This one took me in when I was starving, hid me in their basement, and fed me until I was strong enough to leave. I've maintained the connection. It's not a long-term solution, but they can hide Lazarus and Lot's Wife and discreetly get them the medical attention they need."

The dead soldier's walkie began to crackle again.

"That's our cue to leave," Bathsheba said. "And fast."

Minutes later, the group climbed out of the bunker into the Minnesota winter. Hurrying, they set off for Magdelena's pickup truck, their footsteps kicking up the snow and echoing over the barren land.

***

Bathsheba and Adam waited in the parking lot of Amherst Memorial Baptist, leaning against the side of the truck. The church's limestone façade cast a protective shadow over them. In the truck's bed, Lot's Wife tended to Lazarus.

"We drop them off," Adam said. "Then we dump the truck and look for another car."

The church's backdoor opened. Magdelena stepped out with two men. The first was tall and well-built. The second, shorter, looked at the truck and started over to it.

Magdelena opened the passenger door. "We're good. The church's choir director is a doctor. This is Pastor Michael-John Hope."

The shorter man nodded to Adam and Bathsheba. "Our basement is currently 'closed' for renovations. All access is forbidden, what with the work equipment down there." His eyes sparkled in the waning light. "If our coffers of food should run low at times, well, these things happen."

Magdelena said, "We must hurry. Pastor Hope told me something rather unsettling."

The pastor nodded, his face solemn. "The White House just announced their reparative therapy program will launch next month. To 'honor' Dr. Fisher's legacy. After the State of the

Union, Homeland Security will start sending representatives to schools to identify children to participate."

Bathsheba cursed. Adam willed his rising anger to subside for now.

"We need to stop them anyway we can." Magdelena took Adam's hand in hers and squeezed. "My dear, I know leaving Lazarus is frightening, but you can trust these folks. Not a single person who has gone into that basement has come out with a black bag over their heads, or in cuffs."

Adam said, "We can't stay here."

Bathsheba said, "The fewer of us who hide here, the better."

The taller man, a Deacon, helped Lot's Wife out of the truck bed.

"It's time for goodbye," Magdelena said to Adam. "Hurry."

Adam walked to the truck bed. Lazarus lay pale, wrapped in blankets. Adam took Lazarus's hand and squeezed, then leaned over and kissed Lazarus on the forehead.

"You are Lazarus for a reason," he said, his voice low. "You must, *must* live up to it. I don't know if I'll be back. But if I am...please be waiting for me. Please. I love you." He kissed Lazarus's cool forehead again and then stood back and nodded. The Pastor and the Deacon gently lifted Lazarus out of the truck bed and carried him inside.

Her face pale behind her lace veil, Lot's Wife trembled beside Magdelena and Bathsheba. "I don't know how Heep took those abilities for himself. If Hagar was able to give Adam her telepathy, Heep may have found a way to *take* what wasn't his. Bear that in mind."

Then, squaring her shoulders, she said, "Leave, and don't look back. Not even for a second. Eyes on the prize."

"We won't," Adam said. "I promise."

***

The lights of downtown Minneapolis mingled with urban smog. The cold air and acrid pollution burned Adam's lungs. Most of the traffic had thinned out for the night, at least. And he was near his goal. He only needed the right person. Adam paced the sidewalk.

Bathsheba and Magdelena were waiting back at the tent they'd pitched in one of the city's forested parks on the edge of downtown.

Adam turned a corner and passed a statue of some old television actress on the sidewalk. Adam sat on a metal bench across from the IDS Tower, the city's tallest building, and clenched his glutes as the icy chill of the metal seeped through his jeans.

He cleared his mind and imagined his skull cracking open and petals of brain matter drifting on the wind. Where they landed on people, these petals told him those peoples' thoughts.

Get home before the game, but—and who am I supposed to report to if Bobby doesn't—a few more hours' and I'll—blessed be the meek oh Lord for they—won't make it past the first date if she keeps going on about Beethoven's Ninth, whatever that is, and—vermin and filth, and the sooner gone the better.

Adam latched onto that last thought, finding its owner, a man somewhere near the top of the IDS Tower.

...wants us to get rid of more of the street filth but won't give us more money to do armed sweeps of vagrant encampments. Fucking mayor wants it both ways.

Perfect. Adam waited. The wind died down. The scent of smoke mingled with something frying down the street. Music echoed from one of the alleys.

The man eventually moved—downward, and then through the tower's lobby. Finally, he exited onto the sidewalk. Tall, pale, with a combover and a nose pinched like he'd smelled something rotten. Digging into the man's mind, Adam found bank statements comprising massive sums paid to judges for little favors from the bench, and he found a name.

Adam followed Frank Harper, keeping a respectable distance.

Down Nicollet Avenue, around a corner into a parking garage. Harper hummed *The Battle Hymn of the Republic*. Battle, indeed. Not so much a Republic, anymore—had it ever been? Perhaps in ways. Freedom for some, justice for all who had the means to pay for it.

Harper stopped at a black SUV. Perfect. A Subaru, even better.

Adam cleared his throat. "Frank Harper!"

The man turned. "Who are you? How do you know my name? If you're here from—"

"I'm from nowhere." Adam closed the distance between them. "I'm a nobody from a world that never was."

"What is this?"

Adam drew up to him. *Squeeze.*

"You are evil, beyond the grace of God. Or perhaps it isn't for me to judge your soul, only your actions. And yours make you the perfect candidate for a heart attack."

"I—" Franklin Harper gasped, clutched at his chest, and fell to the pavement.

***

Magdelena said, "You destroyed his SIM card?"

"Yes. Left the phone in his pocket." Adam walked around the back of the car and popped the hatch open.

Bathsheba caressed one of the side mirrors. "I call shotgun. Tell us, was he an awful man? Tell me he was. Oh, I could use a warm bubble bath right now just *imagining* how horrible his last moments were." She moaned, then tittered as she opened the passenger door.

Adam nodded. "Donated to Project Spectrum, back in the day. Paid off judges for things I don't want to talk about. But he died quickly." He turned to Magdelena. "You get the cash?"

Magdelena nodded. "Enough for five tanks of gas, give or take. And food. Let's get the show on the road."

Leaving Minneapolis was easy. Adam had feared a pull over, a police checkpoint, but neither had materialized. Nor did helicopters swarm them. Still, none of them breathed easily until the minivan passed over the St. Croix River into Wisconsin a half-hour later.

They stayed on the interstate until Eau Claire, after which Magdelena directed Adam to turn south on US-53. "Back-roads from now on," she said.

At around 1 a.m., Bathsheba sighed. "I don't think we'll be able to totally steer clear of towns."

"At the very least," Lady Magdelena said, "we stay the hell away from Chicago."

"Agreed." Bathsheba turned the overhead light on and unfolded another map. "We'll cut down through Illinois, then east through Indiana. But I think...yes. Let me do some more mapping."

"Adam," Lady Magdelena said, looking at the backseat. "Keep your eyes out for abandoned cars."

Around 3am, they came across a Honda Civic with 'FOR SALE: CHEAP! $5,000!!!" sprayed in neon green across its back. Bathsheba stood lookout while Magdelena and Adam swapped the cars' license plates. They then drove on.

***

They might have made the drive from Minneapolis to D.C. in about a day, but they'd driven strategically, taking isolated roads through Indiana, Ohio, and Pennsylvania, sleeping in the car or camping in the woods.

In Maryland, they found an abandoned, half-furnished apartment complex on the edge of D.C. The *Starliner Towers: Luxury You Can Afford!* were two five-floor buildings connected by a glass skybridge. Shattered windows on the first floor allowed them entrance.

"Home, sweet home for now." Magdelena tossed a few bags onto the dust-laden covers of a king-sized bed in an acceptable unit on the fourth floor.

Bathsheba went to the bathroom immediately to inspect its condition. She scoffed. "Not nearly big enough for a tub. My emergency bacon won't stick to these slimy walls, either. Still, it'll do."

Adam sprawled on the sofa and wondered whether Lazarus had regained consciousness and whether Lot's Wife was keeping an eye on him. She'd said not to look back, though, so Adam tried not to dwell on it, not with so much to plan.

Instead he thought about Hagar's transfer of power. Somehow, that gift seemed like the crux of everything. It felt like standing before a dozen incomplete puzzles and holding a single piece, knowing it was the key to completing one—but which one?

On their first evening, they sat huddled in the living room eating gas station fried chicken. Adam looked at the photos on the walls. A family, two men and two children, smiled from cracked frames. Where were they now? The possibilities turned his stomach, and he set his chicken down.

"I think it's clear," Bathsheba said as she tossed a chicken bone onto a paper plate, "Heep funded Project Spectrum. He essentially owns the government. That 'big donor' Adam talked about, the one Dr. Fisher wanted to impress, it must have been him."

Adam nodded "I have a vague memory of Fisher talking about the 'donor,' and how he wanted the 'best' results to be given to him."

"We'll give him results," Magdelena said. "The new must do away with of the old by means of the nascent flesh. We were made and remade by Project Spectrum to strip us of everything that made us Magdelena, Bathsheba, Adam—and in place we became what we are now. Yet our core remains."

"Turnabout is fair play," Bathsheba said, giggling, "They changed us, so we change them."

Magdelena said, "The neon-drenched nostalgia dreams of this nation must end. Thankfully, we have time to hone our plan and ready ourselves."

"How much do we make them suffer," Bathsheba said, nibbling a bit of chicken skin.

"Lazarus might have said to hold our peace, and think of other, better ways. Ways that Lot's Wife might approve of," Adam said. He looked at Magdelena, then at Bathsheba. "Once, he might have said that."

Basking her face in the sunlight Magdelena said, "Once, he might have. When the world was beautiful. When all was gold and the world was young, I sat under a tree in a white dress my mother made me because I asked her to; the skies were blue, the grass was green, and the breeze was light and tickled my face. She and I danced under that tree behind our house, Mother and her child who'd been mistaken for a boy but now lived as her Self."

"When all was gold," Bathsheba said.

"Three of us against a nation that wants us dead," Adam said. "We have to try. Before they start finally taking kids to conversion—."

Bathsheba held up her hand, "*Reparative* therapy centers."

"We came to win, not to survive."

Bathsheba said, "A toast, then. To Lazarus. May he rise. A toast to Lot's Wife. May she find them safety. A toast to Hagar.

May she be with us. And a toast to the end of this whole bloody mess."

They raised their Styrofoam soda cups.

Over the course of the evening, they reviewed their plan. A plan that might not work, that might get them killed, with the odds stacked so precipitously against them, but it was a plan.

*****

On the final day of March, the United States House of Representatives, the Senate, the Supreme Court, and the executive branch gathered in the hallowed chambers on Capitol Hill. The wealthiest of the Party's donors had a room to the side where they could mingle and watch from television screens. In the House chamber, cameras broadcast a line of cheerleaders in red, white, and blue bikinis who danced and chanted the President's name. *Jak-Of, Jak-Of, Jak-Of!*

The Vice President, a man whose name nobody bothered to remember because Jakof was on his forty-seventh Vice President, sat next to the Speaker of the House.

Speaker Jett Monsoon, a bespectacled man from Louisiana's 4th Congressional District, clapped out of time to the cheerleaders' chanting. One of his 'special girls,' about twelve or so, squirmed on his lap, wearing pink antebellum lace. The paragon of family values, the congressional face of the Party, he sniffed her blond hair. He then grinned wide as he squeezed the child's waist.

Adam watched this on the screens in the VIP public viewing room. He, Magdelena, and Bathsheba stood at the room's edge. Bathsheba had provided the illusion of suits and lanyards bearing VIP badges. It had been easy to walk right up to the Capitol and fit in with the crowd of wealthy donors.

"Champagne, sirs?" A waiter offered them drinks.

Magdelena waved him away. "Blessed be the fruit of the Lord. We do not partake in alcohol."

"Of course, sir," the waiter nodded and wandered off.

Adam whispered, "Still doing okay, Bathsheba?"

She nodded. "If I need to draw on one of you, I'll let you know."

"We need to make our way to the House chambers," Magdelena said. "Slowly, my dears."

On the television, applause erupted. President Jakof entered the House chambers, wearing a baggy navy suit, a red tie, and waving a small hand at the crowd. A nurse disguised as an aid guided the President and redirected him to the center of the aisle when he started to wander off. Behind them, Obediah Heep jumped around and high-fived members of the Senate and House.

The nurse injected Jakof with whatever kept him temporarily lucid.

Jakof, Heep, and the nurse mounted the platform. Heep looked out at the audience, slapped his right hand to his chest, then shot it out above his head. The cheering became nearly unbearable even in the VIP room.

Adam followed Magdelena and Bathsheba toward the doors leading to the House chamber.

When the applause died down, Jakof took his place at the microphone. Behind him, the dead-eyed Vice President clapped, and Jett Monsoon stroked the little girl's hair and whispered into her ear.

"My fellow Americans," Jakof said. He swept his arms outward as though to gather every listener in his embrace. "This is a beautiful day. The golden age of America continues as we fight to make America the best. They said it couldn't be done. But we did it."

Applause.

Hundreds of millions of Americans would be watching now or at least have their televisions on. The F.C.C. mandated that every household tune into the speech on their Party-issued television. Every ear in the nation, every eye, was attuned to the words of the man who had saved democracy from ruination, from free radicals.

Adam and the others stood just outside the House chambers.

"The gender extremists are gone," Jakof said. He leaned on the podium. "The normal people who want to just be left alone, you know, that's all they wanted. They said, 'Mr. President, we've got to go back to sanity. There's only two genders.' So I made it day one that there were two genders and used my authority to enforce it nation-wide. They said, 'Mr. President, you won't believe what they're saying. They didn't think it could be done.' And it's true. I don't ask for much credit, but I did it."

The nurse pricked him on the forearm. His eyes refocused.

"They said the Gulf of America would never happen, but I did it. I made the Gulf what it is, no windmills. Just last week in California we exterminated a group of gender cultists. We've got a press release all ready to go with the bodies, the pictures of the bodies."

Adam's anger flared. On screen, Obediah Heep clapped and grinned.

"Today I signed an executive order," Jakof said, "to implement reparative therapy centers across the nation, to fulfill Dr. Abraham Fisher's work with Project Spectrum! The kids will love it. We're sending patriots to schools next month to identify any corrupted children, and we'll fix them. My name is President D.T. Jakof, and I approve this message."

Adam said, "It's now or never."

Bathsheba sighed and closed her eyes.

They now looked like Secret Service members. Magdelena led them to the armed guards at the doors leading to the House chambers. She flashed a piece of paper, which looked like a silver badge. "Agent Wehrmacht reporting. We've received a request for more units."

You forgot, Adam sent to the guards, *you have been expecting us.*

The two guards blinked.

On the television, Jakof screamed angrily, and spittle flew from his mouth.

"Understood," one of the men said. The other guard opened the doors.

Magdelena led Adam and Bathsheba into the House chamber. Three of them versus the United States government. The room smelled musty. Heat from nearly a thousand bodies pressed in on Adam. They had to get far enough to make an impact. But the whole government was here. Doubtless, a designated survivor sat in a bunker somewhere. His head ached as they neared the stage.

Jakof said, "I love you Christians. Did you know that?" A bit of drool spilled over his lips.

A few congressmen looked at each other but continued to cheer.

"Adam," Magdelena said. "Hold my hand. We destroy the weapons first." He held her hand. Their power joined together.

Heep jerked his head and scanned the room. Jakof continued to speak. Jett Monsoon continued to stroke the child he'd purchased for the evening.

Magdelena sent a burst of power into the room. Tendrils searched for gunmetal. For bullets.

A Secret Service agent standing at the bottom of the stage yelped then hopped around. He tore his pistol from its holster, then dropped it to the ground. The metal glowed.

"Motherfucker!" Uniformed men around the room tossed their guns to the floor; a few screamed in pain with trembling hands and blisters held up for all to see.

Jakof continued to speak, but nobody paid attention.

"Obediah Heep!" Magdelena spoke.

Bathsheba dropped the camouflage, revealing to everyone in the room and in the nation the three interlopers standing before the podium. Magdelena pointed at Heep. "You are put on notice that we, the survivors of Project Spectrum, know the truth of what you did."

Heep grinned.

Magdelena shouted, "Adam, Bathsheba, now!" Adam and Bathsheba joined hands and projected a vision to all in the chamber; dog-sized roaches made of human flesh and with human eyes rushed under the seats and over the stage.

Congress scrambled. Secret Service men fell back, swatting at their faces and each other.

The oldest member of the Supreme Court stood, clutched his chest, and collapsed. He clawed his way over the blue carpet and soiled his black robes.

The three interlopers walked up the stage stairs.

Jakof rambled on. "And let me tell you, folks, we're going to make China pay, and pay big."

Heep grinned wider. "It's about time you showed up. The nation's been dying to meet you!" He lifted his hands as if in supplication, but a massive wave of energy rippled through the room, blowing papers everywhere, knocking people over.

The President tumbled and fell to the stage floor, where he mewled and thrashed his fists.

Heep said, "You think I wasn't prepared for this? I shall cross the Rubicon tonight, with you three as my boat."

He turned to the cameras and, through them, to every American. "I, Obediah Heep, am stepping in to protect you all. I am called to the Presidency, as is my duty as a citizen of this world. I have attained a level of enlightenment few can hope to ever achieve. With this power, I shall usher in a new age of Manifest Destiny! I shall begin with a demonstration of my ability to destroy these terrorists!" Heep turned to them.

On the House Chamber floor, Secret Service agents scrambled over each other, attacking one another thanks to Bathsheba's illusions. Congressmen and Senators scrambled to escape, but the stampede had been too hurried, and a pile of writhing bodies accumulated at the exits.

Jakof whimpered on the stage floor.

Adam, Magdelena, and Bathsheba stood together on the stage. Adam raised a hand and sent a wave of hot energy at Heep, but Heep batted it away as though it was a mosquito.

Heep laughed. He raised his arms. His blue suit rippled in invisible winds.

"You vermin! Motherfuck! You think you're smart? I knew you were coming here. I just didn't know the when or the how, you clever rats. But I knew, and I wanted it!" He jumped in the air as though cheering. "Stupid motherfuckers!"

"You people have held this land for too long," Magdelena turned to the camera. "Each and every one of you! Every person who voted for Jakof has blood on your hands, the blood of my siblings, of those too poor, too brown, too queer, too *other* to fit your narrow mold! You sold us out for the price of a carton of eggs!"

Jakof whined. "Mine! Bad wokes! *Mine!*"

"Shut up," Adam said. He fired off a tendril of energy, which tried to slither under the President's skin. But he met resistance.

Heep stepped in front of Jakof and raised a barrier of energy.

Adam and Heep faced off.

"He is my pet," Heep said. "And I decide what to do with him. Letting you come this far has allowed me to show the nation my powers."

"Powers you gained through murder," Bathsheba hissed.

Heep said. "Nobody misses a few thousand gender deviants. I thank you quite heartily for your service, but it is time to destroy you." He turned to the cameras and held his arms up. "Bear witness, America, as I destroy this degenerate filth! Know that it was I, Obediah Heep, who saved you! I am your hero! Your *superhero*! Vox populi, vox Dei!" Dramatically, he swept his arms in Adam's direction.

"Now," Magdelena yelled, "together!"

Adam joined hands with the others. Together, they only barely managed to push back.

Heep's power was a juggernaut. He attacked them with a wave of hot, pulsing energy that ballooned outward in a solid mass that shredded paper and skin. The Vice President and Speaker Monsoon both screamed.

Adam and the others pushed back with a barrier woven from their collective energy. The television cameras captured the glowing waves of dueling psychic energy.

The nation of Jakof devotees suckled at the glass teat which had for decades been their only source of news, entertainment, validation. Those who hated the regime also watched, feeling something they hadn't felt for over a decade.

"Adam," Magdelena said, "We'll funnel everything through you!" Adam felt the power of the others swirl into him, as he provided a conduit to push back against Heep.

Adam opened himself to the power of the others.

Heep pushed a wave of telekinetic energy at Adam. Adam pushed back, and their energy flooded the room. Their powers rippled like incompatible tides of oil and water, distorting and bending the air of the room. Everything caught in the crossfire began to distort and fall apart.

The podium splintered. Jett Monsoon screamed and thrashed in his seat. The little girl took her chance and scurried away.

Monsoon's head swelled like a ripe fruit, pale at first but then red and finally blue. His glasses broke and popped off his massive head. Speaker Monsoon stood and stumbled around. He tripped, and his head slammed against the wall. His skin and skull burst like a blueberry; their juices splashed across the American flag.

The Vice-President ran from his seat toward the side door before his body contorted, doubled over, and snapped as bones jutted from the skin and grew more bones. His skeleton scuttled like a spider across the stage, dragging skin and meat with it.

Heep screamed, "You shall not beat me! I am *God!*"

A wave of power hit Adam. Heep's energy edged ever closer. Even with the weight of his family's power behind him, Adam used every molecule of his strength to keep Heep at bay.

The President thrashed on the stage. Jakof squealed as the excess energy swept over him. He thrashed and screamed and squealed like a pig at the slaughter. His clothes fell away, torn to shreds by stray shards of telekinetic power. His hands and feet, pink like a baby's and gnarled like a crone's, beat against the floor. His small member flopped as he rolled. With every squeal he became more slug-like.

Shut up, shut up now and forever, Adam demanded.

The skin around Jakof's mouth fused together.

"Push! Break through his defenses!" The three summoned every drop of collective energy and pushed to break Heep's power, to cut it out of him if possible.

Heep squared his shoulders, lifted his head, and howled. His eyes rolled up in their sockets as he roared, and the whites glowed like the embers of hell. His suit came apart; half of his white tie fell to the ground and disintegrated. Yet Heep stood firm.

Adam felt the blood in his veins boiling. His skin crackled as though it were being fried in fat. He continued to push.

And then he remembered Hagar's gift. How had she given him her power? By sending her energy, her willpower, into him until she had nothing left to give. If it could be freely given, then it could surely be taken. In a better world, they'd ask, but they were not taking *from* Heep so much as taking *back*.

"Pull instead! Take his power!" The three, in sync, pulled at Heep's power.

As though a plug had been yanked from a drain, energy swirled around Adam and the others. Heep's mouth fell open, and his power wavered. It was all they needed. The tendrils of Heep's power flowed into Adam and the others. They pulled, and Heep grasped with his hands at air, clawing at them, but like water through a sieve, his power left.

Blood ran down Heep's face. His skin split. He fell to his knees as Adam, Magdelena, and Bathsheba took all he had.

As the waves of pure energy crashed in on them and swirled like a maelstrom, the fabric of the curtains and the flags lining the chamber ripped to shreds; wallpaper peeled, paint bubbled. The bodies of the government officials contorted and bent, melted, and twisted, forming new shapes, redefining the body politic. The cameras in the room glowed.

The cameras are absorbing our energy! We have too much—it's burning! Adam sent. *Send out the nascent flesh, send it to the ones who wanted it so badly! Our only chance! Together, now!*

Bathsheba shouted, "Enemies of Jakof and Heep! Turn your TVs off! *Look away!*"

Adam and the others filled the cameras with waves of monstrous energy, showing every viewer the truth of what they were, of what America was, what it had been, what it could be. The room glowed. The heat intensified, white and scathing.

Oh god, so much power! Don't stop, not yet!

Across the nation, a howling of rage, fear, joy, anger, ecstasy.

Now!

They let go.

Adam fell to his knees. He looked at Heep and Jakof.

The President resembled a tremendous pink slug with folds of flesh glistening wetly. The thing squirmed, thrashing tiny arms and grunting through its nose. It had no mouth, so it could not scream. A cavernous opening had split from the anus to the bellybutton, and it writhed and gaped as though hungry.

On his knees, Heep babbled and drooled blood onto the stage, little more than a shrunken child.

"Go," Adam said to Heep. "Go back to your master."

Heep, what was left of him, crawled to the massive slug.

"Baby wants Daddy," Heep said, his voice high and cracking. "Daddy love baby, please love baby." And he crawled into the cavernous space and became one with the flesh of Jakof. Heep's face pressed against the thin skin from within the slug's gut, and there it stayed, protruding and squirming like a living tumor.

Adam stumbled, spent. Bathsheba caught him and lowered him gently to the floor. Magdelena knelt with them, crying tears of joy. Fleshy things squirmed and skittered on the floor around him. Jett Monsoon's captive peered from behind curtains. Counting her, only four humans remained in the United States Capitol building.

***

So it was all across the nation. The nascent flesh came to pass like a prophecy of old; a populace which had grown dependent on the screen had changed by the screen, morphed into many heinous little creatures reflecting their true natures. The nascent flesh came to fruition for nearly all, except those who had looked away.

Across the former United States, abominations crawled around living rooms and kitchens. Skeletons danced with chitinous bodies in basements. So it was in the Presidential bunker, where the designated survivor, Jakof's Chief of Staff, had melted into a sentient puddle of flesh and bones, her eyes fused to the television screen.

The word made flesh.

***

Conclusion. Thus you witnessed the might of our power. Thus you saw the President and his followers contorted into monstrosities as their souls were made manifest for all to see. Those of you still able to read know what has come to pass.

They called us monsters for all our lives, and so monsters we became. We five are the Monstrum. Welcome to your new reality. Welcome to the Monstrum.

- Excerpt from the *Monstrum Proclamation*

Mathew is currently the vessel for a traumatized Victorian child. He is also a copy editor based in Minnesota. When he's not working as an editing gremlin, he's jogging, writing, and haunting the wily, windy moors. He's had stories published with Quill & Crow Publishing, Crystal Lake Publishing, the NoSleep Podcast, and others. His debut work, God's Own Country, is forthcoming Summer 2026 from Quill & Crow Publishing. You can find him on all socials @MathewLReyes.

NOT ALL MEN

BY WILE E. YOUNG

Chapter One

One-time decisions have a way of stacking up. Little things we do to break the monotony transform into barely managed habits before becoming addictions you can't imagine the day without.

I had never been a gym rat, One Christmas, my sister had gotten me a skintight pair of gym shorts that were still folded in the back of my dresser. They were more attention-grabber than workout attire, and I thanked her before moving on to the collection of fantasy smut novels my boyfriend at the time had gifted me.

Right when I moved into Thornbend, the pandemic happened, and I was stuck inside wiling the day away between Netflix documentaries and Covid tests. No more night life, no more social gatherings, just housebound and eating my feelings from a breakup.

I woke up one morning and decided it was time to disrupt the cycle of sleep, work, repeat. Digging around my closet produced a sports bra, a pair of shorts, and a band shirt from my obsessive pop-punk days.

The shirt lost its sleeves. An online order delivered a pair of running shoes two days later. I set out the following morning hoping I hadn't wasted money on something I would throw away a week later.

That Thursday morning wasn't too cold; a small rain had fallen in the dark of the early morning but had stopped once the sun crested the hills. The dew reflected droplets like a thousand tiny stars.

I started a light jog before slowing to a fast walk and taking in the sights. I'd moved here about four months ago for a new job.

Work had gone remote once the pandemic had begun, further confining me to my home, so this had been the first time I'd gone out to explore my neighborhood.

That walk became daily, and now four years later was valued routine. I found myself getting to know people. Turns out, my neighbors had been going stir-crazy too

My house was one among many identical homes constructed around circular roads that were easy to get lost in. At odd intervals, sparse trees overshadowed perfectly maintained lawns, lest a homeowner invoked the wrath of the HOA.

Never would have moved here if I had known.

It wasn't the first time I'd had the thought, and it wouldn't be the last. In theory, these covenants made sure the neighborhood maintained a certain level of presentability. In practice, busybodies exercised the pettiest power they could over their neighbors.

But it wasn't just the small tyrants. Each tree stood equidistant from the next one. The lawns maintained all perfect and green. The cars looked like variations on a theme.

Soulless.

I could barely stomach it, though some of the people made it better.

"Morning, Mr. Bobby," I called.

Earl Bobby had lived in our neighborhood the longest, long enough that some of the association codes didn't apply to him, grandfather clauses for a man six times the same.

He pushed his glasses up. The beginnings of cataracts had seen him announce his retirement as a surgeon, and he always said he would get them corrected any day now.

"Morning, Jessie!" his voice reminded me of peat and smoke, warm like he'd just stepped away from a campfire.

"Moving the plants?" I called as I made my way past his mailbox.

He nodded, the warm smile faltering for a split second. "They were Alicia's. Call me sentimental, but I'm not letting them die."

It made me sad considering his wife has passed nearly ten years ago. It wasn't the first time he'd mentioned it on our frequent run-ins.

"Well get to it! The cold waits for no one."

He said he would and that was the end of our interaction. Not the least bit out of the ordinary.

Maybe I should invite him over, see if he likes the yuletide fire and hot cider as much as I do.

It was my favorite time of year and my least favorite weather to walk in. The chill could get under your skin, and I sometimes worried my sweat might have to be chipped away with a scraper by the time I finished.

The snow hadn't come yet, but I hoped it would. There's nothing worse than spending Christmas at a muggy seventy degrees. Still, this neighborhood loses its dismal orthodoxy and comes alive in a show of color and decorations.

The Hollmans lived at the cul-de-sac at the end of the street and every year they adorned their home like kings. Most people in the neighborhood paid for someone to hang their lights, but Jordan Hollman insisted that a man should invest the sweat of his brow in matters of exterior illumination.

Propped on a ladder, trucker cap pulled low over his head to block the wind, the clack of his stapler echoing on the air, Jordan strung a fresh strand above the gutter. Maisey, his wife, inflated a twelve-foot snowman below. The gigantic coal grin emerged from beneath a faux carrot nose, and a friendly mitt waved.

How much money did they spend on this?

Maisey caught my eye. "Quite a sight, isn't it?"

That was one way to describe it. I pursed my lips and nodded. "Does he light up too?"

Maisey laughed, a rare thing...

Jordan leaned off the ladder. Flannel shirt and tan work vest, he looked like he'd just stepped out of whatever fresh offering Hallmark put out this year,. "Thinking about putting a full sleigh and reindeer on the roof for the kids, what do you think?"

The whole thing is a fire hazard.

"If it lights up, I'm sure any kid driving by is going to love it."

He smiled, a melancholy thing that could have milked tears from a dog. "Here's hoping."

After multiple failed IVF attempts they had tried to keep private, the news had spread like wildfire through our neighborhood. We'd brought the requisite tokens of sympathy, but how can you make up for a future that would never be? They would wring some Christmas magic from a world that had less and less.

"I'll leave y'all to it then. I've still got two miles to go."

Jordan waved and went back to his work. Maisey adjusted her dark gloves, featuring little snowflakes on the fingertips. "You're still coming to the party tonight, right?"

I nodded and waved, leaving her and her joy to the world, a baby has not come.

Liar.

It was a scathing thought, but the truth cuts deeper in our minds. These past four years I'd met my neighbors and assimilated into social gatherings I would have preferred avoiding.

I returned to my pace. This early in the morning, most of the usual suspects holed up in their kitchens, steaming coffee slowly bringing them back to life. It was one of the luxuries I treated myself to after this. For now, it was just me and my thoughts.

Hopefully my bonus is better than last year.

Should I go home to visit?

I don't want to spend this Christmas alone again.

Sometimes the answers to my thoughts would come, and sometimes I would ponder the same tomorrow. Those moments of clarity between the sweat and the sunshine felt like a heavy drug, the heady sensation of sitting at my kitchen table with the miles behind me.

I made the circuit to the most northerly part of my neighborhood, turned down Vine Street and headed for home with the last of three miles or so back to my house.

I knew my immediate neighbors, but this far out I usually encountered strangers.

Unfortunately, that didn't keep me from running into someone I'd rather avoid.

Casey Smith served as HOA president and a perennial nuisance. My own fine had come from hanging a flag on my porch advocating the Baltimore Ravens. The flag now gathered dust in my closet and Casey continued his morning rounds for violations.

You could spot him from down the street, usually in someone's yard making sure the flower beds contained the approved species. He drove a white Prius that may as well have had a flashing red and blue light on top.

Today, he stood by the curb taking note of a trailer parked in the Sosa's space, an honest-to-God measuring tape in his hand.

I slowed my pace and crossed to the other side of the street to avoid him. It was no use. In the quiet December morning, my footsteps may as well have been hailstones. He looked up and smiled the unpleasant grin that reminded me of a rodent.

I tried to pick up the pace, but he quickly crossed to intercept me.

"Jessie, Jessie, hey!" he called.

I stopped and forced myself to smile. His high-pitched, nasal voice reminded me of a villain from a Saturday morning cartoon,.

"Morning, Casey," I said, trying to keep my own voice neutral.

He forked a thumb at the trailer. "Rules violation. You know how it is."

I shrugged. "Paid my sixty dollars for a fucking flag."

Maybe I was too aggressive, too bitter, but Casey was a societal ill. A fucking busybody, he used his small modicum of power to make life miserable for others.

The small laugh chittered from his throat was forced, awkward. "Yeah, well uh, it's the rules. Have to the follow the rules."

I didn't return it. "The Sosa's brought everyone fresh cookies when they moved in. Maybe give them a little grace?"

Casey Smith looked like the idea of grace made him constipated. "I wish I could, but that trailer is hanging eight inches out into the road, I've got to cite them for it. Plus, technically, you're only supposed to have your personal vehicles in your drive." The notebook landed in his hand like a pistol as he began fiercely scribbling. "Rules and consequences, have to adhere to them."

Call it the last straw, the dam breaking, or the boiling over of rage against petty abuses of power. I snatched the notebook from his hand and began walking towards the nearest trash can, ripping pages as I went.

Casey trailed after me, protesting, reciting a litany of violations.

I opened the lid and threw in the notebook. Casey began to dig, continuing to spout his bullshit, thinking I was a captive audience.

My walk continued, this time at a jog.

God, he gives me the creeps.

I paused. A shiver that had nothing to do with the cold running through me. What had that been? I'd read about inner monologues and self-actualization. An intrusive thought?

I kept walking, relegating whatever it had been to the minutiae of my mind. It would wither and fade like the plants the association gardener, Billy Chase, tried to keep through the winter. His fingerprints were evident through the neighborhood, shrubbery desperately clinging to life amidst the cold drought, iron plants that had gone brown and now resembled shriveled corn stalks rather than the hardy things they had been.

The flower garden at the entrance to the neighborhood was the true eyesore. Wilted flowers hung from their stalks in disgrace, dropping petals formed a tableau of shame, a beautiful, tragic display in yellow, pink, and purple amidst the red mulch.

How on earth does Casey tolerate this idiot?

The incompetent in question drowned the flower bed from a can, less like a shower and more like a solid column of water. Billy Chase was tall. Every Halloween since I'd moved here, he'd slapped on green face paint and some glued-on electrodes to act out a bad imitation of Frankenstein. His bushy eyebrows furrowed, his long lips pulled into a tight frown as if the drowned flowers still haunted him. He looked up as I passed, setting the can down and breaking into a wide grin which missed a few teeth.

I returned the wave before turning the corner and heading home. I broke into a sprint as I saw my house a hundred yards or so at the end of the row. This was the only cardio I really incorporated, the sudden burst eliciting more sweat than the small perspiration I managed to work up from a steady stride. By the time I reached my house, I panted hard, a stitch developing in my side. I bent over, leaning on my knees and catching my breath.

Behind me, a car honked. I turned to see a devilish and smiling grin leaning out of the truck. "I sure like the view!"

I immediately straightened up and returned the smile. Denim-wearing and handsome as hell, Luke Hopper was the youngest bachelor in the neighborhood. We'd been going around as friends who were turning into something more. Nothing had been said between us other than the indirect flirting... and now an overt cat call.

"Step off a construction site? What the hell kind of comment is that?" I replied.

He shrugged. "Calling it like I see it. How was the walk?"

"Not bad, ran into the regulars. How was work?"

An I.T. guy for a local communications company, Luke worked long nights that often bled into the following mornings,. I didn't envy the hours, but the salary more than made up for it. Luke always said it made him more active in the early evenings and mornings, the best time of day to see the beauty of the world.

"Maybe I'll make it back home earlier tomorrow. Mind if I join you?"

And there it was, the next step, the jump from our light flirting to overt courtship. I returned the smile. "Yeah, I'd like that."

"Deal. And in the spirit of that, I'm going to go get some sleep." He waved as he drove off. His house was three blocks over, a two-story Tudor affair, white and brown paneling with evergreen plants around the flowerbeds.

I returned the wave and turned to unlock my door.

A thought struck me and gained volume until it commanded my attention.

I've read how some people have an interior monologue, the imagined words journeying through the psyche in our own voice. This thought came and the abstract was powerful and not my own.

Oh god… please don't kill me.

Chapter Two

My stomach wrenched and I dry heaved, trying to keep the banana I'd had for breakfast down. Maybe it was the sweat, the sudden temperature difference from the frigid outside to the indoor warmth, but chills ran over my entire body.

Get it together, Jessie. Stranger things have happened.

Except, stranger things had never happened, not to me anyways. I wasn't sure what to think. A panicked giggle escaped me.

Thinking is really the last thing you want to do.

The unknown has a way of drawing out the animal in us, that reptile part of the brain that never left the jungle, the part that wants to hide in a cave until the storm blows over. The vanity mirror in my bathroom reflected my panic.

Steady, breathe, it's over, it won't...

I couldn't even tell myself it wouldn't happen again. That had been proven true within five minutes, and I wasn't sure what *IT* even was. A stray thought couldn't hurt you; I'd had twenty-eight years of them, but this was different. For reasons I didn't understand, I felt afraid.

Staring at your sleep deprivation and sweat isn't going to help anything.

I turned the shower knobs, listening to the water cascade against the porcelain tub. My clothes fell into a pile beside my door and I stepped into the shower, sighing at the delirious warmth flowing over me.

Mama had liked to tell me, in her sobriety between drinks, that I'd spawned straight from hell. With the heat I liked to bathe under, I could almost believe her. Steam poured everywhere, fogging the mirror and the window as I lathered my hair.

By the time I'd gotten to my body, what had happened had slid to the back of my mind. Still there, still waiting to be acknowledged, but for the moment, I was lost in the haze of comfort and the feeling of my fingers running the shampoo through my dark locks.

God, this feels good.

Skye, you deserve this.

My eyes flew open and I slipped. I went down hard, yelping as my head bounced on the stone-lined wall. Stunned, I curled into a ball. The scalding heat of the shower sprayed across my face.

It's hard to explain a violation of the psyche, at least in terms most people can understand. It was like a hand suddenly taking a will of its own; you tell your finger to move, but it dances to something else's tune.

Shivering despite the heat, I sputtered and turned my head to keep from waterboarding myself. The water droplets ran down the porcelain like a thousand tiny eyes. I slid away from the small reflection in each bead.

I finished my shower as quickly as possible, wrapping myself in a towel and blow-drying my hair. My hands trembled and I tried to keep my mind blank, focusing on each strand of hair, hoping commitment would keep the intrusive thoughts from flaring up.

Skye...

I winced at the errant word, accidentally yanking at the wet strand of hair I'd been working on.

It was a name in my heart. I knew it, and like all the thoughts that had come so far, I knew it was a woman.

The only problem? I didn't know anyone named Skye.

***

The next half hour was tense. I finished my hair and wrapped myself up in the rattiest hoodie I'd stolen from my ex-boyfriend. There was no sentimentality attached to the thing, it was just comfortable and good for keeping away the chill of a winter day.

I logged into my computer while I waited for my coffee to warm. When I'd taken this job, I'd expected long hours confined to a cubicle. I'd traded that for long hours confined on my couch with a makeshift desk and far fewer interruptions from some middle management idiot with nothing better to do.

As things were, I finished the majority of my morning queue by the time the Keurig started spewing out my caffeine. I clasped the handle, gingerly walking it back to my desk.

Does Skye like coffee?

It was an honest thought, but I still laughed. I'd gone around the bend, obviously. I'm sure any number of therapists could have prescribed something to ensure it was just little old me in my head.

Like ghosts or demons or the bullies in grade school, just ignore, don't engage. Every rational bit of sense I had told me to enjoy my coffee and get on with my day.

Still the advice didn't stop me from googling the name: Scottish Island, Paw Patrol character, other bits of useless information that didn't satisfy the itch.

Oh god... please don't kill me.

I remembered the thought, the consuming fear, and I typed in "Skye "and "Murder" which brought up several homicides in Scotland.

Sighing, I took a sip of my coffee and whispered to myself, "Girl, you might be losing it."

Indulging this kind of thing seemed a terrible idea. I had a good job, a good home, maybe even love if things with Luke turned out right. There was no reason for me to keep typing, nothing but curiosity, and the vain hope the voice might stop if I proved to it there was nothing to find.

This time I added the name of our neighborhood, Thornbend, to the search. Taking a gulp of my coffee and closing my eyes to savor the subtle flavors, I expected to open my eyes and see another plethora of results regarding Scotland.

THORNBEND RESIDENT, SKYE BURTON, STILL MISSING.

My hand trembled, my mouth went dry, and my heart danced in panic as I read the lurid details in fine print.

<u>OKC Morning Edition:</u> An avid runner, Skye Burton was last seen by her neighbors briskly heading past the neighborhood's entrance on her way towards the cemetery. Her husband, Tripp Burton, reported her missing a few hours after she failed to return. Her neighbor Earl Bobby said she referred to the graves as "her friends," adding "God-willing, she hasn't joined them."

Oh look, he hasn't moved out of the damn bed.

I moaned and clutched my head as her thought came, feeling my nails dig into my scalp like they could pierce my brain and claw the thoughts away. Reason told me a thought couldn't hurt, even one that wasn't mine, but reading this Skye woman's story did nothing to assuage my fears.

Tripp Burton… I didn't know the man, even if he still lived here. Had this been their house?

No, I'd done my due diligence, making sure there were no suicides, burial grounds, or murders. But a disappearance, could they have ignored that?

Steady, Jessica. You're hearing a missing woman's thoughts in your head, that's all. No big deal. Happens to people every day.

Lying to myself about the slightest stress was a bad habit. When my last job had thrown two other jobs' worth of work at me, I'd said I could handle it. When the check engine light came on in my car, I ignored it with the certainty it would disappear.

I could ignore this, had to ignore this, bury my head in the sand, and do my fucking work.

Or you could ask Luke.

"Fuck, fuck, fuck fuck…" I muttered to myself, downing the entire cup of java. Profanity-laced denial or not, I knew what I would do. I just had to get through the rest of my workday.

And I couldn't let my thoughts wander, or anyone else's enter.

Chapter Three

Skye Burton remained quiet, for all the good it did me. But nothing could keep me from chasing my curiosity down the internet.

They never found her, now eight years since the initial report without a trace or a lead, and a trail colder than the ice on Lake Michigan.

It seemed completely negligent, especially in the day and age of the traffic camera. Someone saw something, had to have seen something, people don't just disappear. Tripp Burton had been declared a "person of interest," but he'd stuck to his story.

Slowly but surely, time had relegated Skye Burton to the annals of women forgotten by the public as the cruelty of the world created newer mysteries and atrocities. I wondered if a podcast out there covered this. It had all the hallmarks which true crime junkies salivated over: a good mystery, and a man suspected but never proven.

She's a lot like me.

My mother had once said I had traveling feet and a restless soul, and that's why I liked walking so much, and why I had bounced around the country in various low-effort jobs. I wasn't rooted down. Even my thoughts always wandered.

Had Skye been the same way, a restless soul with wandering thoughts who kept wandering after she had been killed? I didn't have the answers. I laughed at that; only four hours had passed, and it felt like I'd wandered into a funhouse. Reality was stretching to the limit, people couldn't just hear a dead woman's thoughts. I wondered if anyone else could hear her, Luke, Billy Chase, the Hollmans...

Another banner year at the Hollmans' Christmas Adam party, a good idea made by terrible people.

Her thoughts were like lightning strikes through my head and brought with them a good idea. Everyone in Thornbend attended that fucking party, and it was high time I joined the club.

Thanks, Skye.

***

My work let us off early, "a gift from us to you" to celebrate the holidays. What was I going to tell Luke when I showed up at his door?

Hi! I'm hearing a dead woman's thoughts in my head and thought you might be able to answer whatever questions I had about it.

I groaned, lightly hitting my head against my refrigerator door and wondering how many drinks I was going to have to down at the party to silence the voice in my head... both of them.

Deciding at the very least I should look presentable, I replaced my lounging clothes with a green sweater and jeans, then left.

The bitter chill hit me, sending the small flurries that clung to my porch billowing out into the wind. I wrapped my arms around myself.

God, the wind never stops blowing here.

It wasn't as painful anymore, hearing her thoughts, more migraine instead of a lightning strike.

"You said it, sister," I whispered, beginning my walk to Luke's.

An overcast sky had taken hold over the day, and the temperature dropped accordingly. Most of the morning risers were definitely not outside now. Skye's home address hadn't been listed anywhere I could find, and the photo the media had put out could have been any home in this neighborhood.

They had provided a picture of her.

She had dark hair and a coy smile; she'd been at a party or event of some kind. Tripp had done a good job choosing a picture emphasizing her prettiness, and how much fun she had.

I imagined her in every window, some adorned with Christmas lights, like funeral candles around a grave. I paused in front of a home, staring at the tree decorated with ornaments, stockings hung in a row above the fireplace mantle behind. For a moment, I was lost in the dusting of snow and the twinkling of lights. Two kids, a boy and a girl, laughed and watched an animated Christmas special. Their mother sipped a hot drink and scrolled through a phone.

"They're good kids," a voice called.

I nearly jumped out of my skin and turned to see a man climbing out of his truck. He wore a suit and had a small stack of files in one hand, his phone in the other. He had a thick brown beard and could have passed for Santa Claus's younger cousin.

He waved the phone. "Don't tell my wife, but sometimes it's nice to de-stress before going inside to be a dad."

Better hurry, she looks checked out.

I smiled. "My lips are sealed."

He laughed. "I'd offer my hand, but you can see they're full. You're Jessica Logan, right?"

How did he know my name?

He must have seen my discomfort because he immediately spoke up. "I'm on the HOA board. We approve every applicant moving in here. You fit the description, not to mention Casey goes on about your walking habits."

Oh god, that's even worse.

I hoped my smile would pass muster. "Yeah, I see him most mornings. But I don't attend the meetings, so I can't say I know you."

He laughed. "Sorry, sorry, Brent Fischer. I'm the treasurer."

You look better with your shirt off, Brent.

I froze, my head pounding, and I must have looked nauseous. Brent quickly intervened. "Whoa, hey, are you ok?"

My mouth went dry. I coughed into my arm, trying to work up saliva, waving off Brent as he moved toward me.

"I'm good, I'm good. It's a little cold and I haven't had enough water today. I just got a little lightheaded." The words tumbled out of me; the perennial excuse of poor health for a woman wanting a man to keep his distance.

He took a step back, through the grass towards his door. "Well, ok. I need to get inside; I think Alice just noticed I'm talking to a strange woman in our driveway."

I glanced to his window and saw his children cheering to see their father.

Alice looked rather annoyed.

I hope you're a better father than a husband, Brent.

"Hope to see you at the party!" He called.

I gave him a halfhearted platitude and watched him go inside. His kids immediately ran to hug him, but his wife lingered a moment before giving him a cold peck on the cheek.

Do you know what he's done?

His wife turned to glare at me, and, for a moment, I wondered if I wasn't alone in hearing wandering thoughts.

I moved along, but one more errant thought came to me.

For a mother and father who are blonde, those kids sure have dark hair.

***

Luke broke into a big grin when he saw me standing at his door. I shivered and rubbed at my forearms to ward away the bitter chill seeping under the fabric of my sweater.

"Are you going to invite me in? Or are you going to leave a girl hanging?" I asked.

He ushered me inside, and I made my way towards the crackling fire in his living room. Wood burning was attractive in a man, because he took the time to gather the necessaries and not take the easy way out of installing a gas line.

"The temperature took a nosedive!" I said, feeling the warmth slowly spread back through my extremities.

"No kidding. Just means we're probably in for a blizzard," Luke called from the kitchen to my right. He swiftly emerged with two drinks, hot and steaming, and I could smell the telltale hints of cinnamon.

Clutching the mug, I gingerly tasted it and the overwhelming spices of cider swept me away. "Fuck, this is good," I sighed.

He smiled. "Wassail. My family's own recipe. Don't know what it has to do with Christmas, but it tastes so damn good."

I saluted him with the mug and both of us took a long drink. It may as well have been nectar from the gods with the way it settled in my stomach and spread like a comforting hug.

If this works out, I'm going to ask for it every day.

Luke lowered his mug and I realized I'd caught him not at his best. He'd always dressed like he came straight off a romance book cover; his baggy hoodie and matching sweat-pants were a new experience for me. Of course, this might have been his pajamas, working through the night as he did.

He smiled and placed his mug on the coffee table, adorned with a few outdoor magazines that looked well-read. "I didn't expect to see you until tomorrow morning, but I'm glad you came over."

The warmth in my stomach disappeared as I tried to maintain my smile. I'd come for a reason, not a cider date. No matter how much I would have liked to continue it.

An awkward silence hung between us as I tried to approach Skye's disappearance. He took another drink from his mug, waiting.

Come on! Just spit it out!

"Sorry, I don't really know what to say. I read something that rattled me." My words tumbled out of my mouth like snow in an avalanche.

Luke's eyebrows rose and he set the wassail aside. "Oh, ok. I uh, well let's hear it. Though I've never been the best therapist, just to warn you."

I smiled. "I actually doubt that."

He shrugged. "What's eating at you?"

Oh nothing, just the thoughts of a dead neighbor who went missing under mysterious circumstances.

"Ok, well I'm sort of a true crime junkie and I heard a story about a woman in our neighborhood—"

His comforting smile vanished and he said her name. "Skye Burton."

Even though I'd read the stories and had seen her picture, hearing her name spoken aloud made it real to me. I wasn't just suffering a fever dream I was going to wake up from. "I just— It bothers me when there isn't an answer. Like whoever did it is still out there and can do it again. It scares me."

God, you sound pathetic. The only thing you're afraid of are clowns and trains... and weird thoughts running through your head.

Luke finished the last of his drink. He looked away from me to the crumbling logs in the fireplace. He'd been here when it happened, and now he was back there.

His gaze didn't leave the embers as he spoke, "It's something we don't really talk about. The quickest way to kill the mood is to mention her. She's never far from a Thornbend resident's mind."

I let him talk, not wishing to break whatever spell this was.

Luke bounced the empty mug back and forth in his hands. "The truth is, we all failed her. That was a time before everyone came together here as a community before we all got to know each other."

Well, that explains a lot.

"Someone could have gone with her or at least kept an eye out at the cemetery. It's not like the world was any safer seven years ago. Like you said, it's worse that no one could find her, or find who took her."

His eyes grew hard. I'd seen the look in my ex. It was a look of pure determination, all-encompassing, a silent vow to never let anything like it happen again.

He reached over and clutched my hand, and I let him. "We watch out for each other now, share our victories and our struggles, which is why I'd like if you actually came with me to the Hollman's party tonight."

I'd LOVE to.

A small gasp of pain escaped my lips, and I clutched at the corners of my eyes. Unlike the last, this one had come with an intensity tenfold. Luke's hand immediately went to my shoulder, and I heard his concern. "Are you ok?"

Have to lie, have to lie...

I tried to force a smile. "Yeah... yeah, I've just been having these migraines lately and they hurt like a bitch."

Keep the smile up, don't flinch.

Luke nodded, his mouth set in a frown. "This is bringing me back. I was with a girl once who had migraines every other day. She downed more Tylenol than anyone I've ever met." He said the last part with a chuckle I'm sure was meant to put me at ease.

The fire behind my eyes had started to abate, but my heart pounded like it was Seabiscuit on the last lap.

Luke had invited Skye somewhere, and she'd loved to be able to go.

He held up his hands. "Sorry, sorry, I just got lost in the moment there. Should never bring up an ex in polite company. Umm, I think I have some Tylenol if you want some?"

I nodded. "That would be lovely."

He stood and gave a mock bow. "As you wish."

The pain had mostly abated. My request for pharmaceuticals got him away from me for a few moments. A shiver passed over me as an idea passed through the back of my mind. I didn't want to believe it.

He seems awfully guilty for a man who barely knew her.

I didn't know what I should do. What could I do? I didn't want to do anything but to go home and snuggle up under a warm blanket with a Christmas movie I'd seen a thousand times.

But that wouldn't get rid of the voice plaguing my head.

I forced myself to sit; fidgeting and nervous I would let slip something that would turn the warm and caring man into something else. It wouldn't be the first time I'd faked it until I made it out of a bad situation.

He returned, a fresh cup of water in his hand, and two Tylenol. "You can never have enough water."

I nodded and downed the pills. "Thanks, I'm already feeling better."

Luke pointed to the water. "Keep hydrated. The way you walk every morning, it wouldn't surprise me if you weren't getting enough fluids."

"I'm a big girl, I can handle it," I said, an edge of ice trickling into my voice.

He held up his hands. "Not trying to offend, just showing I care."

God, I really hope you mean that.

His voice cut through my thought, "Not to press or anything, but I really would like you to come with me tonight to the Hollman's party. You know Russ, and our 'esteemed' association president. But everyone else, well, you've never really taken the time to get to know them."

I know all I need to know, Luke. I catch half of them staring when I stretch.

Despite the pain, I kept a straight face. Her thoughts contained something else, call it inflection, tone, feeling... She'd had a burning lust for the man in front of me.

Luke hadn't caught the flare up of thought. "So, will you at least consider it? Coming with me tonight? Hell, I'm just going to flat out ask, will you be my date to this thing?"

A few hours ago, my heart would have dropped through my stomach in excitement.

Should I bring a knife too?

"I'd love to," I said calmly.

He smiled broadly, not noticing my lack of excitement. "Well alright then. Can't wait! Oh, and I don't want you to worry about Skye. I promise I'm not going to let anything happen to you."

Why promise that?

I reached over and grabbed his hand, trying to keep my heartbeat from racing straight out of my chest, hoping he didn't notice the line of cold sweat drifting down my brow.

"Thanks. It scared me and well... it's just good to hear that it made our neighborhood safer."

What are you? A fucking PSA?

If he thought anything of the lame response, he didn't let it slip, instead standing and gesturing to the gigantic analog clock he had set in the wall. "Speaking of, I need to start getting ready. Showing up to this thing in my lounge arounds would be the talk of the neighborhood all year round."

I let out a sigh of relief when he turned his back. Hoping he hadn't heard, I hastily headed past him towards the front door. "I think I might freshen up myself."

He opened the door. "I think you look fantastic. I'll stop by your place at five. We can walk over there together?"

"Sounds like a plan." I said.

He returned it and shut the door, "See you then."

I started walking, feeling the hairs on the back of my neck begin to stand. I could imagine him at the window, fogging the glass as he watched me head up the street.

Is he following me?

Her thought nearly sent me tumbling to the frozen street, but I kept my footing, kept walking, kept wondering if I had been lucky to walk out of Luke's house.

Chapter Four

With my previous shower, it didn't take long to ready myself. When Luke said it wouldn't be best to dress down, I was left to guess just how formal I was required to dress. I put away the slinky black number as about seven years and one lockdown out of date, and decided a dress red enough to be blood and a black coat would suffice.

Then I had nothing left to do but wait for my date to arrive.

I fidgeted, trying to keep my thoughts quiet. I'd turned every light in my house off as the winter sun made its descent, bathing the interior in orange half-light. Shadows lengthened. The neighbors' Christmas lights blinked on.

Jolly and bright.

My heart raced as the clock ticked closer. I wondered what Skye had told Tripp Burton about her journey to the Hollman's if that indeed was where Luke had invited her.

Had Tripp been working, too tired to notice his wife was stepping out? Had she even BEEN stepping out?

The doorbell rang and I jumped from my couch, ruffling the folds of my dress and cursing as I grabbed the small clutch and headed towards the door.

Calm yourself, you're going to a party not a murder.

A blurry figure stood beyond the windowpane, as if the world conjured the idea of a man without worrying about the finer details. I opened the door and smiled. "If it wasn't a block away, there is no way we'd be walking in this."

The snow came down in thick flakes that swirled around in miniature cyclones in the wind. Luke smiled. "I don't know, I think there's something romantic about bad weather, the more inconvenient the better. You look beautiful."

I blushed. I couldn't help it. He may be a secret murderer, but he knew all the right words. "Thanks, let's get this show on the road, because my legs are freezing."

He wore dark jeans with a plaid red and black blazer over a deep navy vest and tie. Formal, but fun, and any other day would have had my mind imagining the pictures I'd be able to post.

As it was now, I wondered if he'd chosen the same outfit when he'd taken Skye out.

I reached for the black jacket I'd left hanging on the rack and he reached over and gently took it, opening it for me. The action was pure gentleman. Little more than decoration, the jacket barely drove away the cold. After locking my door, I carefully navigated my drive in heels. He offered his arm, and I reluctantly took it.

I really hope I'm wrong about you.

The snow had started to pile, and the low-hanging clouds reflected the neon festivities of the office buildings a few miles away.

"It's like a poor man's northern lights," Luke said.

Our destination may have only been the end of the street, but I still needed to make conversation. "I've always wanted to see the real thing."

Squeezing my hand, Luke smiled. "Maybe we can go someday? I hear Iceland is a fantastic vacation."

I hoped he thought the tension in my arm was because of excitement. "Hell yeah, I've always wanted to throw something into a lava flow."

We passed Earl Bobby's house, and the older man stepped out, bearing a small gold present with a red bow in his hand. He whistled when he saw the two of us. "Well look at that, about time."

Luke waved his spare hand. "Mind your business, Earl. Nothing official yet. She's just making sure I'm not a lonely sap at the party."

Earl laughed and turned his attention to me. "Jessie, you're a lovely sight. Happy you finally decided to join us for this shindig."

His words relaxed me, knowing the older man would be there made me feel less alone, less vulnerable. "Thanks, Mr. Bobby. You're looking sharp too."

Even under his dark skin, I thought I could see the hints of a blush. He adjusted the bright red bow tie like a peacock preening its feathers. "Alicia always said that a bow tie completed my image, but I always thought they looked silly."

"I think it makes you look smart."

He smiled as he joined us on the walk. "You have a keeper there, Luke."

Please help me, Mr. Bobby.

I stopped dead in my tracks and covered up a splitting headache by rubbing my eyes. "Damn snowflake landed right in it!"

Both men cooed over me, asking the standard questions. I tried to keep my hand from trembling, but Luke noticed. "Are you ok? You're shivering pretty hard."

I waved him off. "Yeah... yeah... it's just freezing. Let's get to the party."

At least it isn't you.

That thought was little comfort as I walked next to the old man who Skye had begged to rescue her. Was she still alive? Where could he be keeping her? His house didn't seem big enough to have a basement...

It was surreal; Mr. Bobby seemed so nice, and gentle, but I didn't have time to dwell on it before we were at the Hollman's. They had managed to finish their display, and now enough inflatable snowmen and reindeer filled out a drive-through light show. Cars filled the street and their driveway.

I stepped to the other side of Luke when he reached out for the doorbell, keeping my distance from Earl.

The chime was loud inside. Even through the door I could hear the muffled din of conversation. A blurry figure moved behind the glass and Maisey Hollman threw open the door. She wore a fur-lined dress and a pair of fake antlers I was unsure weren't meant for a dog.

She smiled broadly. "Welcome! Oh my gosh, Jessie! Hello!" Her melancholy from this morning was completely gone. If I hadn't seen it for myself, I would have thought I was in an episode of *The Twilight Zone*.

She ushered us inside. I only knew a few of the faces in the positively packed house. Luke offered to take my coat and my clutch. I never took my eyes off Earl as he immediately gravitated to an older couple dressed about ten years out of date. I watched him dip a glass into a punch bowl filled to the brim with eggnog. I could see his lips move, but I couldn't hear what he said over the din of the crowd.

A hand grasped my elbow, and I jumped in place.

Maisey took a step back. "Sorry, girl, didn't mean to startle you. Just wanted to tell you how stunning you look in that dress." *I wonder if the rest of these people are body snatchers too...*

"Yeah, it's an old thing. I don't really get out much," I replied.

Maisey laughed. "Now we know that's a lie, I see you out walking every morning."

It was the most asinine point I could possibly think of, but I grinned and shrugged it off as if she'd said the funniest thing I'd heard in weeks. "Well, yeah. I should say I don't make it to many parties."

The woman nodded sagely. "We throw these parties every year, and for eight of those, I haven't taken an ounce of joy from them. We had trouble— well, I'm sure Luke gave you all the gory details."

They want a baby.

My hand jumped to my forehead, and I felt Maisey's comforting one on my shoulder.

"Oh, hey. You alright?"

Lost in Skye's thoughts, I wondered what had caused her to think the Hollman's longed for children. I forced a smile. "Yeah, just having a lot of headaches lately."

She offered me the usual flight of painkillers.

"Some aspirin would be great," I replied.

I followed her into the kitchen, a farmhouse style endeavor with a buffet of holiday delights covering the island. A few neighbors made liberal use of the Hollman's wine selection.

Their medicine cabinet was filled to the brim. Maisey rifled through her miniature pharmacy. "Paid a pretty penny for most of these and it turned out to be completely useless." Her words were bitter, but they were replaced with a manic cheer. "But we found a way."

"You're pregnant?" I asked, feeling an upswell of joy for a woman finally achieving her desires.

"No, but we decided on a different route. You'll find out tonight, just like everyone else."

She handed me the aspirin and I clutched them tight, wondering at her words.

The pills...

My eye twitched and I tried not to drop the aspirin in shock.

Is it even aspirin?

It was an errant thought, but it sent my heart racing and fresh beads of sweat bubbled up from my pores.

"Are you ok? You're looking a little sick?" Maisey asked.

I nodded, feeling a shiver. "Yeah, just getting another migraine."

She encouraged me to take the pills and poured me a glass of water. I stared at the glass like it was a coiled snake. Maisey watched me expectantly and I realized I had no choice. I could give no excuse that would make any modicum of sense.

I had started to get a sense of when Skye's thoughts would invade my mind. I brought the pills to my mouth and knew what to expect.

They drugged me.

The stab of pain was almost nothing compared to the shiver of fear that raced down my spine, and the words I vomited up. "Thanks, Maisey."

Her smile wasn't comforting. "You're very welcome. Now I've got to get back there. Can't host from a medicine cabinet."

I toasted her with the glass of water and watched her drift back into the living room to mingle with her guests. Luke wasn't around and I felt adrift circled by something vast in a sea stained with the blood of someone who'd very recently tread the same water.

I have to get out of here.

You care and you can't run.

I took another drink from my glass, hoping the water inside was only that. After second thoughts, I poured the rest out in the sink.

At the far end of the island were the Hollman's choice of wines. I perused and tried to find one that I thought looked the most expensive, deciding tonight was not the night to pass on the opportunity. It was going to be difficult as it was.

I picked up a black bottle displaying 1982 as the year and poured it in two separate glasses, returning the bottle to the ice.

Earl was nowhere to be seen. Luke spoke to a couple I didn't recognize.

I sidled up to him and offered the second glass.

He took it with a grin, "Digging into the Hollman's good stuff, I see."

"Free expensive wine? Who would pass that up?" I replied.

The stranger gave a rumbling belly laugh. He dressed like he'd just come off a pasture, only cleaner. "Ain't that right? Don't think we've had the pleasure, ma'am."

Luke smiled. "Jessie, this is Jarod and Eileen. They live a few blocks over."

I shook the man's hand, ignoring the cocky leer on his face. His wife was a waif, a ghost of a woman who looked like she had just been released from the inside of a tuberculosis ward. Her words slurred from drinking or medicine I couldn't tell. "It's a pleasure."

Girlfriend, I don't know how much you've had, but you need to have less.

Seeing her husband's demeanor, I should not have blamed her. Jarod slurped down the eggnog, which dribbled onto his shirt. "Shit, that's some good stuff."

Luke looked at me and his eyes pled with me not to leave him alone with them.

Jarod adjusted his hat and looked me up and down, grinning like he was some amazing catch. "Probably think I'm a pig in the kitchen. I'm not used to these kinds of things. Out in the oilfields most days."

Like that's some kind of excuse for being a slob.

"Well, I'm not used to these kinds of things, either. I was just happy I could fit back into this thing. So how long have you lived here?" I said it quick, far faster than I meant to, but this was exactly the kind of man I could trust to run his mouth.

Luke looked at me, but I barely paid him mind. Jarod glanced at Eileen and scratched the stubble of his scruff, "Well, I- uh, don't know maybe ten years or so?"

"So, you would have known Skye Burton?" I asked.

I saw Eileen's eyes widen, but Jarod gave her a sharp look before turning back to me. "Yeah, yeah, we knew her. Eileen spent a lot of time with her."

My mother had developed a perfect system for making sure I knew when I'd stepped over the line. Luke's gaze reminded me of that now.

I ignored him. "I like my True Crime docs and I saw an episode centering around her case. It blew my mind that she used to live here."

Jarod rubbed the back of his head, glancing at Luke. "Yeah, it was quite a ride. A lot of folks around here were scared. No reason to be, it was obvious what happened."

There it was- the weakness in the walls. "What was so obvious?"

Something dark passed over his eyes and I saw Eileen glance down into her drink.

Her husband's words were venom. "She wasn't very *discreet* if you catch my drift. We've got two boys, and we overheard the older describing all kinds of perversity about her."

Luke downed his wine looking like he would rather have been anywhere else.

Eileen stared at the floor like the hardwood contained the mysteries of the universe.

Jarod just smiled coyly. "Not to say me or old Luke here, for that matter, didn't have the same thoughts, but it's different when it's a kid just entering his teen years. They shouldn't be exposed to such things until they can handle it."

He winked at Luke like it was some kind of grand joke and I saw my date bury his face in his hands.

Jarod kept going, oblivious. "Anyway, she obviously finally flaunted it in front of the wrong guy, and he did something drastic."

It wasn't the most sexist thing I'd ever heard; public school and college in the south tended to see frat-bros emboldened to say whatever it was that flowed from the smooth rocks that passed for their brains. Still, it jarred to hear it at a Christmas party.

Eileen looked up from her intense examination of the floor work. "Jarod, shut the fuck up."

I sensed this didn't usually happen, the dynamic of their marriage kept Eileen seen but not heard.

She shook her head, a tear welling at the edge of her eyes. "She was my friend."

You were my friend!!!

Her thoughts screamed through my head, driving me to my knees, and biting my tongue to stop a scream. The wine glass dropped from my grip and shattered on the floor, drawing every eye in the room. I tried to ignore the throbbing agony and when I looked up at Eileen I saw her recoil.

"Oh my god, Jessie," Eileen whispered.

I wasn't sure what she meant until she pulled her compact from the small purse she was carrying.

My right eye had flooded with blood, setting the pupil a black island amid the red sea.

Eileen and Luke knelt to help me up. The crowd around me were a faceless mob of indistinct figures offering sympathy and help. The pain lingered, the intensity ebbing and flowing.

Why is this happening to me?...the cry of the pitiful people who wished it was another way. I wish I could say I was tougher than I was. I was just a girl who liked to walk in the mornings.

I waved them off, trying to stand. Slowly but surely, the people drifted away when they finally heard my protestations that I was fine. Jarod looked squeamish and he pulled his wife to get her away from me.

The pain in my head had barely receded, but I could still feel how Skye had felt: hurt, scared, betrayed.

And my words spat all of that at Eileen. "You were her *friend!*"

Inebriated, drugged up to the gills, it didn't stop the look of intense guilt that flowered across her face before Jarod dragged her into the crowd.

"What the hell was that?" asked Luke, his cheeks pink with embarrassment.

I was livid it was the first thing he asked me. It looked like a complete breakdown followed by a screaming match. I cooly took my arm away and looked him in the eye, hoping he saw the red sea of agony swimming through my sclera.

He looked away and I decided my initial plan had run its course. I didn't know if I could take another bout of Skye's thoughts. that the last one had almost ripped my mind in half.

I ignored his protests as I turned to leave, looking for my clutch containing my phone and throwing out the excuse I needed to go get my eye checked out. It's a hard thing when you realize your attraction for someone is gone. It's an even harder thing when they won't leave you alone.

Luke drifted after me, repeating my name as I pushed through the Hollman's guests. My vision blurred; my right eye was unable to focus through the blood. I'd almost reached the coat rack when Derek Hollman stepped into my path.

"Jessie, Maisey told me that you had an accident, and I just wanted to check— oh."

I put a hand over my bloodied eye, waving my hand as I tried to shoo him out of the way. "Yeah, I think I need to go to the hospital, get this checked out. Thank your wife for your hospitality, but—"

There was a clap and a whistle, and I turned with Luke, seeing Derek's grin widen as he pushed past us. Maisey Hollman stood in the center of the room, smiling like she'd just been given the world.

I wasn't far off. She may as well have been a planet orbiting the star in her arms. A hush fell over the room as everyone stared at the baby sleeping calmly. I couldn't tell if it was a boy or a girl, but it had a strong smattering of black hair.

Maisey spoke. "Everyone, you all know how much we've wanted this. Derek and I have tried and tried, and thanks to Luke... our dreams are finally real."

There was a round of quiet congratulations, smiles, and embraces for Derek as the crowd gathered around the new mother and her baby.

I looked at Luke who bashfully shrugged. "Part of the job, they deserve it. They're good people."

He offered me my coat. "It was the big surprise for the night, a Christmas miracle. I'm sorry I said what I said. I just didn't want the Hollman's night to be ruined."

My anger melted and I took his hand. "You're a good man, Luke."

You're a bastard, you're all bastards.

I didn't even flinch, just kept smiling. The pain had become an old friend.. "You stay here, I'm sure they're going to want to thank you."

Luke looked conflicted, the two wolves doing the right thing and natural desire warring. He settled on natural desire.

"Are you sure you're going to be ok?"

Used to the feeling of disappointment, I nodded and gestured. "Get back in there and suck up your glory."

He nodded and winked. "You know it. Can I come see you after the party?"

No way in hell.

I kept the smile. "I'll call you."

He kissed my hand and went back to the party. I watched him go and quickly grabbed my coat, sweeping out into the dark cold.

<u>Chapter Five</u>

The lights seemed to blink in a morse code warning to me, but my mind was set. Skye Burton had planted a lot of questions about the people in this neighborhood, and they didn't seem eager to answer.

I couldn't believe what I planned. Yesterday I wouldn't have been brave enough. When I was a girl, I'd been forced to attend every Friday night football game with my parents. In the south, it's a town event. I'd always wondered how no one took advantage of the fact that most of our town was there.

As I approached Luke's house, I thought back to the Hollman's cooing over their child. None of that sat well with me; I couldn't recall Luke ever mentioning child services as part of his job description.

I should have gone home and changed, but I didn't know how much time I realistically had before the party was over and everyone would drunkenly stumble back to their homes.

The snow fell harder now, thick drifts of a blizzard replaced the small thin dust of flurries. I deserved to be at home wrapped up under a blanket with a good book and a better movie, with someone who cared. Instead, I was out breaking into a home because I couldn't stop hearing the thoughts of a dead woman.

I didn't want to risk the front door. A hole in the glass next to the door would look too obvious, and his Ring camera would pick me up easily.

God, please let his gate be unlocked.

I opened the gate slowly and poked my head inside, unsure if he had a dog or not. I thanked God or maybe even Skye if my own thoughts could reach her.

Nothing moved and I closed the gate behind me as quietly as I could. The sparse back yard held a grill and small shed. The back of the house had three windows, one looking into the kitchen and two others into the living room.

Standing out in the cold wasn't going to accomplish anything. Discretion wasn't the better part of valor. A pile of bricks lay half buried in the snow, the beginnings of barbecue construction.

The brick was frigid in my hand. Heavy, I probably couldn't toss it more than a yard. Of course, it just had to go through the window.

I threw it as hard as I could and watched my projectile swirling through the air. The wind disguised the glass shattering. Flakes immediately drifted inside to melt on the kitchen floor.

Thankful no alarm blared. I reached through the jagged edges and fumbled for the door lock,

Who doesn't have an alarm system?

I took off my shoes as I entered, my bare feet quieter on the tile. His kitchen looked just the same as I'd seen it earlier, and the parts I hadn't seen weren't displaying signs declaring I KIDNAPPED A WOMAN.

The stone floor froze my feet. I hoped I wouldn't leave footprints as I stepped into the living room. Everything here was the same too.

What am I doing?

I had no experience looking for places to hide someone. I don't think a rational person ever thinks they're going to be on the forefront of trying to find a missing person by themselves. There was the temptation to give up and slink back to my house. I could throw the brick back into the snow and just forget everything.

I halfway turned before I heard the thump, a faint thing. If I had been anywhere else, I would have ignored it without a second thought. Instead, it drew me back through the living room and into the dark hallway which ended at a guest room and the master bedroom.

A small night light burned from an outlet illuminating a guest bathroom and a closet. I clutched the brick in my hand like it was a weapon divinely forged.

I knew the weird sounds of a house, like the touch of the wind whispering through rafters to make them creak, but nothing thumped like this.

How the hell do you have a basement?

Skye's thoughts provided the insight I didn't have. Logic redirected me to the garage, but intuition told me that was too obvious. Luke wouldn't hide his deeds in the garage foundation.

I went to the closet and, when I opened the door, I was surprised by the amount of space, a full walk-in, way more space than necessary for a guest to use. It wasn't bare, there were plenty of clothes hanging from the three walls, and they looked well used.

Another thud echoed, muffled but louder than I'd heard the first time, and it was directly in front of me. The clothes were already pushed to the side, and the stark white wall could have camouflaged itself in the snow banks outside.

There was something off about it which I couldn't immediately put my finger on until I realized the paint on it didn't look as faded as the rest around it. It was subtle, you'd never even know if you weren't looking for it.

And it was the size of a door.

I reached out with a trembling hand and pressed lightly against the wall.

There was a small click and a gap appeared.

I felt a small breeze of frigid air, gently pulled the false door back, and glanced inside. A dim stairwell ended in a spacious cellar. There was a white neon bulb illuminating what looked like a pile of dirty towels.

I could hear a lot more thumping and the faint sound of music playing. I took a tentative step, clutching my brick tight. I was afraid the stairs would bend and announce my presence. They stayed firm so I took another.

I made it to the bottom. A washer, a dryer, and a refrigerator to my left, but the pile of bloody towels pulled me to a stop.

They sat next to a large tub of filthy water, big enough for a person to sit in.

Please give her back to me...

I felt the bile rise in my stomach when I realized what that tub was for, as if the bed with the soiled sheets and full-on restraints didn't lay it out for me in its sickness. An air vent was blowing the frigid air, circulating around the room, and it did nothing to disguise the smell.

The sweet smell of birth is difficult to describe if you haven't been there, a primal animalistic scent, and, in this basement, it was pungent and overpowering.

I should have turned and run. I might have brought the wrath of God down on the sick fuck who lived upstairs, but my eyes found Billy Chase.

He had a mop and bucket. The thumping I had heard was from his moving of a large blue barrel into the corner of the basement. The music came from a pair of Bluetooth headphones in his ears. His crooked teeth were jutted like tombstones. They curved into a reptilian smile. "Jessie." His throat was filled with phlegm; his voice sounded heady, deep, and dripping. Dropping the mop, the handle clanked against the stone floor as he took a step toward me.

DON'T TOUCH ME!

"DON'T TOUCH ME!" I echoed, realizing Skye's words had seized me. And I went to work with the brick I carried.

It left my hand before I even realized what I had done, and it flew quick, catching Billy Chase between the eyes, breaking his nose, and drawing blood, lots of blood.

He fell on his back and I dashed to grab the brick from where it had fallen. I heard him shout something through the blood welling up in his mouth, but it didn't matter, I'd already grabbed my weapon again.

I wept for what had happened to Skye in this basement , new tears for old death.

I was afraid, but Billy Chase was terrified.

I slammed the brick into his face over and over again, listening to his keening curses become wet pleas. I'd never felt bone crunch and give in, or an eyeball pop and leak vitreous fluid, or teeth come loose from gums only to be swallowed in a great intake of bloody agony.

I wasn't sure when he finally died. My arm gave out first. Stained a deeper red, the brick thunked out of my hand, Shivers raced up and down my spine. My entire life, I hadn't really engaged in violence. Even in school, I'd kept my head down and avoided confrontation.

No one would know the bloody thing under me had been named Billy. I could see parts of his skull through the caved-in flesh; the underbite of his jaw jutted at me in a perversion of a smile.

My nausea exploded and I fell off of the body, puking onto the floor as I realized I'd murdered a man. I tried to think as I wiped the bile off my lips.

Self-defense-- look where he is. They can't send you to jail for that.

I should leave, run for the hills and a phone, but the barrel Billy had been hauling caught my eye.

I could not leave until I saw what was inside.

I stood on shaking legs and took a nervous step, helpless to do anything but follow through.

Don't put him there... please...

I took hold of the lid and turned it as hard as I could, a slow and steady twist as it came undone. A caustic odor hit me, and I covered my nose with one hand, smelling the coppery tang of the blood covering my fist.

The lid tumbled to the ground. The barrel contained a lye/water mixture.

The slurry of what had once been skin precluded any insight on how long the tiny thing had been put there. It could have been days... or hours...

My stomach churned and I quickly backed away, knowing I would never escape the sight. Every time I went to sleep from now on, I would see him dissolve in my nightmares.

More vomit would have come if I hadn't already spilled my guts next to a dead man. It was monstrous, inhuman, unfeeling... At least five more barrels squared away under the wooden stairwell.

My will broke and I ran. The stairs creaked under me as I tore up and out of the closet. Luke's well warmed home washed over me like a comforting wave.

I can make it, I can make it...

I heard the front door slam and Luke's angry voice, "What do you mean she isn't there!?"

Luke, why are you doing this!?

I tried to stifle the grunt of pain from Skye's thoughts and failed.

Luke stopped talking, silence settled, and I felt like a deer caught in headlights.

"Hold up, Casey... I think she's here."

The words shot through me like lightning. I panicked and ran toward the master bedroom, barely remembering not to run back down the stairs to hide.

I heard heavy footfalls behind me.

Don't let them get me, don't let them get me, don't let them—

Skye's thoughts thundered like a train through my mind, drowning out everything but the panic.

Luke would have caught me if I hadn't left the door to his hidden basement open. In the back of his home it would've been hard to tell where I had fled. The warm basement air drew him like a freezing dog in the bitter winter. I heard the stairs strain as he descended.

He screamed.

His bedroom was a mess, clothes lying across the floor in piles, food wrappers discarded everywhere, sheets bundled and dirty at the edge of sweat stained sheets. A small moan escaped me. My hope of a backdoor vanished when I saw the enclosed room.

Below me, crashing erupted from the basement as Luke tore his sick/monstrous/horrible laboratory/prison apart. I felt like an animal caught in a trap.

I have to get out of here.

Twin bedroom windows let in the blinking Yule light, and I looked for a latch, tearing the curtains from their hangers and throwing them out of my way. The windows had crisscrossing patterns in the style of an old English cottage.

There were iron bars outside.

I screamed and the crashing in the basement went quiet. I desperately wished I still had the brick in my hand. I looked around for anything I could use as a weapon.

Luke's feet fell heavy on the stairs. He shouted my name.

I looked at his bed, judging whether the room under it would be enough. Then I looked at his closet, open, dark, and inviting, and I ran inside.

Enough of his clothes hung up to hide me and I pressed myself as far against the corner as I could. The clothes had barely stopped moving when I heard him enter the room.

"Jessie? I know you're in here," he said. He had a calm colder than the winds swirling outside.

I'll kill you, Luke.

I gritted my teeth to keep from making a sound, wishing Skye had succeeded.

"I'm curious, what put you on the scent? We thought we'd done everything right. Casey made sure there was an HOA meeting that morning. Billy took down our internet for a bit. I donated the space. Brent made sure no one was around to see him pick her up. Well... except the dead."

He laughed, a short and bitter sound that offered no comfort. "Then today of all days, you started asking questions out of the blue. I wish you could have felt my heart pounding. I was panicking wondering which asshole spilled the beans. Then I realized you didn't have a fucking clue... or at least I didn't think you did until I found you here."

I heard him moving a pile of clothing, then his knees popped as he dropped to the floor, no doubt looking under his bed. "Might as well come on out. There's no way out of here, either the shower or the closet."

My hands grasped at the hanging clothes, wadding them up in tight balls as I tried to control my breathing. I could make a break for it; hope I was strong enough to fight him off if he caught me.

I didn't have a prayer.

He keeps a rifle in the closet.

The thought came like lightning and I reached blindly into the dark, hoping I hadn't missed a safe in my hurry.

His shadow moved across the doorway. "I have to hand it to you; didn't think you were capable of what you did to Billy. I'm going to be seeing that for a while, going to be seeing lots of things. He handled all the nitty gritty stuff like disposal. I thought you may have seen something you shouldn't this morning when he was planting Skye under the flower bed."

I froze, chills running down my arms as his shadow receded. Then I heard the furious sound of the shower curtain being thrown back.

Luke had only one place left to look and I could hear the triumph in his voice as he turned. "If you were trying to rescue her, you're a few days too late. That last one really did a number on her."

The doorway framed his silhouette, a dark shadow looming over the small and searching thing I was.

"And now we have an opening. Everyone has been asking how we could keep things going, and I think I have just the person to take her place in that bed downstairs."

My searching hand closed around something long, cool, and metal. I brought it to me.

Luke murmured, "Are you on the left or the right? And do you like it in the cunt or the ass?" Luke chose wrong, sweeping the hangers to his left out of his way.

I poked the barrel of the gun through the rack, pulled the trigger, and blew his foot from the bone.

His scream filled me. Since this had begun, I was sure Skye's thoughts and mine were the same, our feelings one.

Luke's blood pooled out on the carpeted floor. He grasped at his foot wailing hard enough to rattle the windows.

I didn't know anything about guns. I couldn't have told you the caliber, the manufacturer, anything. But I knew enough to see it had been a shotgun. I fumbled with the switch, cracked the barrel, and pulled the spent shell from the chamber.

He tried to crawl away, whimpering for help. I froze. It had been all instinct and fear, but I didn't know what to do now. He hadn't done this alone, Casey Smith being one of them.

I descended on Luke as he made it into his shower, a walk-in which would drink most of his blood. He tried to fend me off but might as well have swatted at the paws of a predator.

His phone wasn't on him, he'd left it behind in the foyer.

I should've left, gone straight to find it and called the police, but when I looked at this pathetic thing wearing a human shell, I had to know...

Why me?

I squatted next to this paper man and he looked at me with wide, fearful eyes, which matched my own. "Why Skye?"

Hands wrapped around his bleeding appendage; Luke still had enough energy to glare at me. I slapped him. It was reflex, but his glare didn't abate. Seeing his soulless and uncaring eyes broke something inside me and numbed my soul. I slammed the butt of the shotgun down onto the bleeding stump of his leg.

His new screams emboldened me and I began to give the same treatment to his uninjured leg.

I bashed it over and over until the bone snapped. The skin turned an ugly shade of purple and blue as the blood spread inside. His screaming persisted as a distant annoyance, like a fly's wing or a bout of tinnitus, and it didn't stop me from stomping and smashing his hands.

Please kill him, God. If You can hear me, save me... kill him.

Had He been listening? Had He sent me?

He could claim that vengeance was His. Well, here I was ready to substitute until He came back.

I hadn't realized I'd been sobbing until I fell back against the wall and heard the empty gun clatter against the floor next to me. Luke panted and mewed, pitiful noises that could have fooled someone into thinking he had been a harmless, innocent victim.

When I'd caught my breath, I asked the burning question. "Why Skye?"

He nodded fast, defeated, hoping I wouldn't hurt him anymore. "Sh-she was beautiful, liked to flaunt it, teased every man in this neighborhood. We decided to do something about it."

I'd never heard a more evil, selfish, and wretched thing in my life and only the constant torrent of bullshit spewing from his mouth kept him alive.

"Every guy in this neighborhood wanted a piece of her ass. That's what it started out as... then I realized there were a lot of people trying to adopt out there who wait for years in the system. So, I decided we could put her to better use."

My blood went cold and my hand drifted until it closed around the old shotgun. Luke flopped like a fish as he tried to get away with his ruined hands and feet, initiating a fresh round of begging.

"Please don't shoot me, please don't shoot me, please—"

Please, please, please!

I winced and looked down at him through gritted teeth. There was a difference in begging between an innocent and a coward.

"Shut the fuck up," I whispered.

He followed my demand and I pointed at my head. "I hear her, hear what she thought. The day you took her, plenty of days after, through every birth... I FUCKING HEARD HER!"

I kicked his ruined leg and drew a fresh wail. "Maybe she just knew I wouldn't let it go."

He closed his eyes as I hefted the shotgun.

"I'm not going to shoot you."

A sigh rippled through him, he relaxed, and then I turned on the shower. He sputtered as the cold water hit him, crying out when it ran across his broken limbs, looking confused.

I sat down on the edge of the nearby toilet watching him with pitiless eyes.

He tried to surrender. "Please just call the cops."

I refused. "Why don't you just take a hot shower first?"

His eyes widened as he saw the cold-water knob still off and I smiled. "You like it scalding, right?"

I felt nothing at the sound of his petrified wailing. He knew what was coming. The water heated up more and more. I could see the steam beginning to waft.

I'd dated a man who worked building houses. He'd told me to be careful of new constructions, specifically the showers. Most contractors didn't bother putting in safety valves to regulate the water temperature.

I'm not sure when Luke's screaming went from pain to agony.

His skin reddened, reminding me of a steak slowly turning rare under the flame, like his whole body blushed.

Maybe in hell they'd mock him for his screaming.

He would get close to the edge of the shower, and I would nudge him back in with my foot. Eventually, he took a long inhale of breath and lay still.

I left him to marinate under the water.

What am I going to do now? They're dead.

I wish I had Skye's thoughts to comfort me, to let me know that everything was going to be ok. Luke had told me everything I needed. I wasn't going to be some heroic rescuer, no matter how much I wished.

Would her thoughts stop if I found her, or would I carry her wandering mind until I died? Which could be a lot sooner with the kind of men Luke had surrounded himself with.

Stupid.

That thought was all my own. He'd been talking to Casey Smith, creepy bastard that he was. I didn't imagine he would waste much time waiting for Luke to call, not when he had the opportunity for something fresh in the basement.

Ammo... have to find the ammo.

Skye's thoughts set me on my path again. I was sure she was determined to see me finish the course.

I practically dove into his bedroom closet, and flicked on the light switch, bathing the room in a soft orange glow. There were shoes on the floor, clothes that looked like they hadn't been worn in years, and a few shelves' worth of shoes.

In my search, I strewed his possessions into the bedroom to join the rest of his discarded things. My search didn't reveal any ammunition, but I finally pulled aside a pair of dress shoes on the top shelf to find a sharp pocket knife.

Gripping the knife and testing the blade, I decided it was better to call the cops from the safety of my own home.

A pair of headlights panned over the house as I got to the front door. I slowly backed away into the dark of the kitchen. The wind blew an ever-increasing pile of snow through the hole I'd put in the window beside the door, dropping the temperature of the kitchen.

The front door opened and Casey called, "Luke! Where are you?"

I backed out through the kitchen door and into the back-yard, and hurried to the gate, hoping the corpses would keep

Casey occupied. I sprinted out of the yard, the snow under my feet sending spears of cold rolling up my spine. I had one destination in mind.

The Hollman's Christmas party remained in full swing. I was more than sure people at that party were in on what Luke had planned for me. I could see the lights and hear the distant sounds of laughter and celebration. It seemed so surreal knowing what I knew, and the fact I'd killed two people.

I was three blocks away. It might as well have been a world away. My only hope was that some of the people in attendance weren't maggots hiding their perversion and evil from the world.

Light bathed me and I heard the sliding crunch of tires gaining traction on the snow. The black Ford slid in front of me and Brent Fischer leaned out of the cab, "Jessie? What's going on?" He looked around, behind me, everywhere he assumed pursuit was coming from.

I paused and looked at him, remembering Skye's thoughts.

Brent, let me hold him, let me hold him!

The image of his children came to me, their dark raven hair, the strange facial features; it seemed obvious now with what I knew. I glanced at his truck. He'd catch me if I ran. The police wouldn't take much convincing for him to claim he'd lost control and I was nothing more than an unfortunate loss.

Which left me with only one option.

"Brent, you've got to help me! Luke he's- he's—" I devolved into fake sobs, keeping an eye on the man to see what he would do. He looked uncomfortable, reluctant, but certain.

"Come on, get in!" he said firmly.

I ran around to the passenger door, wrenched it open and crawled inside. He eased onto the accelerator and took the turn back towards Luke's house. I turned up the hysterics, "NO! You can't go back there!"

He laid his hand on my own, the one I'd left in resting distance. "Hey, don't worry. Luke's a computer guy; I've arrested plenty of them."

I almost couldn't stand his patronizing tone, as if I didn't know what he'd done and what he planned to do to me.

I was sure Brent had been called away from the Hollman's party, probably by Casey.

Brent drove back to where I had escaped, and my only option was to lean on a man's bias. I covered my face with my hands and pretended to sob. It wasn't long until I felt his hand rest on my back.

"Hey, hey, I'll keep you safe. Don't worry, I've got you now."

I'm sure he thought it was comforting, but it turned my stomach and gave me the opening I needed.

Men like these, they have a certain perception when it comes to women. They assume we are weaker, inferior, that we would rather hide behind someone stronger rather than twist their balls off ourselves.

With one hand I quietly flicked the blade of the pocket knife open, turned and drove it into the soft flesh of his forearm.

I was lucky it had gone in easily. Brent screamed and wrenched his hand away, giving me time to pitch myself out of the truck into a bank of snow. The truck kept going, plowing through a snowman, and into the brick wall of Luke's neighbor's home.

The horn immediately blared. I pulled myself out of the cold and ran to the Hollmans. It was 300 yards down the street, maybe a little more.

Just a little further... I can make it...

My feet flew under me even as I heard Brent's cursing behind me. There were heavy footfalls that I left as I drew nearer the Hollmans' door. All those days spent sprinting the last gasp of my walk had culminated in this.

I crossed the finish line into a house crowded with people. A few screamed, but most looked at me with wide eyes and pale faces. I looked like some kind of feral thing with my dress covered in Billy's blood, more dried on my exposed shoulders, and my hair tumbled over my wide and wild eyes.

I locked eyes with Jordan Hollman who looked like he had seen Skye herself claw out of the grave.

I'm going to die here. No one will know.

The telltale tap of the blood running out of my nose played a metronome of fury as I took one step towards him. It broke the spell and the din around me began, voices of concern overlapping hands touching me which I shrugged off.

Only the man in front concerned me. Jordan didn't hesitate, rushing to his wife and pulling the child from her arms. Maisey screamed, the babe wailed, and I hesitated.

My voice hoarse as it was, may as well have been thunder. "Tell them, Jordan."

He clutched Skye's child to his chest, his lip trembling, but he could do nothing to stop what was coming.

"Tell Maisey how you raped Skye Burton to get a child for her!"

Hark the angels wail, motherfucker.

With a blast of cold behind me, Brent and Casey arrived, both out of breath. I pointed a finger at the bloody tourniquet hastily wrapped around Brent's arm. "Why don't you tell your wife and your kids where that hand has been?"

Their faces were paler than the snow as they glanced around at everyone. Casey looked like a rat caught in a trap, but Brent kept his cool. He nodded to the men in the room. "Guys, she's lost it. She's killed Luke, Billy, and she tried to kill me. She looked up what happened to Skye, and thinks she is her. It's crazy."

How many times have you kept that gas lit, Brent?

Most looked uncomfortable. Some looked at me with sympathy. Others looked at Brent, nodding their heads like everything he'd said made complete sense.

It's hard to fight the urge to believe an officer. They're here to "serve and protect" after all. From the day we start learning about the world, we are taught to believe that a cop isn't capable of bad. They're an honorable service, and any mistakes made are just a good man facing worse people.

"Sure, Brent. Maybe I am crazy. Why don't we all take a walk and see Luke's basement?"

People tend to retreat to extreme reactions when they're pinned, some double down and begin to concoct the most insane stretches of the truth, some run away.

He'll shoot me if I don't...

I barely had time to register Skye's thoughts before Brent had the gun in his hand. The smile gone, his eyes cold and dead, the pistol cracked once. I saw it bounce and I felt an impact against my stomach like someone had hit me. My breath left and I looked down at the blossoming red spread like a highspeed mulberries evergreen in winter.

There were more shots and more screams.

People ran this way and that. The cold didn't seem so bad anymore. It wasn't nipping at my skin but burrowing deeper into everything I was. The only warmth I felt came from my chest and it ran through my fingers faster than water.

Why is this happening?

Why is this happening?

A hand grasped mine, far calmer and warmer than my own blood and, for a moment, thoughts became words, and an anger was whispered to me. Opening my eyes, I saw a woman standing over me, dark of hair and radiant.

I knew her face, knew *her.* We were of one mind.

"You have to get up."

I must get up.

Opening my eyes, I saw Casey Smith rocking on the floor. Rubbing his head with the body of a pistol, Brent stood over him.

There were bodies, there was blood, and it would be a Christmas of mourning. I kept my chest as still as possible. The pain of the bullet in my gut was agonizing, but to make even the smallest sound would see me joining Skye and everyone who'd been in Brent's way.

"Oh shit, oh shit, oh shit..." Casey repeated.

Brent kicked the smaller man, sprawling him across the corpse of a woman I didn't know. He scrambled back and looked up at the sheriff's deputy who glared back.

"Stop panicking." Brent's cool, steady voice was not the voice of a man worried about his life crumbling around him.

I kept my eyes wide and still.

Brent unknowingly stared back. "This is the reason I had us make those bug-out bags. It'll take the police fifteen minutes minimum, so let's get a move on."

Casey shivered. "I don't— I didn't think— it's not fair she's dead. You and Luke promised!" He sounded whiny and petulant, everything a hollow man was beneath the papier-mâché exterior. His eyes remained rooted on me.

Suddenly, the whine disappeared and an excited cold took its place. His eyes dilated when he looked at me, "You know how to survive, Brent. You get your family and do what you have to do. I'm going to stay and get what was promised me."

Brent looked between us. "You're a sick fuck, Casey."

"Says the kidnapper and rapist. Leave me be, this'll last me a lifetime."

Brent didn't have to be told twice, disappearing into the cold night. Casey stood and stalked towards me; I didn't dare blink as his shadow fell over me.

His hands trembled as he ventured under my dress, cooing like a demented dove. "That's right, baby. Just relax, I've waited for this."

Don't touch me... don't touch me...

He pushed the dress up. I could feel the winter wind billowing from the open door. His other hand grasped my head, turning it to look up at him. He smiled down. "You're still so warm. It's going to feel so good."

The pain in my chest was distant, but enough that every jostled movement threatened to elicit the agony I felt. I desperately wanted to scream, but I couldn't. I had to wait for him to follow through.

He fumbled with his pants, looking around at the empty house. "I'm going to go to prison, but I'll remember this, remember you, Jessie. You were more beautiful than her and you don't put up nearly as much of a fight."

His penis flopped out, a limp thing getting harder as he spoke. One hand gripped my head and traced the curve of my lips. I could feel his member sliding up my leg, leaving a trail of pre-cum, and it took everything I had to keep still.

His hand curled around my head. I stayed limp, keeping my eyes still. He wormed a finger between my lips and tapped it against my teeth. He pulled my jaw wider, causing me to twitch in revulsion.

Casey paused, eyeing me with a wary gaze that slowly relaxed as I kept still. "Looks like there's still a little juice left."

He placed his penis in my mouth. I could taste the sweat dripping from his exertions. His finger traced my limp lips and I heard him sigh. "Don't use teeth my love."

What a fucking great idea.

I bit down as hard as I could, sinking my teeth into his stiff, putrid manhood and wrenched back like a dog tearing at a bone. I'd never tasted anything so foul and never heard a scream so high.

He shoved me away out of reflex. His penis came with me. Casey fell back, sobbing, hands desperately clutching at the bleeding stump between his legs. I watched the dark blood bubble through his pants and pool on the carpet, and I stood up, spitting his member into my hand.

There was no walking away from this; he'd die right here. I certainly wasn't going to try to save him. It seemed too little, really. After what he'd done to Skye it just seemed too... quick.

I looked at the severed organ in my hand.

I'd feed your dick to you if I could...

"Excellent idea, Skye," I murmured, staggering over and straddling the fallen rapist. I didn't care about the blood soaking my dress; there was plenty of that already. I just wanted him to live long enough for me to make sure he choked on his choices.

I held the phallus to his face, watching his fresh tears bubble up to the surface, "Say ahh."

Casey's mutilated genitals met my knee as I drove it down. He took a deep inhaling gasp of agony, and...

It was easier than I thought, shoving the hunk of flesh down his gullet. Already weak and choking, a man doesn't want to bite into his own penis. His anguished wheezes as he tried to breathe were music to my ears as they died away in a long, faint rattle.

Eyes bulging and bloodshot, he slumped over. I staggered to the open door, staring out into the cold night. One left to go, as far as I knew.

How many here tonight knew? How many participated?

***

I heard sirens, distant but growing louder as I staggered through the snow. Each step felt like I dragged a weight heavier than my soul. A glance behind me showed blood the blood I left in my wake.

How long can I go on?

There's nothing left.

The thoughts washed over cold skin until they reached a mind grown colder when I reached Brent's home. Warm glows and blinking lights portrayed festive cheer, a veneer of joy over the beastly thing living here.

He'd left his door open; Brent didn't think anyone was going to follow him home.

I appeared like the Devil's own vengeance and found him screaming at his wife, while his children hid behind their mother's skirts.

I couldn't discern what words were being traded between him and his wife, nor could I hear the muffled sobs of his children. All I heard were Skye's thoughts echoing off the neurons of my mind.

Let me go.

LET ME GO.

LET ME GOOOO!!!!

I wasn't sure if the roar was in my head or from my mouth.

Brent stared like Skye herself had floated into his home like the ghost of Christmas past.

It's the present now, bastard. And I'm no ghost, but what's yet to come is damn sure going to be the same.

"I'll give you this," he pointed the pistol at me. "You brought it all down."

"I didn't bring down anything. Skye Burton did," my voice barely above a whisper. I looked at his children, hiding behind his wife, and smiled. "Your daddy killed your mommy, and now I have to kill him."

***

I no longer felt like myself, not anymore. The thoughts in my head were strange, different. When I spoke, it was with a cadence I didn't recognize.

"I screamed for years in that basement. Every time you, or Luke, or Casey, or Billy turned off the light and left me to worm around in the filth of musk and cum, I screamed. And then I cried when you took my babies away from me, the ones I didn't want, but so desperately needed when I saw them."

Brent's pistol wavered.

I took a step forward until I felt the cool metal between my breasts. "You were there when I took my last breath. Did you even pause before you had Billy bury me out in the flower bed? I leaned forward and whispered into his ear. "Would you like me to tell you what Hell is like?"

He ran, despite the pistol in his hand, just like every other paper man who thought themselves brave because they held a gun. Out into the cold of his front door to his truck, Brent fumbled with the keys as I followed.

The snow crunched under my feet and I reached him as he opened the door. "Where are you going?"

He turned and fired a round. The bullet caused a puff of snow to flurry into the wind behind me. "You crazy bitch!"

You fucking bastard.

I lunged and slammed the door, catching his hand in the door frame. I released the door and watched the gun tumble into the white snow. He scrambled from the cab of the truck. I could hear his panicked breathing, but I was beside him already, and the pistol felt solid in my hand.

Collapsing to his knees Brent looked up at me and said deadpan, "Don't kill me." Defeated but not caterwauling. he clung to a last desperate hope that he wasn't talking to the woman he'd murdered.

I crouched, pushing the pistol against his kneecap. "Just lie back and enjoy."

I pulled the trigger, the shot echoing loud in the silence of the snow, but Brent's screams were even louder.

His skin looked like an apple bursting at the seams. The shot had shattered his kneecap and blood ran like waterfalls next to the bits of ruined bone. He rolled on his back. Snow melted beneath him.

The barrel of the gun stayed hot as I pressed it against his other knee, kneeling with my full weight on the length of his leg. With his injuries, he barely noticed the heat scarring his flesh. I thought it was best to make sure he had matching wounds. He didn't pass out from the second shot.

In his screams, he cried to God to save him, cried to his wife who watched from the front door with dead eyes, clinging to his children... my children. They watched with tears, sobbing into the bitch who'd gladly accepted what her husband had given her.

They were my first, across eight years in the dark and seven live births. I didn't want them to grow up and this be the defining moment, the one they'd remember long after I'd disappeared back into the dark.

The sirens were close now. Brent couldn't get away. I could've let him face his crimes. He'd live unless the people saw fit to shuffle him off this mortal coil.

Fuck justice, revenge is certain.

Good idea, Jessie.

I heard the crumpling of bone and the fresh screaming as I dragged Brent, his limp legs leaving red snail trails through the snow. I reached up to the lowest Christmas lights and tore them from the roof.

They blinked festively as I wrapped them around his throat. He thrashed, eyes wide and panicked, but he could go nowhere with the wounds I'd dealt.

I unplugged the cord from the socket. I tied the end of the lights to the rear bumper, and made sure the noose was wound tight.

Brent shook his head back and forth, gibbering, as realization set in. I ignored him and climbed in the truck, grateful to find his keys on the driver's seat. The engine purred to life and I backed out into the street, feeling a light bump as I ran over the bastard's ruined leg.

His scream made a sweet melody as I floored it out the driveway. The tires slid on the snow, fishtailing the truck bed before gripping the asphalt beneath the powder. I saw Brent in the side mirror slide into the street, a line of blood left behind him, hands desperately grasping at the cords around his neck.

In the rearview mirror, I could see the police as they came screaming around the corner, sliding just as I had. I wondered what they thought when they saw the man being dragged.

Did they rejoice? Did they pause for a moment, considering if they should allow it? Justice is accommodating to the undeserving. Deciding he was worth saving, they followed. They could save whatever smear was left if they wanted.

I swerved hard and watched him fly into the curb, hitting the sharp edge of a brick mailbox, hard enough to break his spine. My foot eased the accelerator faster and the truck roared as it rocketed through the silent night.

His body hit cars, pavement, sidewalk. Snowmen watched impassively, huddled faces peaked from behind curtains, and the steady procession of sirens behind me masked the torment of the condemned.

Street after street, I didn't stop, didn't pause, not until I saw a house, a familiar house...

Her house.

The other thoughts, her thoughts, the one who'd heard me calling.

I pressed onto the brakes slowly, looking at my home, and the For Sale sign, blowing lightly in the breeze.

It wasn't for me anymore, none of this was for me. I was a memory. And those memories were where I had to stay.

I killed the ignition and stepped out of the cab. The police swerved, exiting and drawing their weapons, shouting their impotence.

Brent Fischer still lived, barely. His teeth gone, his face smashed, one eye rolled, he focused on me while sounds only I could understand spilled from his broken throat. They were the same words that had poured from my own mouth when I felt death's grip.

I grabbed his bloody hair and made sure he could see the house, where we were.

"I'm home, Brent, but I can't stay. Don't worry, you're coming too."

He died and the winter wind took his last breath out into the quiet.

And I went with it.

***

I came to in a hospital room, unsure of where I was, and alone with my thoughts.

They said, "Fugue state" from the moment I'd taken the gunshot wound until the moment I woke up in the hospital. They were her memories, not mine. They grilled me, shouted, asked all kinds of questions I couldn't answer.

I could only remember my own thoughts, and those were just words shouted into the void. No one could explain how I'd survived the gunshot. The word bandied around was "miracle," and the phrase, "stranger things had happened."

In those quiet days alone in my head, I only had one thought:

Not likely.

There had been others. It turns out Luke's house wasn't the only one outfitted for evil. Four sets of remains were found, and there was no telling how many children had been given or to whom. Brent's wife stepped forward to testify on my behalf, claiming he'd been threatening her. All of it was enough to keep me from being charged with murder. It broke the dam of silence, plenty of wives started to come forward, including Maisey Hollman.

She wouldn't get to keep her baby.

Luke, Brent, all of them had not kept records. I don't know if it was intentional, a misdirection to throw off the scent of justice if it came calling, or if they simply hadn't cared.

They dug up Skye from the flowerbed, after I told them where to look. I felt guilty I wasn't there to see her pulled from the dirt, and I wasn't well enough to attend the funeral, but I received the letters from the grieving families that had held out hope their lost ones were still alive. They called me brave, they thanked me, and all it did was make me feel worse.

When I got out, I put my house up for sale. The late February snow whipped around my car, loaded with everything I thought worth taking. I had decided to keep driving until I found a place I hoped would feel like home after I passed the city limits.

But I had a stop to make. I turned off on an old county road on the outskirts of the city, following it all the way until I saw the dark gates and the graves.

I pulled onto the black service road that ran in a long ring around the center of the cemetery and parked closest to where I would find the one I looked for. If Skye's wasn't the newest, it was close enough, and it gleamed like a beacon amidst the weathered headstones.

Chiseled with decorative flowers and shining suns, I read the summation of her life:

SKYE BURTON

1993-2025

Loved for all time, never forgotten, her soul wanders free

The last few words stuck with me. I hadn't told anyone, not even the mandated therapist, about Skye's thoughts in my head. Conversely, I didn't have anyone to talk to about the loneliness that came without her presence. For twenty-four hours, I'd lived the closest thing to another life, and, in my quiet moments, I could still feel how she had.

"I came to say goodbye. I didn't think I would, but I feel like I owe it to you."

The wind blew and I sat completely still, hoping for a moment that she still wandered nearby.

I heard a crunch of snow and turned faster than a snake could strike, pulling the small pistol I'd purchased.

Earl Bobby stood a few feet away, a bouquet of flowers in his hand. "Thought I might see you here eventually."

I didn't lower the pistol. "Keep the hell away from me."

He didn't approach. "I had nothing to do with any of them, girl."

His assertions didn't mean anything to me. I'd heard his name in Skye's mind. I'd had time to think it over. Her cry for help may have been something silent the old man had no chance of hearing.

Or it could have been something she'd spoken to his face as he stood over her.

I stood up and kept the pistol trained on him. He sighed and walked forward; free hand raised. "You want to shoot me, go ahead. I'm too damn old to care anymore. Especially when you find out you haven't seen the evil around you."

He laid the flowers down and I stepped away, refusing to respond.

"For what it's worth," he started. "I'm sorry you went through it. Not all men are like that."

I hated that platitude, that nugget of privilege thrown out as if it could atone for the wounds committed by awful people. Who was Earl Bobby to apologize for all men?

"Not all men, but it always is," I answered.

It was a kernel he'd have to live with for the rest of his life. Seven decades in this world seemed long enough and I couldn't take the chance he was nothing more than an innocent old man.

Help me, Jessie.

I pulled the hammer back.

Red was a good color on her tombstone.

Wile E. Young is from Texas, where he grew up surrounded by stories of ghosts and monsters. During his writing career he has managed to both have a price put on his head and publish his southern themed horror stories. He obtained his bachelor's degree in History, which provided no advantage or benefit during his years as an aviation specialist and I.T. guru.

Fuck Your Thanksgiving

By Judith Sonnet

One

He wanted to call himself "The Puritan," but the newspapers dubbed him "The Gobbler." He didn't like the moniker much. It was tacky and reeked of '80's cheese. When he felt really sour about it, he reminded himself that one didn't have the privilege of choosing one's own nickname, but also he should be thankful for what he had. That was why he did what he did: to give thanks. Thanks... for all he had and all he took.

It was Thursday the 24th, in the year 2022. The Gobbler prepared to strike again. Gingerly, he donned his mask, a creation of his own making, fashioned from a wicker cornucopia. Looking like a beige triangle, it sat over his face with its top point curled to the left. He had affixed a snappable strap, so he could wear the mask without worrying about it tipping off his head. He had also drilled eye holes into the front.

The cornucopia mask rasped against his shaggy hair, and he had to readjust the whole operation to see through the frayed holes. He looked at his reflection in the mirror and admired its uncanny terror. He looked like the real deal, in terms of freaky slasher villains. That was good. He wanted to strike terror into the hearts of the guilty when he approached them.

He wore a frilly blouse and a tight pair of pants, secured to his cumbersome hips with an oversized silver buckle. Not exactly what the pilgrims wore, but a close enough simulation. When a victim ran in fright, they wouldn't stop to analyze his get-up for inconsistences. Nothing mattered when you were covered in blood and gore.

He left his bathroom and strolled into the living area of his doublewide trailer. It had been eighteen years since he had last celebrated Thanksgiving with his family. They had been taken from him because he hadn't offered enough thanks to God. The holiday was, for Him, a sacred event. The Gobbler had been calloused toward it and had insulted God in the process.

With pitch perfect clarity, he could recall the way he had rushed through his meals so he could watch the football games on his crappy television. He had convinced his wife that it would be better to spend Thanksgiving at the trailer and not join the rest of the family in Florida.

He was also reminded that the year his family had died... they had forgotten to say "grace" before cutting into their turkey.

For The Gobbler's stupidity and hubris, the God who so loved the world that He sent His only son to die on the cross... had taken everything from him.

He had come home to find the trailer's door wide open. When The Gobbler walked in, what he saw changed him.

Laura-Bell, laying in a pool of steaming blood, her face battered in and jism drying on her naked rear—

Spike, his head cranked so hard to the left a delicate bone protruded from his broken throat— Baby Rose, her crib swabbed with gore, and the still snorting chainsaw beside it—

They never found the killer, but it almost didn't matter. He already knew who had killed his family: God. Maybe Jesus had given the Ol' Man a helping hand. God came into the doublewide trailer, broke his wife's face, raped her corpse, killed his son, and butchered his daughter with a chainsaw.

Before returning to His heaven, God had said: "And let that be a lesson to you!"

It was.

The Gobbler didn't need to hear the lesson twice.

He spent the first year in misery. He wailed and wept at the perceived injustices of the world, but deep down, he knew that the extermination of his close family was his own doing. The Gobbler had betrayed them with his lax attitude.

Thanksgiving came back to him with a vengeance, fueled by rage, and anger, and—most of all—a desire to please the God he had insulted.

So, The Gobbler was born. Twisted by his convictions, he set out to do the Lord's work, to prove to Him that he understood the lesson God wanted him to learn. Eighteen years later, the Gobbler had become as much a tool to God as a bolt of smiting lighting. Every Thanksgiving, he donned his outfit, and he found someone who needed to learn the reason for the season.

The holiday brought no rest. He saw no friends or family—not that anyone wanted to bring the holiday up in his company, ever since "the tragedy." Instead, The Gobbler selected a house and ensured its occupants understood that God did not reward the ungrateful.

Before leaving his trailer, The Gobbler took an axe from his coat-closet and hefted it against his shoulder. He whistled on his way to his truck. His wicker mask muted the tune which was okay with him. He sang to his God and to no one else.

Behind the wheel and no need to rush, The Gobbler carefully drove away from his driveway. This year's pupils had already been selected...

Two

"Max Peterson said The Gobbler would get us this year!" Troy Fitz admitted to his mother as she busied herself in the kitchen.

"Oh yeah?" She humored him, even though the whole Gobbler mythos disturbed her. "How come?"

"'Cuz of that." Troy pointed at the faux-turkey patties in the oven. "Max said that The Gobbler gets people who don't celebrate Thanksgivin' the 'Traditional Way.'"

"Max watches too much TV." Tig rolled her eyes and ruffled her adopted son's head. He batted her hand away playfully. Tig and her partner, Norma, were both proud of him. Tig often wondered if her motherly love influenced her opinion or if her little boy happened to be special.

Even at eight, he had a firm understanding of social cues, like the way grownups talked. You couldn't slip a fast one by Troy. She didn't feel the need to keep her true feelings away from him but if someone had a problem or a secret, he'd sniff it out like a truffle pig. Tig's own parents had been reserved, prudish, and always shocked whenever she asked important questions. She wanted to foster Troy's curiosity in any way she could, even if it meant having to talk about... *The Gobbler.*

Tig shuddered at the thought. Words like "morbid" and "grotesque" felt tame in comparison to The Gobbler's crimes. Norma often brought her police work home with her—always out of Troy's reach, thank God. Tig had the misfortune of spying a folder filled with crime-scene photos.

The Gobbler had murdered a family of three last year, and he— assuming The Gobbler was a "he"—had made a "human punch bowl" out of their young daughter's head. The gory details had been hard to avoid. The locals had discussed the specifics liberally and with mad relish. Since Norma had witnessed the awful crime scene, Tig felt obliged to picture the grisly scene.

The poor parents of the girl had been forced to eat a cranberry-brain mixture, before taking turns drinking from their daughter's cranium.

It was sick and disturbing. Tig could hardly conjure the proper emotions. To think it had happened not thirty minutes away from her own front lawn! Tig thought herself an optimist, but such events put her philosophy on trial. She struggled to imagine a person committing such deeds, much less making a yearly "thing" of it. Yet, The Gobbler struck without fail every Thanksgiving.

Tig felt another wave of revulsion stitch its way through her flesh. She looked down at Troy and said: "The Gobbler won't get us, because Mommy will protect you."

She believed with her heart. Norma was stronger than any woman Tig had known in her entire life. A female sheriff—and a lesbian to boot—in the state of Missouri? You had to have some *balls* to put up with the sort of shit Norma dealt with on a near daily basis, and this did not factor in the yearly dose of homicides enacted at the hands of The Gobbler!

When Norma catches the son of a bitch, we'll all sleep a little better, Tig thought.

Tenacious, and voracious, Norma would bring The Gobbler to justice. Tig felt vulnerable and sensitive, and Norma always held her steady when the world seemed extra sharp and toothy. Even now, as she and her son stood in the kitchen of their suburban home, Tig felt *something* amiss. Tig couldn't say what but the moment Norma walked through the door it would be all better. Like a kiss on an "ouchie" from your doting mother, everything felt right the moment Norma came inside.

Three

Norma didn't know how to tell Tig the truth anymore. As she inhaled a lungful of wispy smoke, she looked over the backyard and wondered if the truth even mattered. They had a kid now; she couldn't pack up and leave. Besides, Norma didn't hate Tig. The mere thought repulsed her. The truth was...

What was the truth?

Was Norma simply bored with domesticated life? In her late thirties, she figured a mid-life crisis waited a way off. She could find no other basis of comparison.

Tig... I don't want to sit around and watch reality shows with you. I don't want to battle through parent teacher conferences, and recitals, and... God it sounds like I hate my own kid. Norma loved Troy. Though she never really felt as if Troy was "hers." Attached to Troy at the hip, Tig insisted on being a stay-at-home mom, which relegated Norma to the able-bodied breadwinner.

To afford their middle-upper-class house in their dainty suburban neighborhood, Norma felt strong-armed into working the most ungodly hours imaginable. Norma had wanted to travel. When she and Tig had married, they promised to visit Europe. Eventually Norma would be able to quit her job at the Sheriff's department. Instead, Norma found herself promoted.

Working for the police had been her father's idea. Norma had always resented it but saw no alternative. Now, she resented Tig, and worse yet... she resented Troy.

I was supposed to be my own person. Norma thought with a steely frown. *Fuck it. I'm just another blue-collar mom now, aren't I?*

She shook the selfish thoughts out of her head and refocused. Norma stamped her cigarette out on the ashtray precariously placed on the patio rail. She turned and peered through the window. Tig and Troy laughed in the kitchen, which did bring Norma joy.

Worried with lines, Tig's face had matured but had never lost its spark. Norma knew she was lucky to call such a pretty woman hers. Yet, as she watched Tig pull a sheet of ridiculous vegan turkey patties from the oven, Norma thought: *Wouldn't we be happier apart?*

Stern-faced, auburn haired, and short, Norma felt like the total opposite of Tig, who had blonde-white hair and stood six-feet tall. Small and plump, Troy bore dusty brown hair.

They all looked so different. Those differences bothered Norma today.

She wondered if Tig would make *everyone* eat a vegan Thanksgiving dinner this year. Norma looked at her watch and hoped that Bill and Lucy would bring something edible.

Four

"I still think it's rude." Bill said from the front seat. In the back, Lucy held a crockpot filled with her homemade turkey-chili. "We didn't ask if they wanted us to bring anything."

"Norma can't cook for—for poop." Lucy glanced toward the passenger seat, where their five-year-old daughter sat. Hollie looked out the window, watching the world whirl by. Doubting the child paid any attention to her parents, Lucy still refused to swear in front of her baby.

Bill adjusted his coke-bottle lenses and sighed. "Granted, your chili is amazing."

"You'll get an extra helping. You don't have to butter me up." Lucy smiled.

Five

"They're here!" Troy shouted from the living room. Norma strolled up and looked out the window with gratitude. Lucy lugged a crockpot with no help from Bill, who stared up at the sky with gawking wonder. Bill and Lucy had been friends of the family for ages. Since Lucy's parents had died a few years back and Bill's lived in Ireland, they spent Thanksgiving with the Fitz's.

"Oh, now what did she make this time?" Tig huffed as she joined her wife and child at the window.

"Food!" Norma joked, nudging Tig's arm.

Good humoredly, Tig rolled her eyes and sulked back to the kitchen.

Troy ran to open the door, smiling down at Hollie when she walked into the house.

"Troy!" Hollie cheered, giving the older boy a hug. They often acted like cousins rather than kids lumped together for the benefit of their parents.

Norma's brother would be along soon, bringing his nine-year-old with him. It would be good for Troy to have someone nearer his own age in attendance. Norma didn't like to fret whether or not the children had enough entertainment, especially when the adults already made a handful.

Norma helped Lucy up the steps and into the house. "God, it smells good in here!" Lucy declared.

"It smells better in here!" Norma knocked her knuckles against the roof of the crock-pot.

"I can hear you!" Tig shouted jovially from the kitchen.

Everyone laughed, the children included. Bill and Norma settled into the living room.

"I'm honestly surprised we're even having a Thanksgiving this year." Bill admitted.

"How so?" asked Norma.

Bill scanned the room and only continued after he felt assured the children had left. Troy had taken Hollie outside to play at his new swing set, which Norma had installed.

"With all this 'Gobbler' stuff going on, it's hard to feel safe around the holidays."

Norma shrugged. "We don't know that he'll strike this year."

Tig had told her to put up an optimistic front. *No one wants your doom and gloom, Norma.*

"He hits this town every Thanksgiving. Puts a real sour note on things." Bill echoed Norma's internal sentiments.

Norma's deputies were on the prowl for The Gobbler. They hoped to catch him before he committed another holiday-themed atrocity. A few longed to catch him during his malicious act, so they'd have an excuse to fill his face with holes.

No one knew The Gobbler's identity. Even though he usually left behind a few witnesses to detail his vile deeds, no one had ever seen his face. Meticulous, he never left a strand of hair or a fingerprint in his bloody wake. Like a ghost, he selected an unfortunate family, taught them a bizarre "Thanksgiving lesson," then went into hibernation for the rest of the year. If you didn't celebrate Thanksgiving *his* way, then you wouldn't celebrate Thanksgiving at all. With a singular and dreadful purpose, he didn't care about any other holiday and he had no sprees during the offseason.

"Are you at all close to catching him?" Bill asked. "I mean, do you have any leads?"

Norma frowned. She hated this question, and she faced it routinely. There was no correct answer, and there certainly wasn't a satisfying one.

"Sorry, I don't really wanna talk about work. You know?"

"Sorry." Bill blushed.

"Nah, you're good. Want a beer?" Norma jerked a thumb toward the kitchen.

Bill nodded—a bit embarrassed but easily placated by the promise of alcohol.

While Norma grabbed two Corona's from the fridge, a knock came at the door. When she answered, her big brother immediately embraced her.

"Hey, Norm!" Ralph said, his breath smelling of onion dip and his bulk compressing her a bit too tightly. Ralph's big bones had only gotten heavier with age. His jolly face encompassed Norma's view, and her heart warmed over. Yes, as long as Ralph stayed around, their Thanksgiving had no chance of turning sour.

"Where's Patrick?" she asked.

"He heard Hollie and Troy in the backyard and circled around." Ralph patted his sister's back. "One of those for me?" He indicated the beers clinking from her grip.

"Nah, they're both mine." Norma joked.

"Is that Ralph?" Bill called from the living room. "Send him back!"

More laughs and playful digs. Norma retrieved more beer. If they weren't careful, they would all be sauced by the time Tig served dinner.

Tig and Lucy kept busy in the kitchen and Norma made sure she was in and out quickly. She didn't want to impede her wife in any way. Norma often thought she was in charge of earning the bread, but Tig bore sole responsibility for baking it. Besides, Norma kept the men energetic—but not too hyper—and entertained.

She popped the cap off her beer and pocketed it, then took a long swig. The acrid taste calmed her frayed nerves.

Ralph beamed at her, his teeth foamy. Ever since his sweet wife had passed from Ovarian cancer two years after Patrick had been born, he had been every bit the best father he could be. Somehow, the large man took in stride being a single parent.

Would Tig thrive or flounder if something happened to me? Norma thought with a shudder. *Jesus, where did that come from? No bummers allowed, Norma. You calm your tits and enjoy your beer.*

"God, I've been looking forward to this all week." Bill said. "I'll be honest, Thanksgiving is the calm before the storm. My folks are coming to visit—"

"From 'The Old Country'?" Ralph joshed.

"From Ireland, yes." Bill laughed. "God, they're making such a big deal over Christmas. Not a day goes by without a pestering phone call. I mean, God love 'em! But what'll it be like when they're here in person? It might sound awful of me, but I'm used to seeing them on a computer screen."

"You'll be happy when they get here." Ralph shrugged.

"Yeah. I bet." Bill scoffed.

"So, what was in that crock-pot Lucy brought in?" Norma asked.

"Oh, thank God Lucy cooked something!" Ralph interjected.

"Turkey chili. Figured we deserved a 'carnivore alternative.'" Bill's grin fell away. "I hope that's not rude of us—"

"Not at all. If I had to eat one of those mushy tofu patties with white gravy, I'd string myself up with next month's lights." Norma whispered, conspiratorially.

Six

Patrick came around the house and saw Troy pushing Hollie on the swing. Caught entertaining the baby, Troy looked embarrassed, but he continued anyway.

"Sup?" Patrick tried nonchalant. He stuffed his cold hands in the pockets of his hoodie and strolled to the other kids.

"Troy was tellin' me about The Gobbler!" Hollie yipped as she swung back and forth.

Patrick froze. "The Gobbler, huh?"

"Yeah. Said it's a monster tha' gobbles up the turkey's every year!"

Patrick looked toward Troy. The slightly younger boy communicated via raised brows.

The little girl had asked Troy about The Gobbler. Rather than traumatize her with the truth he had been quick on his feet and had fabricated a kid's story, just to please her.

"That's why our parents are so worried 'bout it. Cuz he may gobble up the turkey 'fore we get any! *Too high*!" Holly shrieked.

Troy quickly stopped her by grabbing the chains of the swing and towed her back.

Her feet dangled above the ground and her head wobbled dizzily.

Again, Troy communicated to Patrick by giving him a smirk and raising a brow. This look said: *kids, huh?* Having to watch out for Hollie made both boys feel like grownups. They would never admit it, but they enjoyed the responsibility.

It hadn't snowed, but the air felt cold. The grass crunched loudly beneath Patrick's feet. He walked toward the edge of the yard, where manicured lawn met tangled underbrush. "We should have a sleepover sometime." He said when Troy walked up by his side, moving backward so he could keep his eyes on Hollie.

The little girl hummed lazily, moving her hips so the swing rocked side-to-side.

"Yeah?" Troy asked.

"Yeah." Patrick responded. "Get a few guys and maybe convince your moms to let us camp in the woods?" He indicated the foliage. "That'd be cool."

"We could roast marshmallows!"

"And weenies!" Patrick added.

"We're makin' marshmallows?" The utterance of her favorite treat had conjured Hollie like a magic word. She kicked herself off the swing-set and dashed over toward the boys.

"Nah, sorry to get your hopes up." Patrick ruffled her hair. "We were jus' talkin'."

"Ah." Hollie nodded vigorously, trying to appear as if she understood exactly what the big boys discussed.

"Seriously, though, Troy. We could do it. Get a few of your friends and mine together. We could rough it for the night. I have a few sleeping bags stowed away."

"I've got a tent!" Troy said, victoriously.

"Wait? Am I invited?" Hollie cautiously asked.

"Nah. Guys only." Patrick said. "Besides, you don't wanna go camping. There's gonna be bugs and bats and—"

"EW!" Hollie proclaimed with a grimace.

"You don't like bugs?" A voice surprised them from the woods.

The three children turned around, more perplexed than frightened.

A bizarre character stepped out from behind a bare tree. Surrounded by autumnal hues, the man with a cornucopia for a mask looked like a Fall spirit.

Patrick realized that the term he was looking for was "mascot." This fella was a representation of autumn, like he would teach children about the science of falling leaves or the changing of the seasons in a school program.

"W-who are you?" Troy asked.

The man did a polite bow and spoke with a calming lilt, "Your parents hired me to entertain you before the big feast!"

"Like a party clown?" Hollie interjected.

"Yes!" The man snapped his fingers. He wore white gloves. The guy looked almost clownish with his garish outfit, his weird mask, and his giant silver belt buckle.

Patrick, at nine, knew that if his father had hired an entertainer, he would have forewarned the kids. Besides, why had he been hiding in the woods?

"Just like a party clown!" the costumed man reiterated. "And I have a whole lotta magic to show y'all!"

"I dunno," Patrick said. "Maybe we should check with our parents first."

"Yeah," Troy said.

"Very wise!" The mascot said, hands against his hips and eyes gleaming through the holes in his mask. "Very wise indeed!"

How does he know my name? Maybe our parents did hire him! Patrick thought with the brand of wish fulfillment that was only afforded to the young.

"Why don't we go together?" The mascot said, reaching behind the nearest tree. "That way you can see how well your folks and I get along!"

Patrick nodded and turned to lead the strange man toward Troy's house. Troy and Hollie stayed close to the older boy. None of them saw The Gobbler draw his axe from behind the tree.

<u>Seven</u>

The back door swung open, leading directly into the kitchen. Tig and Lucy busily prepared dinner. They had laid out stuffing, cranberries, flat noodles in a mushroom broth, mashed potatoes, sweet potatoes, yams, and even stuffed mushrooms buffet-style on the island.

They did not celebrate the holiday the "right" way. Blood boiling, The Gobbler considered this another strike against them. *Thanksgiving must be served AT THE TABLE.* He seethed. *It may as well be served in a goddamn, fucking feeding trough! Are pigs thankful for their slop?* If it had been this one offense, The Gobbler may have left the Fitz house alone, but multiple reasons drew him to them.

He followed Tig's social media account from a burner profile she had friended without question. She intended to feed her guests *fake* turkey. She may as well have spat in God's face, telling him she didn't care for bird meat, despite the fact He had created them so lovingly. You could be vegan all year long so long as you ate a proper bird on Thanksgiving! If he simply spelled this out to them, they wouldn't understand. The lesson must be taught in a way which challenged the student.

Just as I learned. Just as I faced challenges... when my family was butchered. Nightmare visuals flashed before The Gobbler as the children led him into their house. He saw the baby crib spattered in blood and the roaring chainsaw vibrating on the floor.

The chainsaw had stirred Baby Rose up like butter. Only a few months old, her fingers landed all over the place, because she had reached up to push at the encroaching blade.

The Gobbler's knees went weak, but he steadied himself. He let the door shut and waited for the adults to notice his presence.

"Mom!" Troy said, going up to Tig and pulling at her apron.

"Lucy, would you check the fridge and see if I've got any green beans? I totally forgot to—"

"Mom!" Troy was more adamant. "Mom!"

"What? What?" Frazzled, Tig whirled around.

Lucy looked over too.

Patrick and Hollie stood by Troy. The three had become connected at the hip while they walked, and their invisible leash still tied them together even in the warmth of the kitchen.

Unsurprised, The Gobbler hefted the axe and adopted a batter's stance. Children often perceived danger preternaturally, though unable to respond accordingly. The Gobbler waited with pregnant breath, glaring through his eye holes.

"Mom, do you know him?" Troy pointed.

For the first time, the adults both saw the intruder. Tig cocked her head in confusion. Lucy released a startled gasp.

In that moment, the children recognized the uncomfortable feeling in their guts and knew it was too late to do anything about it.

The Gobbler swung the axe.

Eight

The axe's head cleaved through the air. Tig stooped down, hearing the blade as it whooshed by her cranium. If she hadn't moved so quickly, it would have bitten deep. She grabbed the children and dragged them back. They moved like liquid, pooling around her for safety.

"Bill!" Lucy called out. "Bill, come quick!" Her screams couldn't convey her true terror.

Norma and Ralph still laughed amiably while Bill ran into the kitchen. "What's going on?" he asked before noticing the masked maniac and his axe. By then, it was too late.

The Gobbler pivoted, swung the axe low, and buried it directly in-between Bill's legs.

Tig didn't have balls, but her groin tightened with pain as she watched crimson blood spew from the crotch of Bill's pants.

Lucy had been muted by fear, but Bill trumpeted impending doom. Bill fell to his knees. His legs tightened around the axe and dragged it out of the maniac's hands.

Confused, The Gobbler stood empty-handed, watching as the man hobbled backward on his knees.

Bill clutched the shaft of wood protruding like a comical phallus from betwixt his thighs. Blood rained on the tiled floor. Bill spritzed the walls with crimson splatters when he swung his hips in agony. He screamed in a high-pitched tone foreign to his stature.

The axe dislodged and plopped wetly against the ground. Bill scrabbled with something at his pelvis. *Something* slipped from his struggling, wormy fingers and smattered against the floor with a soft detonation of blood-- one of his balls. Pulped and deflated by the axe, a chewed-up olive rather than a stone, a frayed cord hung from its rear like a pig's tail.

The Gobbler picked up the blood smeared axe.

Tig hadn't thought to turn around and grab a piece of cutlery from the countertop. Instead, she prioritized Hollie's safety.

The girl wailed, her face red and her eyes so large they looked like tennis balls crammed into her sockets. She screamed, "Daddy!" on repeat.

Tig covered her eyes and pulled her close. The other boys sheltered Hollie, barricading her in a wall of nimble limbs.

Lucy held her hands over her mouth. Bill's blood had flecked across her face.

The Gobbler lowered the axe, as if deciding where to hit Bill.

The poor man was stammering, his glasses askew and his eyes brimming with tears. "D-don't... k-k-kill me-e."

The Gobbler threw his whole body into the next chop. The axe slammed against Bill's head with a hollow *thunk*. Instead of burying itself in his skull, the axe bounced back in The Gobbler's grip. The result proved no less explosive. Blood spouted from the crevasse torn through Bill's hairline. A congested wave fanned particles of brain matter.

Bill jittered in place before tumbling back. Leaking from the top of his head and from the inseam of his jeans, he lay dead on the floor, his arms and legs spread.

Tig couldn't believe she had just witnessed the death of one of her beloved friends. It felt unreal, like a nightmare.

The Gobbler set the axe against his shoulder, turned toward the huddled bystanders, and spoke in a whisper, "He was lucky."

What the FUCK does that mean? thought Tig.

<u>Nine</u>

Just as Norma was about to ring her coworkers, the masked man wheeled around the corner. He held an axe to Troy's bouncing throat.

"Ah-uh!" the man sneered. "Don't touch that dial!"

Frozen with panic, Norma and Ralph had heard the explosive death of Bill. Even with her training, Norma hadn't known what to do with the terror located inside her own home. She considered running upstairs to retrieve her gun, but she kept it stowed under her bed in a lockbox. She had taken her cellphone out, only to note the low battery. By the time Ralph had handed her his, a madman clutched Troy.

The Gobbler.

Who else could it be? Thanksgiving, after all.

"Oh, sweet Jesus!" Ralph said after seeing the blood splattered slasher.

The Gobbler laughed at this before shucking his shoulders. "You both are wanted in the dining room. Follow me."

In the next room, he released Troy and pointed at the table. Glad to see her son out of the maniac's hands, Norma found the possibilities for rescue unpromising. If he confidently released a bargaining chip, The Gobbler didn't care about his own safety or he knew no one would dare fight him.

When he pulled a gun from his back pocket, it confirmed Norma's fears.

"Sit down, everyone." The Gobbler said.

The family and their friends obeyed. Norma sat where she had expected, at the head of the table. Tig sat beside her, holding Troy's hand tightly. Patrick was next. Then Ralph took his place at the table's end. Across from Patrick, Lucy shook like a whippet. She held Hollie to her chest. The little girl had become catatonically silent.

The maniac pulled a Ziplock baggie filled with zip-ties from his pocket and tossed it on the table. "Patrick," the fiend hissed, "are you the eldest?"

"Y-yes." Patrick nodded, uncertainly.

"Then you have the biggest responsibility here." The Gobbler whined. "You get to make sure none of the grownups get out of their seats."

"Wh-what?" Patrick sounded flummoxed.

The Gobbler didn't take kindly to questions. He thumped the back of Patrick's head with the butt of his grimy gun.

"Hey!" Ralph stood, but the weapon swiveled through the air and pointed right at the larger man's nose.

"You wanna taste lead, fatso?" The Gobbler chortled.

Chastened, Ralph settled back into his seat. He looked toward his son. Patrick wept, but he held in his sobs with wet hands.

Norma would bet money that The Gobbler could have knocked the kid out with a tiny bit more force. His blow had been harsh, but it was controlled. It sent a clear message: *When I say something... do it!* "Why are you doing this?" Norma spoke in a raspy tone as Patrick worked. He started with his dad, securing his hands to the armrest of his chair. Ralph's meaty hands turned blue with his circulation cut.

The Gobbler snickered. "I'm doing this for your own good."

"Is it always like that? Did you do this to the Yearling family for their own good?"

"Norma!" Tig hissed, wanting her wife to avoid provoking the gunned maniac.

"They didn't keep the holiday pure," The Gobbler said. "They refused to celebrate because they believed that Thanksgiving is built on genocide." He chuffed. "They deserved what happened to them."

Norma remembered the photos. The Yearling's looked connected to an invisible maypole by their bowels. The killer had pinned them to opposing walls, pulled their organs out, and tied them together in the middle of the room. This madman had left their son, blinded and "I'm ashamed of my heritage" scratched into his stomach with a knife. The lettering had been exact. The Gobbler hadn't wavered as he carved the epitaph into the ten-year-old.

This guy is capable of anything. While he killed Bill in my kitchen, I tried to figure out what to do about it. Christ, I never wanted to be a sheriff... or a protector... or the strongest person in the room. What the fuck am I doing? Norma couldn't afford to have an existential crisis at the moment.

Norma nodded at what The Gobbler had said, "What did we do wrong? Just tell us, sir, and we'll fix it."

The Gobbler responded with a snarl. He reached up and tugged at his cornucopia mask. His whole body shuddered with anger. "You won't get it if I have to spell it out for you."

Patrick had tied Lucy down and worked Norma's hands into place. Two zip-ties secured her to her chair.

The children remained unrestrained.

"Now their feet." The Gobbler tossed a second baggie of zip-ties onto the table.

Patrick gulped. Taking the ties, he settled onto his hands and knees and got to work.

Pointing his gun from one tear-stained face to another, The Gobbler walked behind Patrick. Every time the nose of the gun sniffed a victim, they mewled with fright. Lucy shrieked the loudest when the cold barrel touched the first knob of her spine.

"Shhh." The Gobbler said while wiping Lucy's hair away from her sweaty brow. "It'll be over soon. Most of you are going to live through this. Don't cry."

Hollie whimpered from Lucy's chest. The little girl hugged her mother like a koala against a tree. The Gobbler reached down to ruffle her hair.

"Don't touch her!" Norma shouted.

The Gobbler turned the gun toward Norma and fired.

The bullet plowed through the top of Norma's scalp, searing a red river through her hair. Blood fell from both sides of her skull and dappled her shoulders.

The adults screamed. The children howled.

Norma gurgled as her mouth filled with blood. The bullet paved a clear path through her skull. She lay back in her chair, jerking against her ties.

"NO! NORMA! OH GOD!" Tig wailed.

"Momma!" Troy shouted, his voice cracking. "*MOMM-MA!*"

The Gobbler laughed. The noise around him sounded like a symphony.

Ten

Troy couldn't believe his mother was dead. He looked at her corpse, watching her eyes roll up. Her jaw fell slack and her blood ebbed. His eyes fuzzed over with tears and his teeth seared through the tip of his tongue. Tasting iron felt like tasting his mother's blood. Troy looked at his mother's slayer.

The brute laughed, like a day at the circus for him. His gun still released smoke, which reminded Troy of Norma's cigarettes... *Only a few seconds ago her heart beati and she loved me, and now Mom and I are alone. All because of the man I let into the house, It's my fault. It's all my fault.*

Troy's tears flew from his eyes. Snot slicked his lips. He wept loudly, covering his face in his hands and wailing into his palms. The Gobbler laughed, mocking Troy's trauma .

Tig turned her panic into rage. She threw curses at the intruder, "You fuck! You fucker! I'll kill you, you *fuck*!"

Troy had never heard his mother swear so profoundly except when she had accidentally dropped a hammer on her thumb while building a birdhouse, but that wasn't at all comparable.

Tig's violent anger had been stoked in flames and blood, the opposite of who his mother *was*. Norma protected and provided while Tig nurtured.

Clogged with tears, Troy gasped for breath as The Gobbler turned toward Tig and raised his gun once more. If he fired, Troy thought his heart would stop from shock.

Instead, The Gobbler spoke, his voice a snake's rattle, "Shut the fuck up, cunt."

Everyone tried to hold their noises. Lucy hiccupped. Ralph seethed. No one spoke.

"The children will come with me now," The Gobbler said.

"No. No. NO!" Tig started.

"I SAID SHUT THE FUCK UP!" The Gobbler raised the gun.

"Don't hurt my mommy!" Troy blurted, standing up and holding his hands above his head. "I'll go with you! Just don't hurt her!"

"No! No!" Tig shook in her seat, tearing her arms up and down. The tightened zip-tie cuffs scratched her wrist open. Troy saw blood welling up along the white line of plastic.

"Good, son. You understand." The Gobbler said. "When I say something, you do it. If you don't, more people will die than necessary."

"No one should have died!" Tig interjected. "NO ONE!"

"Please, mister." Lucy looked up woefully. "Not our babies!"

Hollie hugged her tightly, and her soft little face nuzzled like a kitten into the crook of Lucy's neck.

The Gobbler grabbed a handful of Lucy's hair and pulled. "The kids will come with me and, if you all behave, things will go smoothly."

"What are you going to do with them?" Ralph asked, detached from the events laid out before him. "What do you want our children for?"

"That's for me to know and for you to find out!" The Gobbler mocked.

"I'll go," Troy walked around the table. "I will! Just don't hurt anyone else! Please!"

His jeans soaked in urine, Patrick stood by his father like a statue, holding his hands over his front.

"Troy, pull the kid away from the bitch." The Gobbler said, pointing to Lucy and Hollie. "Separate 'em!"

Troy waddled over, keeping his eyes glued on the serial killer. When he came to Lucy and Hollie, he whispered to this child, "It's okay. I told you he only eats turkeys. You need to come with us."

Hollie nodded, bleary eyed and traumatized.

Troy attempted to peel Hollie away from Lucy. She clung like Velcro, shaking her head and whimpering

"C'mon!" The Gobbler insisted.

"Just give him a second!" Ralph snapped.

"Shut the fuck up!" The Gobbler roared.

Hollie cried again.

Troy wiped her tears with his hand, smudging red lines across her puffy face. "It's okay. We're okay. Everything is going to be okay." The child told the child. Troy wished he could believe his own words, but they tasted arid in his mouth. Eventually, he had Hollie bundled against him. He dragged her away from Lucy.

"Not my baby! Please, don't hurt my baby!" Lucy cried.

"C'mon, kids!" The Gobbler led the way. "Follow me!"

Troy hazarded one last glance at his dead mother before rounding the corner into the kitchen.

Eleven

Tig pulled at her restraints. Patrick had tied her tight. She had lost feeling below her ankles. Her fingers had turned a bruised shade of purple. The pain and irritation meant nothing in comparison to her emotional turmoil. She couldn't help looking at Norma's corpse.

Her wife had received a merciful death compared to Bill, but that didn't lessen the trauma. Every time she saw Norma's uprooted scalp and bloody streams, Tig re-experienced the shocking act of violence. It played in her brain like a demented movie on repeat. The Gobbler raised the gun and fired. Then the bullet sucked back into the weapon's throat only to be coughed up onto the same trajectory.

"What's he doing with our kids?" Ralph asked with a whimper. "Oh, God, could someone have heard the gunshot? Is help on the way?"

Tig would have liked to believe so, but their next door neighbors had left for the tropics and the other house stood vacant. The "for sale" sign hadn't moved in months. She didn't mention these woeful observations, in order to preserve what little hope Norma's brother clung to.

"If he touches Hollie, I'll kill him," Lucy seethed. "That bastard. That motherfucking bastard."

Tig felt another wave of sorrow fall over her. She glanced toward Norma and asked, "What should we do?"

Usually so reliable when it came to solving problems, Norma had no answers. *This is more than your usual household issue, Tig. This ain't a leaky pipe or a burned-out bulb. This is something none of us could have prepared for.*

Time rolled by slowly. It moved in a slog, as if the very air had turned into a seeping mold. Tig felt her thoughts wind down into vague aphorisms and prayers.

Lucy spent the duration of their wait muttering to herself, "If he touches Hollie, I'll kill him. I'll kill him. I'll kill him."

The Gobbler came around the corner, still wearing his cornucopia mask. He had removed his frilly shirt, revealing his chest grizzled with wiry hair. His torso and hands were soused in blood. He carried a turkey baster, drooling with warm liquids.

Unceremoniously, he walked to Lucy, grabbed her hair, and cranked her head back. She opened her mouth in shock. Lucy gagged when The Gobbler crammed the baster into her orifice before squeezing its rubber rear. A blast of fluid filled her maw. She sputtered violently.

The Gobbler stormed away, leaving Lucy to retch and howl. Whatever he had coated her mouth with had been foul. Lucy vomited. Raspy croaks escaped her throat between expulsions of chunky bile-syrup. Her spew quilted the placemat and empty dinner plate before her.

The Gobbler returned from the kitchen, repeating the process with Ralph. Before he retched up the juices forced into his gullet, he gasped, "What the fuck is that?"

Not answering, The Gobbler left the room. When he came back, the baster oozed even more fluid. Humming as if on a merry chore, he strolled to Tig. He held her head back, slammed the baster into her unwilling mouth, and squeezed. Worse than anything she could have imagined, the wet sauce ejected into her mouth. Acidic and slick, it coated every inch of her trap, leaving nowhere for her tongue to escape the offensive fluid.

Unlike the rest, The Gobbler made sure Tig swallowed. He tossed the baster aside, pinned her mouth shut, and squeezed her nose with a gnarled hand. "Gulp!" he commanded.

Tig had no choice but to obey. Comparable to enduring the taste of a hard medicine, she forced the confection past her throat. The repulsive stew immediately wanted to bounce back up. Tig forced it to stay down.

Satisfied, The Gobbler released her face and stepped back. "Do you want to know what that was?" The Gobbler asked.

Tig shook her head, "No."

"That was the contents of Bill's tummy. I opened him up. I filled the baster with his stomach acids, his bile, and his bowel-juices. I even put the baster up his rectum and sucked up as much of his shit as I could. Then I poured it all in a bowl and mixed it with my own piss. There's some left over. Anyone want seconds?"

After making such a show of holding down his awful offerings, Tig vomited. The explosion of puke flew out of her like water from a storm-drain. She burped gutturally after the flow tapered down.

"What are you doing to our kids?" Lucy screeched. "Please, don't hurt my baby!"

"You can't do this to us!" Ralph called from the table's end. "You can't!"

"Do what you want to us but let our children go!" begged Lucy.

"No!" The Gobbler growled. "You must all be taught a lesson!"

"Please! We'll learn! Whatever we did, we'll do better!" Lucy pleaded. "Just let my baby go-o-o-oh!" Her voice broke into sobbing gulps. "*Please!*"

The Gobbler rushed to Lucy's side of the table. He smacked her across the face with a hollow w*hap*.

Lucy's cries continued unabated.

"I'll teach you to be quiet!" The Gobbler pulled a steak-knife loose from a folded napkin.

Tig imagined he would cut Lucy's throat, so The Gobbler surprised her when he curtly severed her bounds and hefted her up from the chair. He tossed her over the table, bending her at the waist. Roughly, he towed her skirts up. Lucy's cries increased in tone as he tugged her panties away. The sound of the fabric shredding was deafening.

He held her to the table by the nape of her neck, then he reached across the table and retrieved the baster.

No. No. No. No. No, Tig thought.

"NO! NO! NO! NO! NO!" Lucy wailed.

He used the baster to slurp up the vomit Lucy had expelled upon her dinnerplate. The yellowed fluids congealed around the baster's tip.

"Stop it! For the love of God!" Ralph cried. "PLEASE!" Lucy begged.

He shoved the baster into her from behind. Tig heard Lucy's skin shred as the Gobbler forced the intruding instrument as far up her anus as it would go and began to pump. He giggled gleefully as Lucy's panicked cries turned into yips.

"I'll teach... *you!*" The Gobbler said. "I'll teach you *all!*"

<u>Twelve</u>

After violating her with the turkey baster, The Gobbler used another set of zip-ties to secure Lucy to her chair. Her face was red with humiliation, confusion, and pain. After losing her husband, not knowing what had become of her child, and being sexually assaulted, Lucy's brain had put up a "Do Not Disturb" sign.

Tig respected the request. Instead of reassuring Lucy with hollow words, she worked against her restraints. They dug into her flesh, but she didn't care. If Tig wound up degloving her hands, she'd consider it the price of her freedom.

"This is crazy," Ralph stated the obvious. "We can't die like this. It's not fair. It's just not fair."

Tig ignored him. Looking at Norma's cooling corpse, Tig wondered if every family attacked by The Gobbler had gone through such existential disorder as they endured his whims. More than "crazy," The Gobbler was evil incarnate. *What did we do so wrong that God sent his most vile agent after us? What was it?*

As if to answer her query, The Gobbler came from the kitchen. His mask smeared in juices, blood dribbled down his throat and filled the bowl of his clavicle.

"You deserve what's happening to you," The Gobbler said. "You upset the balance and you deserve this."

'What did we do?" Tig asked, her voice breaking. "Please, just tell us."

"You eat turkey on Thanksgiving," The Gobbler said, "not fake meat."

The three adults sat in silent agony.

"T-that's why y-you're doing... *this*?" Repulsed, Lucy sounded ready to vomit again.

His eyes steely behind his mask, The Gobbler turned his head slowly toward her. "Yes, because when you ignore tradition, you deserve to be punished. Thanksgiving is a special holiday. I'm tired of seeing it besmirched by people who *think* they know better. I thought I knew better and God punished me for my transgressions. Now, I'm punishing you, so God doesn't have to."

I wasn't too far off the mark, Tig thought. *He's on a mission from a puritanical God, a God that doesn't take lightly to slights against His plan. And his God wants us to celebrate Thanksgiving HIS way, not our own.*

"You're supposed to have meat at your table," The Gobbler said.

"We do!" Lucy said. "I brought a goddamn turkey chili!"

"An abortion of the tradition! A deformity! A perversion! A supplement to make up for this one's crude sins!" The Gobbler pointed toward Tig. "You brought this upon your friends and family, Tig! You!"

Tig shook her head. "You're insane. You're a crazy freak who does this for–for *pleasure*! You justify it with tradition and religion but you aren't pious! You aren't *right*! You're just a pervert! Just a perverted fucking piece of shit! Fuck you!"

The Gobbler chuckled, as if Tig had told him an inside joke.

"Just because we don't celebrate the way you do doesn't mean we deserve to suffer!" Tig snarled.

"Oh, Tig." The Gobbler hummed. He turned briskly and walked back into the kitchen. As he did, they heard the oven beep shrilly. He puttered quietly in the kitchen.

The adults all listened, hoping their children would give them a signal that they were okay, that The Gobbler had, for some reason, spared them from misery.

The Gobbler came back into the dining room, wearing oven mitts, He had employed Tig's largest baking sheet. In an ode to his brute strength, he carried his payload without faltering.

"Tig, you wanted to celebrate Thanksgiving without the bird God provided you. I assure you there will be meat at this table today!"

They screamed when he set the baking sheet in the center of the table. An amalgamation of limbs and burned flesh steamed on its top.

Patrick had been sliced open down the middle. His clothes had been removed and his arms had been sawed off. His legs ended at the knees. A widened cavity, his torso stretched so far apart that his splintered ribs pointed like white fingers toward the heavens. In his center, Troy had been shoved. He had been cut apart so all that remained was his head, his trunk, and the nubs of his shoulders. He had been de-boned, so his lower portions could be folded and crammed into Patrick. Blackened with burns, Troy's head rested right beneath Patrick's chin. Hollie's head glistened in Troy's guts. A tangled loop of intestines plugged her open mouth, like the apple in a pig roast.

They had been cooked individually, then compressed together. The Gobbler had used thick strands of twine to secure them so they wouldn't fall apart as he walked them from one room to the next. The actual butchering had taken place outside, leaving the backyard a mess of discarded limbs, loose bones, spattered blood, and neatly folded clothing.

"Ladies and gentlemen! Boys and girls! I proudly present... THE HUMAN TURDUCKEN!" The Gobbler proclaimed with a flourish.

His audience applauded with screams.

Lucy wailed louder than any of them. Her daughter's eyes had dehydrated into crinkly crisps, yet Lucy swore Hollie looked right at her! Hollie plead with her burned eyes, asking her mother, *Why couldn't you keep me safe?*

Quieter than anyone at the table, Ralph couldn't believe that his son had actually been butchered so offensively. It made no sense to his frazzled, traumatized brain, so he simply refused to believe that the display before him was real.

Tig cried out in horror. She recalled every memory she could of Troy. Earlier, hadn't they been talking in the kitchen while she cooked? Hadn't he been tugging at her apron expectantly? Hadn't he been... *alive?*

The Gobbler clapped his hands together, cheerfully laughing as his captive audience wept in agony. Their tears nourished his cold heart. The cacophony of brutality that surrounded him paid off all his efforts in triplicate.

A gunshot cracked through the room. Blood sprayed from The Gobbler's wounded throat and rained against the tabletop. He stumbled backward, tripped over his own feet, and slumped against the wall. He gazed across the room and saw a deputy from the Sheriff's department standing in the entryway.

Green-faced, the policeman's hands trembled. He squeezed the trigger once more. This bullet chomped into the center of The Gobbler's chest.

The villain's lungs detonated from the intrusion. Weakly, he keeled over and lay simmering against the ground. Not dead yet, he leaked profoundly. More blood gushed out of him than he thought possible.

The adults hadn't noticed their savior or the gunshot. They fixated on the mashed remains of their children. They cried and bellowed and made promises to God that they would be good if only he'd make it stop—make it stop, oh, make it stop!

"Oh, Christ!" The deputy vomited as he caught sight of the distorted horror laid out on the table.

Of course, the deputy probably came by to check on Norma, thought The Gobbler. *The sheriff probably updated the department on her day since they looked for The Gobbler—for me. When she stopped responding to their texts, they sent this jackass out... and he had to go and ruin everything.*

Before passing, The Gobbler remembered a morbid memory, what he had done to his own family. The Gobbler had such fun breaking them to pieces and playing in their gore, the messes and the stains they left behind.

Worst of all, The Gobbler thought, *I shouldn't hold onto this memory. If I do, I might do something really bad. I might hurt someone else. It's one thing to kill my own family, but another to go after strangers.*

Then, The Gobbler's thoughts quieted and his heart stilled in his battered chest. For him, Thanksgiving was permanently over.

For Lucy, Tig, and Ralph, the screaming was only the tip of the iceberg. They pulled at their armrests and unified their misery into one long wail, as wild as that of animals in line to be slaughtered. Roars of pain bubbled from the dining room and didn't ever want to stop. As the deputy continued to vomit, the three survivors continued to scream,

God sat high in His heaven. There, amid the clouds, the angels, and the souls of the dead, He laughed.

Judith Sonnet is a trans woman who lives in Utah, where she writes stories, collects vintage films, and hoards massive amounts of retro paperback books. Judith also believes in ghosts, UFO's, and Bigfoot.

Night's Near With Much Undone

by Craig Brownlie

Come then, night's near with much undone
And Time's fine sand too swift doth run.
-**Defiance**, *Ivor Gurney*

***

"Giuseppe Arcimboldo," read Louis Stern off the label on the wall. "*Four Seasons in One Head*, on loan from The National Gallery, Washington, D.C."

Louis sat on a bench in the British Museum. The CBS radio network had asked for a story on the art loaned to the Brits by the Americans and now held "hostage" by the Germans. The

Nazis had taken London three months prior. Louis' editor in New York had used the word "hostage" inaccurately since the Germans had not yet taken notice of all they now possessed.

Eric Sevareid, one of the three CBS reporters senior to Louis, had dodged this assignment but did offer a brief primer. "Arcimboldo is the fruit face guy from the Renaissance. He painted different fruits so they formed human heads and the like. The painting you'll be looking for will be an assembly of seasonal growths, like citrus and berries."

Eric had been right about the assemblage part, but he missed the boat on the specific items. This creature contained apples, plums, sticks, grapes, flowers, fungus and more. Rather than the amusing picture Louis expected, this painting appeared downright somber, as if an elderly goblin had sat for the artist.

Louis jotted a few notes sufficient to babble into a microphone for the brief piece expected overseas. He had another appointment, less innocuous, at German Headquarters with Obergruppenführer Reinhard Heydrich.

***

Louis Stern did not speak German. He knew Auf Wiedersehen, Schnitzel, and not a lot more, which limited the conversation with his driver. Heydrich may have assumed Louis spoke the language because of his last name or perhaps the Nazi officer preferred to limit Louis' chance of interviewing the young man. Either way, Louis wished he could say the words for "slow down" and "where are you going?" because the driver clearly had never been to the English countryside.

After two rain-drenched stops to consult a map which the driver kept to himself, they arrived at Down House, a large, brilliant white house set amidst a swirl of gardens. Even in the dreary weather, the estate looked like a pearl set in an emerald oyster.

Wearing black uniforms and carrying umbrellas, soldiers walked in the yard. When the car arrived at the main entrance, the young driver leapt out but failed to reach Louis in time to open the passenger door. Louis stood beside the car as a familiar face approached, reaching out with an umbrella.

"Greetings, Herr Stern," said Heydrich, glaring at the driver for his ineptitude. "As you can see, the weather in England is not what brought us across the Channel."

Louis wanted to ask if anything specific had, but he preferred to wait and watch. No one in the bar at Claridge's Hotel had the slightest idea what the Nazis had going in Kent, but a number of bigwigs had an interest. Even Ed Murrow, Walt Cronkite, and Sevareid had no specific information, though they offered Louis all sorts of contraband in exchange for taking his place in the English countryside.

Murrow offered two cases of American cigarettes and a half-empty bottle of Jack Daniels if Louis arranged for Edward to hide in the trunk of the German car. Louis had not bought his own drinks for the last three nights and had fought off all sorts of bribes in which every newspaper reporter in London insisted Louis post his first copy with a one hour window before transmitting it across the Atlantic. No longstanding professional wanted to be scooped.

"But where is your luggage? No worry, I will have the servants lay out one of our spare uniforms for you. And the radio room will be prepared to transmit your story to North America each evening." Heydrich smiled. "Here is Andrew. He is particularly good at the job of butler, I believe."

"This way, sir," said Andrew, dressed to the last detail to serve an aristocratic weekend at an English country house.

Louis followed the servant into the house, which turned out less grand inside than expected. The smaller rooms did not lend themselves to large gatherings, though they appeared warm and cozy for a well-to-do family.

At the top of the stairs, Andrew finally spoke, "You have been assigned one of the four bedrooms, sir." Leading the way, he stepped into a pleasant accommodation with a single bed and not much else.

"I confess confusion, Andrew," said Louis. "My fellow correspondents from America told me Charles Darwin and his family resided here."

"So it is, sir," agreed Andrew. "He and his wife lived here happily for forty years. Their children ran among the gardens and assisted their father in experiments."

"Shouldn't it be larger?"

"Mr. Darwin lived the comfortable life of a country gentleman, sir. Not what Americans or Germans, if you pardon me for speaking out of turn, consider the life of an English Lord."

Louis gestured at the sparsity of the room. "Surely not like this though?"

"Mr. Darwin died many decades ago, sir. The estate passed through other hands in the meantime. When I arrived, I found the furnishings in a state similar to most of the country cottages in the area."

"Deserted?"

"The war and this aftermath. Many left in a hurry, sir—those who had the means. When we arrived, Down House had been empty for a few weeks at least."

"Where did you work prior to this, Andrew?" Louis asked.

"I served at the pleasure of His Majesty," said Andrew. "My brother served in the land defense force. Our guests detained me in Dover while the royal family evacuated to Dublin."

"Canada, now, I hear," said Louis. "Along with the cabinet." Louis looked downtrodden for all of England while Andrew retained his composure. "You were in Dover to bury your brother?"

"Many of our lads required seeing to, sir," said Andrew, showing the first cracks in his official capacity. He moved toward the door.

"Any advice for me, Andrew?"

"I can't say what they're up to, sir, but it's not God's work," said Andrew before stepping into the hall. Passing boots in the hallway prompted Andrew's tone to change, "Dinner at seven, sir, per the Obergruppenführer's habit. Until then, please enjoy the gardens."

Suddenly alone, Louis's mind flipped through pages of questions. The most useful advice given by Sevareid had been to memorize his notes. The Germans had proven mercurial in every interview, prone to second thoughts, and fond of intense oversight. By the time you made it to the exit of a building, you might be summoned back into the bowels and told to turn over your notebook. A visit to the Tower awaited anyone unable to sit quietly while some Aryan ripped pages free and tore them to shreds.

Louis cleared his head with a rapid walk in the garden. Eyes followed him, but no one engaged the visitor until his driver materialized to warn him dinnertime approached.

Surprised to be seated at a small table with three officers in addition to Heydrich, Louis expected a grilling about America, journalism, or any number of dangerous subjects. Heydrich introduced Gruppenführer Hofmann, Gruppenführer Müller, and Obersturmbannführer Eichmann.

"Schöngarth and Klopfer prefer to dine in the mess with the men," explained Heydrich.

Louis nodded as though he recognized the names. He struggled to keep track of the major figures up and down the militaries of all sides, but the constant shifting of roles made it a futile exercise. His primary experience with the British forces suggested most enlistees and many officers expressed surprise at the lack of definition in their duties. A rare man expressed a certain appreciation for the flexibility.

Like dinner back home, the conversation during the meal focused on the weather and shared interests. Eichmann made a particular effort to involve Louis: "How is the weather in the Americas?" "How many children do you have?" "Have you visited Germany?" "Did you like it?"

Louis confessed to growing up in Chicago but had no familiarity with the current weather, though he assumed his hometown faced its standard windy and cold. From then on, he deflected and then deflected more.

After the last course, Hofmann could take no more banality, "Reinhard, we ought to review details before tomorrow."

"No, Hofmann, I will not. We have an honored guest present and I for one have no intention of ruining his evening." He raised a glass of port in toast to Louis, "To future friends from distant lands!"

Louis studied the eyes on every face before raising his own glass.

***

Waking in darkness, Louis went in search of a late night mind-easer. The Germans and the staff slept, most outside in tents and other makeshift beds. Louis opened a window and listened to the shuffling of feet in search of the latrine, but little else sounded in the shadows.

Downstairs, the kitchen might have something stronger than the empty liquor cabinet offered in the sitting room. Clean and neat throughout, he hesitated to open the stores. His attention went to a thin book on the kitchen table. He poked it open and discovered a collection of poetry. Focusing on the page, he turned in time to see the outer door open.

Andrew walked in and stopped, examining Louis. "The servants' loo hasn't worked in ages as near as I can tell," he explained. "Pardon the familiarity, sir, but...," the butler shrugged.

"I'm an American and needs must," said Louis. "Yours?" He held up the book.

"I served with Mr. Gurney in the Gloucester Fifth at the Somme in 1916. He scribbled everywhere. Even paid the locals to let him use their piano to compose his songs."

Scanning a stanza, Louis, said, "He writes a good line."

Unprompted, Andrew recited, "'One died on the wires, and hung there, one of two--/Who for his hours of life had chattered through/Infinite lovely chatter.'" Andrew unlocked a high cabinet and poured them each a little sherry. "I brought this with me." They raised their glasses. "To my brother in arms, forever immortalized by Ivor Gurney."

"L'chaim," Louis closed the book. "Have you word of Mr. Gurney since the landing?"

Andrew shook his head almost imperceptibly. "You mustn't use such language, sir, not here. This is not London."

Youth encouraged Louis to declare Heydrich must have known whom he had invited to the country. A Jewish American journalist must be safe if any Jew could be, but Louis' tongue refused to protest the older man's wisdom.

"In 1937, sir, Mr. Gurney died in the psychiatric hospital," Andrew said as he carried their glasses to the sink.

***

Louis woke with a start. Sun rays made crosses out of the window panes of his room. A man screamed.

Doubting his ears, Louis waited for a second outburst before hurrying to the glass. The wail came from the tents beyond the greenhouse. From here, the grounds looked horribly trampled. The soldiers had avoided ruining the front lawn but obviously cared little for anything other than the approach to the house.

Another yell encouraged Louis to pull on his clothes and rush downstairs. Breakfast waited on the dining room sideboard, but Louis headed out through the garden doors in the sitting room.

Everyone wore black or dark gray, matching the dreary clouds floating overhead. A few men glanced at the man important enough to warrant a room in the house.

No one screamed.

Louis picked a likely looking low-ranking youth and drew him near. "Did I hear a voice calling out?"

The young German raised an eyebrow. "Sprichst du kein Deutsch?" A few passersby watched their conversation. Louis examined their faces for a person willing to admit they spoke English. No one looked helpful.

Holding up his hands, Louis went back into the house and headed for breakfast.

While he had stepped outside, Eichmann had taken a seat at the table. "Good morning, Herr Stern." He watched Louis make selections from the sideboard. "I understand you Americans invented the coffee break. Your city of Buffalo had a profusion of coffee beans and employers wanted more from their workers, so they offered them ten minutes each morning to smoke and drink this marvelous beverage. A German discovered the magic ingredient, however."

Louis settled into a chair and saw the lone cup before his companion. "Is this your coffee break?"

"Indeed," smiled the German.

"Your English is very good," complimented Louis.

"My job has entailed a great deal of travel," said the Obersturmbannführer. "I report to Obergruppenführer Heydrich, but much of my work involves meeting with Jews from around the world."

Stern lowered the fork from his mouth, as if suddenly realizing who sat across the table.

"Don't let me interfere with your breakfast, Herr Stern," said Eichmann.

Louis had neglected coffee and went to the side table for a cup. He sensed the other man's eyes on his back. Louis took a moment to steady his hand while dissecting his own reaction. He wondered if this presaged the crumbling of his personal sense of invulnerability. He placed the thought in a sealed room inside his mind.

"Buffalo served as a major trade hub at the time, earlier this century. Now the Erie Canal and the railroad are not quite as brilliant." Louis returned to his seat with a full cup.

They sipped and studied one another.

"You will find this interesting, Herr Stern. I visited Palestine in 1937," said Eichmann. "A lovely country populated by a fascinating people. These Zionists occasionally have incredibly promising ideas, wouldn't you agree?"

Louis studied the face across the table. "You have a very disarming demeanor, Colonel."

"I appreciate the compliment, Herr Stern."

"You present one desire written everywhere about you. You want to be my friend more than anything. Am I right?"

Eichmann managed to make a bleaker expression. "You have uncovered my greatest fault, Louis. I do want to be friends, but not at the cost of your respect."

Louis wondered where respect and fear intertwined. "Why did you want to tell me about your visit to Palestine, Adolf?"

Eichmann waved his hand at the foolishness of the question. "Aren't you a Zionist, Herr Stern?"

While a voice in his head screamed, Louis gritted his teeth and said, "All Jews are not Zionists."

Eichmann swallowed the last of his coffee, "You must agree it is a most unfortunate thing, Louis?" He picked his gloves off the table and walked out of the room.

Louis let his left forearm tremble until it ached.

Back in his room, a note awaited: "Your presence is required in the meeting hall at precisely 13:00. This is the reason for your presence, Obergruppenführer Heydrich"

Louis spent the remainder of the morning scribbling shorthand notes in the small datebook he carried in his pants pocket.

***

After wandering outside and repeating "Meeting hall?" to anyone nearby, Louis learned the name applied to a large tent at the back of the campsite. As Louis waited beside the closed entrance until the appointed time, he watched a military transport drive around the corner of the house and cut across the lawn to a small cemetery.

The truck stopped and four men climbed down to be met by their superior officer who had been in the cab. They extracted a coffin from the rear and set it on the ground. The truck drove off to the motor pool to the east of the house. The Germans had converted the old barn into a vehicular garage.

The soldiers stripped off their coats and grabbed the shovels which lay on the ground. After brief discussion and finally a decision, they selected a spot and dug.

"You're observing Reinhard's little project, my friend?"

Louis recognized the voice of Gruppenführer Hofmann and turned to see the officer standing beside him. "And what project is this?"

"Reinhard would be very distressed if I ruined the surprise and we can't be distressing Reinhard on his big day. It would be an unbelievably bad idea." Hofmann grinned like a child with a new toy. "Come," he gestured toward the now open flaps on the meeting tent, "it is always best to be a little bit early."

Louis recognized the editorial meeting ambiance immediately. An empty chair waited for the man in charge. Direct reports and others with special roles filled out the large round table in the center of the room. Satellite gophers, junior officers, and a few random players hoping to be noticed circulated in the open space along the canvas walls.

Hofmann took his seat near the head and pointed to a chair and tiny table in the corner which apparently anticipated Louis. Once situated, a clerk brought Louis a small folder of papers. A quick glance made it clear everyone else in the room had received much thicker folders.

Louis waved his binder and asked the clerks "Why so thin?" but found no one to answer until he approached Hofmann.

"You suspect censorship, my friend?" responded the Gruppenführer. "Heydrich only informed us of your invitation two days ago allowing not nearly enough time to translate all the documents. You have enough to begin. Ask me anything during the breaks."

The conversation ceased abruptly as the entire room rose to attention. Heydrich walked to his chair and sat. Louis moved quickly to avoid being the last man standing.

Then, the ordeal began. All German all the time in the meeting. Occasionally, an individual at the front table caught Louis' eyes and commiserated, exuding a sense of a shared understanding. Louis played along in the hope of a translation, but the only visitor to his corner proved to be the young soldier overseeing the water pitcher.

Fearful of staring off into space or falling asleep, Louis sought any snippet of sense. After a half hour bathed in consonants and run over by syllables, Louis' elbow jostled the unopened folder on his table. Others in the room had spread out their papers. Desperate for information to hold his attention, Louis opened the folder and read.

The first page listed the contents, all official documents, seemingly from Eichmann's arena of repatriation of undesirables, officially *Head of Report IV B4 of the Gestapo*. The initial documents outlined a history of the department's activities. This must have been provided for Louis' use, as the other attendees must already know these details.

The Nazi goal of freeing their lands of those they deemed inferior had been going well. Jews and others had been shipped eastward within controlled territories, primarily Poland. The numbers staggered the mind. However, many exceptions had been made for those who could establish long-standing citizenship within their home country. Where arrangements could be made, Jews had boarded ships for the

Americas and Palestine—anywhere willing to trade gold for the unwanted. In certain communities, Jews left on their own, surrendering all they owned for the privilege. They could not always travel far enough, but the Gestapo could not be blamed for local persecutions.

Seduced by the hard, cold print of it, Louis marveled at the administration capable of so bluntly documenting the manipulation of so many people. Here, they admitted lying to whole communities of undesirables in terms brimming with efficiencies gained and in columns overflowing with numbers.

Looking around the room, Louis recognized the rhythm of other meeting he had ever attended. Heydrich sat in the middle of a whirlpool while people rattled off data in startling counterpoint. On either side of the man in charge, Hofmann and Müller interrupted with interrogatories, drilling into details until satisfied.

Intoxicated by the clamor, the closeness of the room, the unexpected warmth, the sheer inability to latch onto any hold for his mind, Louis rose.

Suddenly, Heydrich leapt to his feet, forcing the entire room to rise. Reinhard's eyes strayed toward the American correspondent. With a nod to Hofmann, Heydrich announced in German and then English, "Let us move to the gardens for our service. Then we will adjourn for an hour."

Catching his breath, Louis watched the senior officers lead their subordinates out of the meeting. He took a moment in the cooling room to regain his equilibrium before weaving through the empty chairs. Outside, in the stiff air, Louis watched the entire party make their way to the small cemetery. He debated turning toward the house.

Andrew appeared at his side, "I believe they may be waiting for us. Word arrived last night. Everyone who is not required elsewhere should attend the planned service. If I may be so bold, sir, to confess a certain curiosity."

"I don't suppose you speak German?" asked Louis.

"I'm afraid not," admitted Andrew. "However, there may be aids to translation in the library."

Eichmann met them at the edge of the gathering and led Louis to a chair. A dozen seats in three rows ran along one side of an open grave. The casket which Louis observed earlier lay on supports waiting to be lowered.

Heydrich stepped to the front and smiled, making a self-deprecating comment which cheered the men. He then launched into an emotional speech referring to Charles Darwin.

The stranger seated beside Louis kept glancing his way, trying to share in the wisdom, humor, and utter humanity of the Obergruppenführer's eulogy. Surrounded by such unanimity of feeling, Louis imitated the reactions of his companions the best he could.

Heydrich paused and announced he would say a few words for their English-speaking friends. He studied Louis until the reporter took the hint and withdrew his notebook from his pocket.

"It is a supreme honor," declared Heydrich, "to restore Charles Darwin to his preferred gravesite. Others wished to see him buried in Westminster Abbey. His religious wife preferred to see him at her side in the local church graveyard. After much consideration and in consultation with the Führer, we decided to return the great man, this great inspiration, to the place of his greatest achievement. Forever more, he shall rest in the birthplace of evolutionary theory, where we first learned about the true nature of progress. Today, we celebrate the man who taught us how to differentiate between species, who taught us to acknowledge the superiority of specific genetic types and showed the way for the survival of the fittest!"

A familiar voice objected from back in the crowd of standing men.

Heydrich paused before giving voice to a smattering of German. Switching back to English, he concluded, "This gesture is for all our friends wherever they are found, but today I especially have in mind New York City, Chicago, and Washington. Consider how sacred we, as National Socialists, hold our creed. Let today ring in the hearts of all who strive for the betterment of humanity."

A brief salute and Heydrich made way for Hofmann to conclude the service and dismiss the men.

Louie examined the nonsense he had scribbled in his notes only to catch his neighbor looking askance at the wild lines. "It's a shorthand of my own invention," he whispered. Surprisingly, he received a learned nod in return.

Four men took hold of the ropes and lowered the casket.

***

Louis found lunch on the side table in the house only to realize after eating that all the Germans had dined together in the mess tent. He stopped by the kitchen to share thoughts on the reburial with Andrew. The cook said the butler had been detained after the service.

More of the same during the afternoon session in the big tent. The discussion turned serious; number crunching intensified. References to various inferior people multiplied so it became manifestly clear they occupied the primary topic of conversation.

As he paged through the documents in his English folder, Louis identified the missing information: for all the background provided, nothing discussed Nazi plans going forward. Louis had not learned his German verb tenses, but he strongly suspected everyone in the meeting spoke in future perfect.

A junior officer in a distant corner stood and addressed the senior officers, going off on a rant of support. To Louis' ears, the voice rose in tone, chanting "Juden, Juden, Juden." Louis' mind slid into a hole too close to Darwin's dirt hole not a hundred yards away. Louis heard a pencil snap and saw he had blunted the lead with his own hand repeatedly dragging back and forth on the table. He studied the groove which he had excavated and wondered how the Nazis treated misbehaving guests who carved the furniture.

Once the subaltern sycophant wound down, Hofmann staggered to his feet, embodying Louis' exhaustion. He spoke along the lines of "You have your assignments. Do them and we'll talk more tomorrow."

Louis watched the room empty. Once bodies ceased moving across his line of sight, Eichmann materialized into view, still seated. He smiled at Louis and nodded. After a few more minutes, no one else remained.

"These days can be very long," said the Obersturmbann-führer. "I remember negotiating with a Senior Rabbi in Budapest, or perhaps Vienna, and he wanted a lower price or more ships. Either way, I could do nothing for him, but he sat an entire afternoon because he wanted to do his absolute best. That is the way today felt. We have decided what we are going to do, but we must talk about it long enough to demonstrate our seriousness."

Louis wanted to leave. He longed for the solitude of his bedroom in the main house. He would have to broadcast a story eventually, but he craved a bed in a dark room devoid of a German accent. "Is this why I am here? To validate whatever you intend to do?"

"You misunderstand me, Louis. We have validated. We have demonstrated our seriousness. You bore witness to all of it."

"But I don't speak a word of German!" Louis' voice cracked.

"The beauty of Herr Heydrich's idea. We are a bureaucracy engaged in important work. We do not wish to hide from our potential friends in America, nor do we wish to bore them with inanities. Invite the radio reporter and show him how we toe the civilized line better than anyone else, show him how we debate amongst ourselves, and demonstrate how we formulate the best viable solutions to our issues. Only don't bore him or his audience. You are our Plato, emerging from our bureaucratic cave to inform humanity the National Socialists are here to save the world."

Louis stopped himself from responding. In interviews, he had learned not to correct every misquotation and logical error. Even without recording equipment in hand, Louis did not want to turn off the leaking spigot of Eichmann's drivel.

Eichmann headed for the exit, "I am to invite you to join a small gathering at the cemetery before dinner. I understand we will have a small fire for external heat and French wine for internal warmth."

***

Rested, but no more content, Louis added additional layers prior to venturing to his appointment at the graveyard. Before he could broach the subject of leaving Down House, he needed to fulfill whatever expectation the Nazis had about a radio broadcast across the Atlantic. He required a story to file once he returned to London. The news department in New York, let alone the gang at Claridge's, would never let him off the hook for returning from this event empty-handed. Louis would attempt to work on both goals at this gathering before supper.

More of the regular military nodded to Louis as he passed, having become a familiar figure since the tent meeting. Louis resisted checking if Andrew had turned up. He had adapted to the rigid English divide between servant quarters and residence before the Germans arrived. They added a degree of threat to inappropriate closeness. Louis had crossed the line before, but now he needed German beneficence for a ride to London, while Andrew would be staying at Down House with the Nazis whatever Louis did.

His dinner companions from the previous night awaited Louis in fine chairs carried from the house. Placed in a half circle around a contained fire set beside the fresh grave, Louis stood beside the empty seat.

"Sit, sit," said Heydrich.

The others had draped their lap rugs and held warm tins of hot wine. Louis settled in time for a recruit to appear with a pitcher and a warm mug. Even as Louis accepted the drink, the young man faded from view.

"You have instilled in your men a remarkable sense of their position," said Louis.

Müller chuckled. "The young man is a sinecure. Eichmann found him in a theater in Berlin. At times it is best to mold the clay, though I confess a certain fondness for pruning the tree as well."

Heydrich raised an eyebrow as if to warn Müller the time for chitchat had passed. "Louis, do you find England dreary? You must if America is as beautiful as your songs suggest."

"Have you seen Bavaria?" asked Hofmann.

Louis declined the bait, "This emerald isle has a great deal of history."

Heydrich thrust forward, "Exactly right, Herr Stern. And it birthed one of the greatest minds ever to grace the world. I speak of our host, of course."

Louis glanced at the grave, wondering if the Germans expected Darwin to join them. "Is that why you transferred him here?"

Snuffling and harrumphing went around the fire while Heydrich adjusted his position on the chair. "The work of my repatriation monkey," he gestured at Eichmann. "I fear you will never understand the importance of this man lain before us, who much influenced the philosophy of our Führer."

"Charles Darwin lived the life of a scientist, not a philosopher," contended Louis.

The officers chuckled.

"Science began as a philosophy," proclaimed Hofmann.

"Nein," Heydrich raised a hand. "Not one of your tedious lectures, Otto. This man is an American reporter. One or the other should tell you he has no patience, but both should warn you to drive right to the point."

Everyone grew silent. They studied the insides of their mugs. They removed their gloves and blew on their hands. They examined the contours of the freshly piled dirt.

Heydrich sighed like a man who must do everything himself. "We have reclaimed the homeland of the man who proved Darwin's theories. Gregor Mendel did his greatest work in Moravia. I do not hesitate to tell you I hosted a dinner party the day we reclaimed Brno.

"Darwin had absolutely no idea how traits passed from one generation to the next. He took it for granted it happened, perhaps you could say he took it on faith."

"Faith in science eventually finding the method," offered Eichmann only to receive a hard stare from his senior-most officer.

Heydrich continued, "With all due respect to our deceased host, I am personally grateful for the knowledge genetics is destiny. This is the foundational idea of the Third Reich. Your American eugenics movement, Louis, predates even the Führer's magnificent book, so do not tell me you do not see the wisdom in a world which at best rewards the fittest and at worst removes those who present obstacles to the flourishing of the human species."

Someone said, "You're insane." In the ensuing quiet, Louis realized it had been his own voice.

The Germans chuckled.

Heydrich raised his mug in toast to Louis, "They said the same of Darwin. They merely ignored our beloved Mendel.

"Herr Stern, I like you and I want your cooperation. Tonight, after dinner, you will go to the radio room and contact your editor in Manhattan. Otto will give you the story to file. No, I am not corrupting you. Edit it as you see fit. Today must have been difficult as you strained to follow the proceedings."

Louis thought Heydrich far overestimated the popularity of the German tongue.

"File your report later. In the meantime, while we sit here bathing in the chill air of rural England beside a great dead man, let us tell you what you witnessed today." He motioned to the others who all turned their attention to Eichmann.

The junior officer quivered as he reveled in the attention. "Before I begin, may I say today blossomed like a revelation. We engaged in the Fatherland's work, but I had no expectation we had the blessing and direction of the Führer in such explicit..."

"Enough, Adolf," interrupted Müller. "Our American friend is not interested in the chain of command. That is history." He finished as though laying a trap, "Summarize for Herr Stern your understanding of today's meeting."

"Nothing less than the resolution of all my work over the past few years," smiled Eichmann. "We have been sending the malcontented and the unassimilable to places where they become problems for other people or, at a minimum, much easier to manage. We have experimented with permanent solutions, often following the lead of others, notably the Romanians."

"What are you saying?" asked Heydrich. "Perhaps you would prefer to lock these Jews, Mincéirs, homosexuals away in train cars and ship them around the countryside until they suffocate and starve and die of thirst. This may be the Romanian way, but it is not the way of the National Socialists, Adolf."

Hofmann intervened, "Herr Stern, my friend, understand we now propose an efficient program for the eradication of those undesirables for whom even Obersturmbannführer Eichmann cannot work his miracles to find a new home."

Müller added, "Today we presented plans which have been refined by experimentation on the Eastern front. We tried processing the injured at the front lines by bringing portable facilities on site. We learned a great deal through the graces of our scientists, medical corps, and martyrs of the German military. Supply and transport being primary issues, we established the need to set up centralized processing. In short, bring the overflow to an industrial location rather than trying to drive our factory to the consumer."

Eichmann's eyes looked drunk and probably mad, "Don't you mean the consumed?" He laughed at his joke.

Heydrich carefully set down his mug and walked to Eichmann. He stared into his inferior's face, gently removing his gloves, and struck him across the face, raising a cold crack into the air. "You are intoxicated. Retire to your quarters." The Obergruppenführer returned to his seat.

Silence reigned while Eichmann skulked out of view.

"I find all of this distasteful," commented Heydrich to the hearty support of his direct reports. "All this bureaucracy, this table talk, this logistical planning—all of it obscures the important scientific work we have done and will continue to do. We work for all of humanity, based on the soundest principles. Everyone has always known and we have demonstrated the truth of it—" he waved his gloves at Louis, but his voice went quiet.

After the pause lingered, Louis leaned forward, "What does everyone know?"

Heydrich's nose wrinkled, "We take the measure of a man as we learned from Herr Darwin. We dismantle him and we determine whether he satisfies. Should he contribute to the future? Should he contribute to the present? Or was he nothing in the past, nothing in the present, and nothing to the future? In which case, he belongs on the trash heap with all the other dead ends. He exemplifies nature's failed experiment, not ours. We simply perform the work which nature would handle across generations."

"You make these determinations based on what? Observation? Testing?" insisted Louis.

Müller hissed, "On common sense! Walk down any street in London and you will see dozens who offer nothing to improve the species. Men who frequent the most disgusting purveyors of filth, men who spend their days in synagogues expecting others to wait on them, caravans of homeless with no sense of duty, ... I laugh at testing such obvious disappointments."

Heydrich held up his hand to stop the outpouring, "Herr Stern, you have seen physical catastrophes, have you not? Would you have them reproduce? If we could identify those who are equally damaged inside, then should we not act? Have you read history? In his wisdom, the Führer has declared the obvious failure of other evolutionary dead ends. Make your broadcast after dinner. Tell your audience you have found a better way."

Hofmann raised his glass and led the Germans in a toast, "Heil Darwin! Heil Hitler!"

***

Louis dined alone in his room. No one came to him with a preferred script for broadcast. No knock at the door summoned Louis to the makeshift studio. He retired to bed at sunset and listened to the military camp as the men bedded down outside his window.

Vacillating between how to avoid a broadcast, how to return stateside as soon as possible, and how to understand men who countenance mass murder, Louis could not sleep. Convinced leaving the sanctity of his room would lead to danger, he listened desperately to every creak and voice inside while jumping at every howl of wind and each mutter of a disgruntled guard.

When Charles Darwin appeared beside his bed, Louis proved cogent enough to tell the great man, "So this is a dream."

Darwin leaned over to study Louis' face, "Indeed it is."

Louis Stern had seen photographs of Darwin as recently as the afternoon. Otherwise, he would have struggled to recognize the man. Darwin's head consisted of an iguana for his forehead, pigeons for a beard, one eye a baby tortoise and the other a barnacle. Mockingbirds for cheeks, and bees filled out the rest, with worms wiggling and burrowing from hidden depths. Feathers fluttered and the iguana kept turning and looking, independent of where Darwin's weird eyes focused. When the scientist spoke, ants skittered from his mouth to circumnavigate his lips before returning to the cranial interior via the nearest seam between creatures.

"Your breath is like honey and bird shit," commented Louis.

"Look at me," said Darwin, twisting his head from side to side to grant a fuller view of the turtle shell at the back. "Nothing about me is natural or selected except inside your mind, lad." He bent to Louis' ear and exhaled, "I will not be ill-used."

Louis' cheek burned where breath hit like hot steam. His hand rushed over the skin, seeking bee stings or wounds inflicted by beak or claw. "Am I awake?" He sat up in bed and scratched his skin to test this dream which might be otherwise.

Darwin towered upright. "Could it be so?"

Louis slid out from his blankets. The floor scratched rough beneath his feet. He extended his hand toward his guest. "Can I touch you?"

Darwin reached out and shook the outstretched offering. "An honor to meet you, sir."

"And you," admitted Louis. "What am I saying?" He pulled his hand back and touched it with the fingers from his opposite side. "It's my hand. I'm not dreaming. Your face is animals, but your hand is normal."

"You sound like a man who has retired early after an excess of drink," commented Darwin. The left mockingbird flapped its wings.

A dream would be better than insanity, so Louis decided to plunge forward. "So, you're aware of the Nazi intentions regarding your legacy?"

"They misapprehend me!" thundered Darwin, exciting all his head creatures, great and small. "My notion of change by descent has become the survival of the fittest individual or society, race, or business. Don't talk to me of sociology or economics!"

"Why come to me?" asked Louis. "Aren't you better off taking this up with Heydrich or one of his men?"

Louis' room had one chair and Darwin sank onto it. "These men are lost to me." His mouth drooped. Worms crawled from his tear ducts and slid down his cheeks. "They have corrupted my writings, and then they have used those corruptions to justify the most heinous acts." Darwin's voice became a wisp so quiet Louis could hear the buzzing of his face bees.

"They brought your body here to venerate you," said Louis.

"Look outside," Darwin went to the window.

Louis stood beside the apparition. "Who are those men gathered in the graveyard?" Torches illuminated a handful of dark uniforms.

"Reinhard claims to pay obeisance while secretly hoping to raise my body or my spirit. By bringing my body here where much of my research happened, he has merged me with my work."

Louis reached over, "May I?" With permission, he touched a barnacle which formed Darwin's left ear. "It's alive."

"I should hope so," muttered Darwin. He turned to face the American. "I did not speak often enough about the importance of asking good questions. For example, is there a more direct path? Another favorite query: what does not belong?"

Louis nodded, "I understand."

"You don't," continued Darwin.

"What?" said Louis.

"When I looked at this military camp and asked who does not belong, you were the obvious answer."

"What difference does it make?" Louis studied the floor. When he raised his gaze, Darwin's chin rested on his hand while worms wove through his fingers.

As the great scientist sat up straight, his chin worms dangled until they pulled themselves up and into his lower jaw. The death of conversation hung heavy in the room as Darwin shifted, avoiding Louis' eyes.

"What are you doing here? In this room with me?" asked Louis.

"I'm here to warn you. I suggest you leave." Darwin pushed out of the chair. "I believe in observation and quality reportage. So, you should not go far. The Flannery's have a lovely home about a mile toward church. Tell them Charles sent you."

Louis did not want to tell Darwin the only house still standing on his way here currently served as a detention camp for British officers. "It is the middle of the night. I can go in the morning."

"Remember how I told you this has to stop. No more using my name in vain." Darwin scratched a beetle which had landed on his cheek. Caught between his fingers, he studied the tiny creature before carrying it to the window and holding it outside to fly away. "Leave first thing in the morning."

Louis lay in bed, more certain this had been a dream or near enough. "I'll need to arrange transport." The reporter fell asleep telling himself to remember this strange encounter.

***

The pillow against Louis' face caressed his skin. He could sleep until the Germans lost patience with him and sent him back to London. Then he could book a boat home. He opened one eye.

A bird egg came into focus as his eyes adjusted to being awake. He unsteadily nudged the blue with brown splotches egg. It tumbled toward the edge of the bed. Louis leapt upright and reached out, only to see the egg shatter on the floor.

Leaning over the mattress, Louis wondered what his dream or his discovery signified. He replayed his overnight conversation and decided whatever else he might believe, the advice to leave appeared sound.

A knock on the door brought all his anxiety to the surface.

Andrew stood in the hallway when Louis answered and let him in. The butler could barely look at Louis as all his attention focused on the window.

"What is it?" asked Louis.

Andrew pointed, "You have a mockingbird on your sill." The beautiful creature flew away as soon as Andrew finished calling attention to it. "What's this?" He pointed to the broken egg beside the bed.

"From my pillow. I knocked it off before I could pick it up."

Andrew smiled grimly, "Eggs are designed to be dropped. When you go down to breakfast, your room will be cleaned."

"If you don't mind my asking," said Louis. "Where have you been? And what are you doing here?"

Andrew motioned him over to the window and pointed across the grounds. An oversized truck parked between the last tent and the graveyard.

"Where did the vehicle come from? Why didn't I hear it arrive? Not there last night." Words tumbled from Louis. He stopped to catch his breath. "What is it?"

Andrew shifted his eyes to Louis and then turned his head to confirm Louis had no guess. Andrew stepped back from the window and scratched the back of his neck. "If I guessed, sir, then it is one of the mobile killing vehicles they used on the Eastern front. Or rather a retooled English truck for their evil purposes."

"They were just discussing trucks for gassing," Louis stumbled back to the bed and sat down. "Britain is still a sovereign state. They agreed not to institute any of their policies while negotiations proceeded about the future. This the Prime Minister said."

"Maybe it's a delivery truck for food. Could the Nazis have lied?" said Andrew. "Which do you believe, my American friend?"

Louis stared at the floor, flooded with thoughts about his overnight visitor. Or dream. Or nightmare. He needed to leave. How could he sit still? Every bone in his body ached from fear, from confusion, from this awful bed. "Out!" Louis looked up and saw the shock he had inspired in the butler. In a lowered voice, he said, "You have to go. I'm sorry, but I need to dress."

Andrew stopped himself from responding and found the door handle. Back to his butler skills, he disappeared from view without a sound, so quietly Louis checked the hallway to see if Andrew had in fact departed the area. Then Louis dressed quickly. He bypassed breakfast and went out the front door. No one interfered with his progress as he proceeded down the driveway a hundred yards.

The house loomed large, and the only road in view made him question which way toward civilization. Louis stood very still, hoping the planet might make a few hundred revolutions and deposit him in the future in a safe bed where world and war did not so easily go together. When the Earth failed to accommodate his desire, he trudged back to the house and walked straight through to the rear patio.

Louis bumped into two soldiers while making his way past the tents. The first glared, but the second had seen the earlier misstep and gave Louis a slight shove on his way. He did himself no favors walking to the truck, even bearing the mantle of an American reporter. He stopped fifty feet from it, noting the freshly made tracks in the mud and snow- they led around the tents and the side of the house,.

Eichmann appeared at his side, like a ghost or a valet. "It is a fearsome vehicle, don't you think?"

"What is it?" stammered Louis.

"It is a modified Bedford QLD lorry. Such a delightful word 'lorry.'" Eichmann outlined the cargo truck with his hand. "Can you believe it used to be a kitchen? In truth, Hofmann found it and realized how perfect for our needs."

"What needs are those?" asked Louis.

Eichmann ignored the question. "Have I told you how fascinated I am by America?" He stepped back toward the tents. "Walk with me. I have a thing to show you."

Losing all expectation of escaping any time soon, Louis followed the German but refused to engage in conversation.

Eichmann led him into the meeting tent, all but deserted except for Müller seated and Hofmann standing, both with backs to the entrance. Moving closer, Louis heard an American voice he recognized and saw its owner seated opposite Hofmann.

"Good, you are here," stated Müller. "This man claims to your acquaintance."

Louis nodded, "Hello, Walter. What are you doing here?" He meant the question for the Nazis as much as for Walt Cronkite, who looked ill-used, but not injured in any permanent way.

"It's good to see you, Louis," said Walter. "I've been explaining to these gentlemen how Murrow felt it would behoove us to see how you made out."

"This does not explain why you did not arrive at the front entrance of the house. Or why we found you hiding in the trees." Hofmann picked a passport up off the table. "We granted you permission to remain in Britain for business purposes, which could provide cover for a thousand deceptions."

"I'm a reporter, like Louis," explained Walter. "We even work for the same radio network. We both report to Edward Murrow. Surely you've heard of him!"

"I have listened to his broadcasts," announced Heydrich from behind Louis. "Would you say you subscribe to the same biases as Mr. Murrow? I would not consider him a friend of the Reich. Are you a friend of the Reich, Mr. Cronkite?"

Walter looked at Louis with desperation. "I'm a reporter. Reporters are no one's friend when they're doing their job," Walter grew sadder as he spoke.

Louis pled with the most powerful man in the room. "Walter came to see if I needed any assistance filing my story. They must be growing anxious in London since I did not file."

Heydrich stepped up to Louis, "Not only London, Louis. When you did not appear at our makeshift studio, I personally experienced disappointment."

"I took ill," said Louis. "I can send the story now."

"The sun has not risen in New York, as yet" said Heydrich. "The ideal time will be midnight tonight, when your countrymen sit down to their steaks and potatoes." He turned his attention on Eichmann. "I worry our American friend did not find your script to his liking. Perhaps you can work with this Cronkite to improve it. It would be a tragedy for German American relations if we miss this opportunity again. We long to extend an olive branch across the ocean." Heydrich studied each man, "Are we all in agreement?"

Enough grunts of affirmation filled the room for Heydrich to leave. Hofmann took Louis by the elbow and guided him out of the tent and toward the house, "You look like a man who skipped his breakfast."

***

Louis spent the morning escorted by Hofmann until the day's gathering in the large tent. Hofmann left him at his small desk, but this time a young man in ill-fitting Gestapo gear stood behind Louis. His neck itched, and Louis kept glancing at the young German, who refused to meet his gaze.

Louis could not focus on the proceedings. He had seen no sign of Walter since leaving him earlier. Andrew did not appear at breakfast, and Louis had no opportunity to contact him. When he could force his brain to concentrate, his priority focused on his radio script. Louis tried to care about the topics at hand, but he felt like a man fallen down a well and hearing German words echo from above.

After an hour passed in the stifling tent, Louis examined his notes, which proved to be singular: "My life has become an oubliette." The soldier behind Louis had apparently not read it or did not understand English. Louis scratched out the sentiment.

The papers provided this day outlined the solution mentioned by the firepit yesterday. Louis resisted engaging with the details because the entire program looked absurd on its face. Even if the Nazis intended to commit mass slaughter, the scale surely had limits.

Paging through the document, most of it covered transportation details, specifically the financials. As near as Louis could tell, costs dominated the topic of the day. Secondarily, communication and coordination appeared on the agenda. The Germans intended to place liaisons everywhere they had control, though these would be different from the officers assigned to work with government officials. These liaisons would work with the targeted communities to expedite transfer of populations.

The last few pages showed estimates of personnel requirements by region. Louis rubbed his eyes and asked the young German to bring him water. Louis had to be mistaken, but the words on the page did not change no matter however he shifted the paper or rubbed water on his face. The final paragraphs covered England, Wales, and Scotland.

***

"I need to run right out of here, Walter," hissed Louis across the dinner table. After dinner with the senior officers, they had been left to work on the radio script.

"I agree, but we can't go back to London without the story," said Walter.

"I don't care. I want to go home," insisted Louis, struggling to control his voice.

"If you mean New York, then you'll have a tough time making it. The Germans have restricted flights and ships, especially for Americans. They mean to keep us here until Roosevelt comes to heel." Walter nervously tugged his eyebrow.

"When did this happen? I've only been out of London for a fleeting time," Louis sounded desperate.

"Sevareid is losing his mind," said Walter. "He believes the Germans are going to imprison us to make sure we don't leave. They already have the military observers under observation. Also, the observers are under house arrest."

"Gallows humor, Walter?" said Louis. He studied the two pieces of paper before him: one the script provided by the Nazis and the other the blank page he and Walter had failed to write on for the past hour. "All we can hope is these Gestapo boys will grant us exit visas if we do their damned broadcast." He sketched in the corner of the German script.

Walter's eyes turned inward in serious contemplation before he finally spoke, "I covered the rally in Madison Square Garden, one of them anyway. You might remember?"

"I don't keep track of all your stories, Walter," smiled Louis.

"When the American Nazis gathered and filled the Garden."

"A farce," said Louis.

Walter sounded angry, "Go look outside and say it again, Louis. How ridiculous is it while we sit here talking about sending home a report about these German invaders suggesting... the unthinkable." Walter waited for a response, but Louis kept drawing on the paper. "What will they do with the lorry out there? What about when the first similar truck rolls off a Detroit assembly line?" Walter studied Louis' artwork. "Is that a lizard?"

Louis frowned. "It's supposed to be a face, like I saw in the museum." His eyes shifted toward Walter. "It's possible I'm losing my mind."

A dozen possible responses traversed Walter's face, but he said, "Then we had better proceed to business before you're no use to anyone."

***

Eichmann found the American pair asleep at the dinner table when he came to retrieve them for their broadcast. He slid the two versions of their script from beneath Louis' arms. The journalists could write no better than he could. However, their effort would satisfy Heydrich.

Eichmann kicked a chair leg under each, startling them awake. "We go to make your broadcast, schnell."

The two men staggered to their feet.

Eichmann smiled, "Perhaps I should suggest to Heydrich how nothing should stop the German navy from considering a North Atlantic strategy of hopping from Iceland to Greenland to Canada and heading down the East Coast of the continent." He shoved both scripts into Louis' hands and led them through the house toward the motor pool.

No one in the camp considered the radio network in New York might have their own ideas about what constituted a reasonable approach to reporting live from England. Host John Daly did not let Louis proceed two sentences into his script before interrupting. Daly asked about conditions outside London and prodded for any information on German intentions.

As soon as Louis alluded to the Gestapo plan to dispose of undesirables, Daly asked about the possibility of a Vichy England, like the French had created. Even as Daly guided, Louis' stomach twisted in knots. All four senior German officers stood nearby and their fury filled the air.

Louis pressed the earpiece tighter as he struggled to hear New York. Moments passed before he realized the noise nearby had increased. He scanned the room only to see Walter erupting in bursts of laughter. Louis glared at him. His mind raced, trying to identify the repercussions if Cronkite did not regain his self-control.

Müller strode forward and rapped Walter across the face with the back of his hand.

Louis rose to his feet.

Müller walked around the table bearing the radio gear and disconnected Louis from the States.

Tossing aside the mic and headphones, Louis demanded, "What did you do it for?"

"This sideshow is finished," declared Müller. "I will not stand by while you use our resources to make idle chitchat."

The ensuing silence broke when Heydrich groaned, "You and everyone here will do exactly as ordered. Exactly as I follow decrees from above, you will do precisely as I say. We faltered in fulfilling our goal tonight of winning the minds of those in North America already sympathetic to our ideals. Who are you, Herr Müller, to have an opinion on the American mind?"

Flummoxed, Müller stood at attention, holding his tongue.

Eichmann moved behind Heydrich. "You are correct, sir. My visits across the Atlantic highlighted how many Americans will listen if only we speak to them with a voice which they can understand. I gained a great deal of experience in my travels..."

"Stop!" shouted Müller. "Reinhard, I cannot listen to him prattle on like a schoolchild. You are a fountain of information while little Adolf is a spray against an alley wall."

Heydrich moved aside and studied each man in turn. Without another word, he swiveled and walked out. Looking small and alone, Eichmann dashed out of the garage.

Louis arranged the equipment before him, returning pieces to their boxes until the temperature in the room lowered. Then he walked around the table and looked for Walter to join him.

Müller summoned guards, causing Louis to cringe and Walter to shake. Müller looked at Louis, "Return to your barracks."

Automatically, Louis replied, "I'm not in a tent. I'm in the main house."

"You are dismissed," Hofmann spoke for the first time. "Retire to your room."

Before Louis progressed, Walter spoke his name.

When Louis looked back, Walter stood though the soldiers had placed themselves on either side of him.

Hofmann placed a hand on Louis' shoulder and guided him to the door. "Sleep tonight and look for your friend in the morning at breakfast. If you must lay awake, then decide how to make tomorrow night's broadcast better. We can all agree it cannot go much worse than tonight, and it would be quite tragic for all of us, indeed, my friend?"

Louis shifted under Hofmann's guidance but found himself outside in the frigid air despite his efforts to stay with Cronkite. Longing for one of Murrow's cigarettes, he stood and listened. Louis had spent a night on the roof of their hotel helping Murrow transmit his live narration of German bombing. They stayed warm by rationing Murrow's cigarettes, even as Louis took over the broadcast when Edward's voice failed. After half a pack each in freezing air, no one in the States noticed any difference in their stricken voices.

Realizing his hands clenched painfully, Louis took his first steps back to his bed since no cries had emanated from the garage. By the time he arrived at the manor, Louis had a powerful thirst for sherry. Detouring to the kitchen, he dragged a chair and thumped a basin but then stopped trying to draw attention from the servants' quarters.

Careful searching of the cabinets demonstrated the absence of Andrew's sherry. The poetry book did not turn up either, though it would likely be with the butler in his room. Louis prepared a whiskey and soda, then studied the glass at the kitchen table. Sagging, he cursed every German in the camp and in the country.

***

Terrified, Louis sat up in bed. The bombs must be falling again. The pounding sounded more repetitive, rhythmic, and he realized knock came at his door. Not in his hotel, he lay in Kent surrounded by Nazis. "Yes?"

"The Obergruppenführer requires your presence at the rear of camp, sir!" came an unfamiliar, youthful voice.

"I need to dress," said Louis not nearly as loudly.

"They warned me to expect such a response, sir, and to tell you your friends await you. Also, I received orders to escort you."

"I'm not opening this door until I'm dressed," replied Louis.

Five minutes past when the young soldier thought to inquire, "You are not attempting to crawl out the window, are you, sir?"

Louis considered the idea and wished he had thought of it first. "No," he sighed. His shoes had become a mess and he struggled into them. Randomly, his thoughts turned to the Darwin apparition. Why couldn't it have appeared in his latest dreams?

Louis opened the door and looked into the face of a teenager dressed in a villain's costume, black, draped with symbols of piracy. "I left my coat in the kitchen."

The German produced the coat and helped Louis into it. "I wouldn't mention about being in the kitchen last night, sir, not if you want the morning to go smoothly."

Before they stepped outside, Louis stopped his guard, "How is it you speak English so well? I understood none of you Nazis did."

"I arrived last night, sir," said the youth. "An officer from the Staatspolizei came to the barracks and wondered if anyone understood American English. I have family in Wisconsin and I spent two summers in Milwaukee. Have you ever been there, sir?"

"What's your name, son?" asked Louis.

"Werner, sir, Werner Becker. Three of us rode down from the barracks last night and they set us up in a tent with these uniforms. Mine is a little loose." Werner shifted his shoulders to demonstrate.

Louis wondered how much more this trip could feel like a Lewis Carroll story with added horror. "I see." He followed his escort out the back and through the tent line. Within a few steps, he saw they headed for the gas truck. Camp chairs sat in two rows facing the death lorry.

"Coming, sir?" said Werner.

Recognizing he had slowed, Louis caught up to the soldier, but he struggled to pump his legs. Black clad figures occupied a few of the seats. Louis suddenly identified the one person out of place because of his street clothes. "Walter?" he exhaled.

Even if Louis' voice had been too soft, Walter turned and saw him.

Louis picked up his pace, passing Werner, who stopped before the inner circle of chairs. Louis took the empty seat beside Cronkite. "What happened to you, Walter? Your eye?"

Walter looked over Louis' shoulder as he answered, "I fell and banged it. I may have broken a rib, also."

Louis admonished him for lying. Instead, he searched for one of the senior German officers. Hofmann stood at the far end of their row. Louis met his gaze and wanted to demand they send Walter into town for treatment. He wanted to insist they return to London immediately. He wanted to go home.

Hofmann walked around the back row and came to stand beside Walter.

Looking down, Louis saw Walter's hand shake. Walter tried to suppress the movement, but it only spread to his core.

"You're cold, Walter," said Louis. "Take my coat."

Walter hissed at Louis and glanced at Hofmann. "We need to understand our role. We are not guests here." He finally turned his entire face to Louis. His eye looked red and hideous. The ear had been burned. "We are at this juncture at the sufferance of these men, Louis, and we need to fulfill our part of the agreement."

"What part is that?" asked Louis, unable to prevent desperation from creeping into his voice. Behind them, the entire camp had stepped from the tents to watch the proceedings at their end.

"As I understand it," Walter looked at Hofmann, "we make a broadcast to their specifications and we go back to London."

Hofmann stood to attention and everyone around the Americans followed suit.

Reinhard Heydrich stepped around the truck and raised his hand to put his men at ease. "Good morning." He alternated between German and English, turning to Louis and Walter when he spoke their language. "We had hoped to hold this demonstration after a first comprehensive broadcast to the United States, in order to offer our radio personalities two fascinating stories to share with their listeners. Because of technical difficulties and a need for medical attention, we offer this spectacle to convince our American friends of the seriousness of our position, as well as theirs, America's, and the world's."

Heydrich smiled.

Louis' chest burned as stomach acid filled his mouth. He coughed and gagged. Everyone looked in his direction with disapproval. Louis spit onto the ground and watched the icy earth soften between his feet where his former insides spread. When he straightened against the back of his chair, he held stiff, sensing Walter grow rigidly upright. Louis desperately ignored the angry eyes focused on them.

Heydrich must have paused. Now, the Obergruppenführer turned and paced back and forth as he spoke. "I have it on good authority many Britons welcome us with open arms. They resent the scourge of a failed monarchy which has toler- ated deviant behavior, corrupt influences, and aberrant ideas. Men and women of moral and political rectitude have looked across this Emerald Isle and watched as it has declined in power, in moral rectitude, and in respect.

"Their very leaders fled, but not before recognizing their own failings. They deserted many of their royal entourage, not because of their need to depart in a hurry or because of a lack of room, though indeed they did rush off, afraid to look the Führer in the eye. No, they left behind those who they could not trust, could not rely upon, and did not consider worthy of saving. They left their detritus for us to clean up!"

All around Louis and Walter, the Germans cried with outrage.

Two large soldiers emerged from the nearest tent. They stood on either side of Andrew, arms bound. They had left their great coats behind and wore greys and blacks.

"We took this man into our employ here only to learn of his inclinations," Heydrich twisted the word so it rang tunelessly. "Still, we might have returned him to London as long as he agreed to report to our offices on a regular basis until we could implement our system of management here in England. But before we could confront him, he attempted to run away last night.

The soldiers led Andrew forward. The butler's face twisted side to side, seeking out familiar faces. Once he saw Louis, he exhaled, "Help me."

The beefier soldier punched Andrew in the stomach, doubling him over. Andrew wretched blood.

Heydrich stopped his pacing directly in front of Louis and Walter. "Yes, Herr Stern, why don't you help the butler? Were you aware of his deviance when you spent time alone with him in the kitchen late on your first night? Why did you seek him out on multiple occasions since then? When I requested your attendance this weekend, I knew you to be a Jew, but I had no idea about your... What did you tell me they call it here in England if they're talking about their aristocracy, Eichmann?"

"Eccentricity, sir," said Eichmann, standing to speak.

"Are you eccentric, Herr Stern?" asked Heydrich.

Louis spoke too softly and the Germans called for him to stand. He rose to his feet, "I'm a married man. I have a wife!"

"Good for you!" cheered Heydrich. He turned to Andrew. "Take the butler into the lorry."

Andrew pushed against the ground until his legs gave out and soldiers hoisted him halfway up the stairs.

A group back by the tents suddenly cried out.

Everyone turned to see what the commotion might be. Except Heydrich, Louis, and the three men on the steps of the truck did not.

Louis pushed past the front row, all distracted by the noise away from the main event. Andrew neared the back door of the lorry. "Obergruppenführer Heydrich, whatever is happening, you have to stop what you're about to do."

Heydrich turned to Louis and then noticed the lack of attention focused forward. Quickly evaluating the situation, he slashed the air, bringing Andrew's progress to a halt shy of the chamber in the rear of the truck. "What do you propose?"

Before Louis could speak, Hofmann appeared and spoke into Heydrich's ear. The German grew louder as more outcries erupted among the men by the tents. Heydrich directed Hofmann and strode off to address the disruption.

Louis searched for Walter, but he had moved in the direction of the news story. Planning to follow Cronkite momentarily, he turned to see Hofmann herding Andrew and the two guards into the back of the lorry. He ran to the Gruppenführer's side, "You can't put them in there!"

"We don't want anyone running off, do we?" responded Hofmann. He threw the latch, securing the cargo doors. "Would you like to see the madness which has disturbed our melodrama?" Without another word, Hofmann pushed into the crowd of soldiers, cutting a path for Louis to follow.

As they approached the center of attention, the turmoil grew more subdued. The soldiers formed a neat circle with seven men standing in the open space. Heydrich held one of them by the chin, shifting the head back and forth and studying his subject closely. All of these men grunted forlornly.

Walter appeared beside Louis and translated for him.

"And you say they didn't look like this before?" Heydrich directed his question at a lower ranking officer.

The answer came through chattering teeth, "No, sir. Buchner was a good looking lad, even, and the others did not look so..."

"Are you certain these are the very same men?" demanded Heydrich.

The faces on the soldiers looked like nothing anywhere else in the camp, and likely not in the country. Their jaws protruded and their noses flattened. Dried blood formed crusty mustaches. Their brows had become bony and pronounced. The whites of their eyes had gone pink. They struggled to speak. Malformed expressions displayed pain more than disobedience.

Heydrich dropped his grip on the soldier and stepped closer to the unusual face. He stared into the eyes. "I don't believe you. These men are impostors, spies possibly. I ask you again, Sergeant, are these Neanderthals yours?"

The Sergeant studied the ground at his feet before looking back at the most powerful man in the camp and possibly the country. "I don't see how they could be."

"Hofmann! Have these partisans brought to the truck! Let's put the butler back to work with a warning. Louis Stern! Where are you?" Heydrich headed back to the lorry, and Louis fell in beside him. "Do you see what I have to deal with, Stern? Don't disappoint me tonight and we can all leave this cold, wet mud for London. In the meantime, keep your friend from the servants' quarters on a tight leash. After this demonstration for the men, I will need to have more cannisters brought down." He paused and tapped Walter on the chest. "We do however still have plenty of bullets. Now if you'll excuse me, I have to stress proper diligence among the troops."

Louis and Walter walked ten yards back toward the house before Louis grabbed Walter's shoulder. Turning around they watched while the sergeant who had lost his men unlocked the cargo door on the gas truck. The soldiers staggered out, dragging Andrew. Back on solid ground, they dropped the butler who landed hard.

On the walk back to the house, Walter and Louis wished they could block their ears to the cries and uproar from the soldiers and not-quite-soldiers. They resolutely ignored the muddle of a foreign language mixed with sounds almost simian behind them. Before entering the house, their journalistic curiosity caused them to turn and observe the proceedings.

Andrew's former guards forced the so-labeled "Neanderthals" into the chamber at the rear of the lorry.

***

Louis and Walter argued in Louis' room until Walter fell asleep. Louis had insisted they stay and make the broadcast. They had no chance of hiding in a country overrun by Germans, especially an island with no transportation in the midst of poor weather. Too badly off to argue further, Walter tilted slowly onto Louis' pillow.

The soft knock at the door an hour later did not disturb Walter. Louis drifted away from the window where he stood, staring at clouds, wondering how the sun managed to stay so bright in the sky. He carefully opened the door to see Andrew standing in the hall, in full livery, like the first time they had met. Louis stared at the purple bruise at his temple. "Come in."

Andrew motioned him to silence. He extracted a familiar book from inside his jacket and passed it to Louis. "Mr. Gurney has family in Maryland, I believe. See they have this, please." He raised his hand to forestall any response.

***

Louis helped Walter dress for dinner. If they could not run for it, then they ought to present a united front. Word came they would once again join the senior officers, proper attire expected. Both Americans felt at a loss until dark suits arrived.

The chambermaid explained how the neighboring homes had been scoured for clothing. Locating a trove of "fancy dress," the Germans decided to "do the English way" for the evening. Walter insisted on being left alone to finish with his jacket and tie, so Louis headed for the garden door downstairs.

Louis noted the decrease in camp activity and chalked it up to the horrifying display in the morning. Heydrich straddled a fine line between discipline and dissolution. Walking a few yards off the patio, Louis noted the first tent on his left had an open flap. The men sat on their cots, half-dressed, lost in desultory thought. They contemplated their own hands.

One of the soldiers looked out and saw Louis. By the time the young German reached the opening, Louis recognized him as the man who had visited the States and spoke English.

"Sir," the young soldier sounded downcast, "could you give me a hand?" He ran his hand over his unbuttoned shirt.

"What's all this?" asked Louis, confused even as his mind acknowledged something looked strange when the German moved. "Werner, is it? Have you injured yourself?"

Werner shook his head. "I don't know what it is." He moved his hand over his buttons. "I can't hold them anymore."

Louis watched as Werner struggled to bring his thumb and index finger together to clasp the button on his shirt. The thumb proved too short to meet up with the index finger in any sort of grip. "You're playing tricks, Werner, and I don't like it," said Louis. "It's been a terrible day and I'd rather not..." A twitch in the young man's face made Louis stop. "Let me look at you." He grabbed Werner's wrist. "I don't see how you could ever dress yourself with fingers like that," commented

Louis before examining Werner's other hand. "Why don't you do whatever you've always done?"

"Sir, I lay down for a nap and this is how I woke. My fingers always worked before. I can't understand it." Werner's voice grew more desperate.

"Have the other men in your tent to help you," Louis definitely had other worries.

"The same thing's happened to all of us, sir," said Werner.

Louis went to the flap and studied the men inside. Werner had not lied. Louis backed up until Werner stood before him again. The young man held up his hands which now looked grotesque and misshapen with overlong fingers and a thumb which appeared utterly unhelpful. Dark hairs sprang from the back of every digit. "The joints hurt like my grandfather described his arthritis. But this doesn't happen overnight, does it?"

Louis shook his head, held up his hands in refusal, and returned to the house.

"What are we to do?" called Werner.

Back on the patio, Louis studied the military compound. He could not step back inside. Since leaving London, the Nazis had orchestrated this descent into madness. He had no idea how or why. Stories had circulated of cruel experiments by German scientists. Perhaps it explained the deformities, though putting them on display for the very reporters whom you hoped to persuade to your side defied all logic.

He searched his pockets for cigarettes before remembering he wore the clothes of another. Perhaps he had a pack upstairs or Walter did. Reluctant to subject himself to dinner with the usual tormentors, Louis surrendered to the inevitable and stepped through the garden doors.

Darwin stood inside the door.

Louis cried out and stepped back.

They both paused and looked about. As no one approached, they both relaxed.

Since the light shone stronger, Louis watched the animals shift on Darwin's face, forming his expressions. With less shadow, he found the peculiar movement of the creatures less frightening, and more random. The slugs traveled at random yet avoided disturbing the great man's visage.

Keeping his voice soft, Louis asked, "Does it hurt?"

"What do you mean?" Darwin's voice sounded rough, though fully human.

"The animals...," Louis sketched the fluctuating animals with a finger.

"Stop blathering," ordered Darwin.

They studied one another, as if meeting unexpectedly at a corner shop. "What are you doing here?" asked Louis, when he meant to ask how such an apparition could exist with Louis fully awake.

Darwin considered for a moment, "The Tories and the clergy, they drove us to it." He noticed the confusion on his companion's face. "Emma and I realized the pursuit of my work would present difficulties. People with influence ostracized or did worse to anyone who asked questions or challenged their orthodoxy. We had little money and thought it was best to find a country home. We turned our little box into quite a charming home."

Louis nodded, "It's lovely, though I daresay it can't have been quite like this in your day."

Darwin shook his head, "Time changes everything."

Louis listened for a moment to ensure they remained alone. "I should have listened to you and left when I could. You knew these men for charlatans and villains."

"They stopped reading at the first chapter of my book," agreed Darwin.

Louis agreed vaguely, "Yes, I see... would be the one on..." He struggled to identify any details from *The Origin of Species*.

The pigeons on Darwin's face cooed their disappointment. "Artificial selection."

"During the Scopes trial, it became big news," said Louis.

Darwin ignored this. "I read the Teutonic plans. I listened to them talk. They dream of a master race. They wish to develop a species through selective predation."

"Exactly," said Louis. "People aren't dogs."

"In the chapter which you struggle to recall, I wrote about my experiments with selective breeding of pigeons. When expanded to geological history, it became apparent..."

"Yes, evolution!" Louis cried out. "I remember!" Louis' cheeks flushed with chagrin as he saw Darwin's terrible eyes focus on him. Every time his expression shifted, beak clicks, reptilian blinks, and slimy slithering goops accompanied the movements. "I read your Beagle book on the boat coming over, from the ship's library."

Darwin chewed his lips, "Appropriate to read about one long excursion at sea while making another." He rose to his full height, which seemed greater than anything the scientist reached in life. "Artificial selection is a remarkably effective means for removing variability, both in combination and in available options, from a species. Natural selection prepares a species for what nature throws at them. I choose to teach these false scientists the cost of their choices."

Louis made the leap quickly, "Are you the one who has been...?"

The patio doors opened. Louis stepped between the entrants and the apparition.

Eichmann led Walter by the elbow. "There you are," said the Nazi. "Walter and I had the most wonderful chat imagining where you might have gone. I'm glad to see Walter had the better guess." After a long pause during which all three of them failed to look comfortable, Eichmann added, "It sounded like you spoke with another?"

Louis gave the area around them an exaggerated scan and saw no one. "Envisioning the broadcast tonight."

Eichmann nodded, "Good, good. It pleases me to hear. Shall we go in to dinner?"

***

Müller did not join them at the table. Heydrich explained he had complained of not feeling well, but he expected a little rest would have him ready for the radio show later.

During a dessert cake with a dark liquid nothing like coffee or tea, they heard a gagging voice coming down the stairs.

Before any of them could stand, Müller stood in the doorway, shirtless. His hands held in the air, palms covered in blood, he moved his mouth, but no words came out, only blood in a small wave.

Walter, Louis, Heydrich, Hofmann, and Eichmann all sat still, blanched.

Müller stepped into the room.

Hofmann pulled his Luger and shot Müller in the chest, staggering him. Hofmann fired again. The noise and the smell shook all five men, but they kept to the chairs and watched Müller spasm on the floor, forcing more blood out of his mouth. Then he stopped.

Heydrich placed a napkin over the dead man's face, leaving Louis with a last impression of blood coating the still cheek like an irresistible threat to all of them. Heydrich rang for the servants and ordered them to carry the body to the garage.

After they left with their burden, Heydrich retook his chair. Slowly, he turned from face to face until he stopped at Eichmann, "Am I a fool to you?"

Eichmann's eyes grew, but he kept himself together, "No, Obergruppenführer!"

Heydrich repeated his question to Hofmann, who echoed Eichmann. Walter shook his head and studied the tablecloth.

When Louis' turn came, he responded, "I want to go home. We should all leave."

"Do you want the truth, Amerikaner?" Heydrich lit a cigarette. "The work we do here is the most important work the Reich has ever undertaken. The people of the world may not be grateful for our military endeavors, but one day in the future, they will look back and say, 'What wonders they started at a little house in Kent! They could have met in a villa outside Berlin or a hotel near Paris, but no, they charted a new course for humanity in the very home of the man who showed the way.'"

Darwin stepped into the doorway behind Heydrich and looked at Louis. A slug moved across his forehead. Ants made a trail along his neck on one side and down the other. In this light, Louis admired the apparition's tailored Victorian suit. Beneath the cloth, ripples roiled as if hidden creatures moved in their own patterns.

Louis shook his head, "No one will ever think so."

Heydrich's left hand shot out suddenly and grabbed Walter's wrist. He pulled Walter's hand close and ground out his cigarette on the back, driving the burning tip into the skin until the flesh darkened, giving off a noxious odor. Walter gasped at first before pulling his face tight. His eyebrows clenched against the pain.

The cigarette fell to the tabletop as Heydrich released his grip. "Do you see? Your friend accepts whatever I do to him? This is what men are reduced to when surrounded by mediocrity."

Darwin raised his arms as if to grab the Nazi.

"Do it!" shouted Louis.

"What is it you would have me do?" asked Heydrich, smiling playfully. "Do you imagine what else I believe? I do not believe like my men that we have been the victims of a trick, or an occult phenomenon. We are being poisoned."

Louis examined the contents of his cup and then confirmed that Darwin remained within view. "It's ridiculous," he said unconvincingly. He closed his eyes and drained the liquid. When he looked again, Darwin had departed.

Heydrich had his Luger in hand, "The hotel where our officers first barracked has a library filled with English books. Most of it is... claptrap. But the English do write a good mystery. So, was it the butler? Or the last foreign arrival at the country manor?"

Heydrich stood, causing everyone around the table to follow suit. Then, he pointed the gun at Walter's chest. "What do you say, Louis? Herr Cronkite or the butler?"

Terror engulfed Walter. He raised his arms in surrender or placation. He quaked twice before lowering his arms and gaining control of his body. He stuck out his chin and blinked at Louis.

"The butler," said Louis. He had never heard anything as loud as the firing of the Luger.

Walter staggered before realizing Heydrich pointed the gun at the ceiling. Still, he checked his body for wounds.

Louis' eyes watered as he strained to hear the words Heydrich mouthed. Everyone else reached for cups or sat down. China jiggled silently for him. They could hear, so why not him? "Walter? Walter?"

Cronkite resumed his place at the table. Pale, but visibly relieved, Walter nodded to Louis.

When his hearing returned, Louis heard himself repeating "Walter."

"You sound like a lovesick young man on one of these British soap operas, Herr Stern," said Eichmann.

"Be kind," said Heydrich. "We might have damaged our radio man. Are you all right, Louis?" He feigned interest, but moved on quickly, "Let me thank you for volunteering your information. I will be certain to inform Andrew who deserves credit for his arrest. Your westerns always feature sheriffs in search of bounties. Louis, what reward do you seek, I wonder?"

Louis pictured the inside of his own skull as though an unseen hand had first poured in broken pieces of china from their dinnerware and then added a few of the animals populating Darwin's face. A pigeon pecked at the inside of his temple while a saucer turned to dust. "Let us go home."

Walter placed a thick hand on Louis' shoulder. "Louis needs rest before our broadcast. Won't you excuse us?"

***

Walter and Louis never made it to the garage for the broadcast even though they left the house with adequate time to cross the grounds.

Louis carried his pack. "We should climb into one of the cars when we're done. We will already be in the motor pool." He heard Walter respond, but Louis stopped walking.

Darwin stood in the opening to a barracks tent. His head bore a significant dent from which an iguana had migrated to his shoulder. When he met Louis' gaze, the iguana scrabbled up the back of the dead scientist's head and settled into the gap. Darwin's arms held the tent flaps apart, revealing an interior of sleeping men in cots.

Growing impatient, Darwin motioned Louis over.

"Where is your mind?" Walter finally interrupted Louis' daze by stepping in front of him.

Louis veered and Walter did not follow. Darwin widened the entrance and Louis entered the barracks.

The men slept. They snored. Most had tossed their blankets aside. A few more legs bent into the air than one might expect. Their ears looked dark, like the eye of a hurricane—no, it was blood, a little crusty.

Louis stepped softly closer to the nearest sleeper. Without waking, the young man reached to the side of his face and scratched. He inserted a finger into the ear hole and itched vigorously. The finger withdrew and the hand relaxed onto the cot.

Louis stared at the hand. Blood and more covered it. Fresh, crimson, and gray... the German had pulled out eardrum or deeper tissues?

Louis turned back to Darwin to ask, "Is that brain?"

Darwin had left.

Louis repeated his question with a stronger voice, as if Darwin stood right outside the entrance. The sleeping Nazis stirred but stayed on their cots.

Louis located a lamp and carried it to the ground beside the sleeper who had excavated his own head. Louis scrabbled until illumination filled a globe within the tent. The young man turned away from the light, pointing his bloody ear at the tent roof.

Louis watched as small blobs of blood, wax, and matter more important mapped a trail along the back of the man's head. Unable to stop himself, Louis watched his own hand reach out and touch the brain effusion.

The soldier's eyes flashed open.

Louis fell backwards onto the ground.

The soldier leapt into a crouch on the opposite side of the cot. He yelled, "Waaah! Oooo!" His voice trailed off to silence as if the sound of it surprised him. He experimented with a few vowel sounds, like a boxer after a bout seeking a way back to coherence. Except he made no progress.

By this time, every other sleeper in the tent had roused. They stood by their cots, not quite upright. They all watched.

"I'm sorry, lads," said Louis. "I meant nothing by it. I heard someone fell sick and thought I should check." Rising to his feet, he studied their faces for understanding. "I don't suppose anyone here speaks English?" He backed toward the flaps while noticing how many of them shared the first soldier's affliction. How much change could a human cell tolerate? "I'll tell them to send in a doctor, all right? You probably ought to stay in here, for everyone's sake."

Backing through the tent entrance, Louis stumbled into Walter.

Walter grabbed and held him steady, "What are you doing? We're not going to survive another screw up. That's the way it is."

"Don't say it like that, Walter," responded Louis. "Those men in there..." He stopped and nodded but soon saw Darwin by another tent. He walked beside Cronkite a few steps. Darwin gestured urgently. "I'm sorry, Walter. Last time, I mean it. I won't let this take more than a minute."

Darwin held the tent open until Louis stopped in the entrance.

The men inside no longer slept. Distressed, they stood in any available space, tearing at their clothes. They had changed into sleepwear, though much of it lay in rags all over the ground. Each soldier moved in his own chaotic dance, groaning in pain, scratching at his skin.

"What in God's grace is happening to them?" Walter had walked up behind Louis.

"We need to leave," said Louis.

"Absolutely. We do the broadcast and hightail it," agreed Walter.

"We shouldn't stay."

"Louis, they can make us disappear." Walter tugged Louis around. "We have no way out of the country. If we've learned anything being over here, there is a certain degree of attention which comes along with our jobs, but we don't need to make ourselves into the primary focus of a military vendetta, certainly not one of these Gestapo Nazis."

Louis watched Walter walk toward the motor pool, before peeking into the tent again.

The naked men itched frantically, bloodying their skin as hair sprouted all over their bodies. A few wrenched the fresh follicles out by the roots. They screamed at the pain, drawing attention. Suddenly the men ripped the hair and skin on one another. The dozen soldiers formed a bloody, yelling, agonizing, naked mass, shifting from side to side of the barracks. They tumbled over cots, rolled in the mud, passed out... perhaps died.

A man shoved Louis aside, and an older officer stepped into the tent. Standing outside the closed flaps, Louis heard howling which ceased with the firing of a gun. The silence lasted a few seconds before a group of men responded with anger. The fight resumed, peppered by Luger shots. Then, it subsided. A few voices moaned as the tent flaps opened.

The officer stood still, not blinking. Slowly, his head turned as he focused on Louis. His gun pointed at Louis and he pulled the trigger. He had exhausted the ammunition on his own men. He talked but stopped before any words came. He staggered away.

Louis looked through the vacated opening. Dead soldiers lay in a twist of hairy bodies, oozing pus, leaking blood, and displaying surprise at their fates.

One survivor caught sight of Louis. His legs lay trapped under three dead men. Mud caked his back. A youth had torn off a swath of his chest, revealing pink skin. He motioned to Louis for aid. He begged for help. He dug his hands into the muck and pulled ferociously, pointlessly.

Louis looked to see how far away Walter had gotten. His friend hesitantly entered the barn.

Back inside the tent, the soldier's face pleaded with Louis. Unwilling to spend another thought on this vision, Louis let the flaps fall closed and tied them shut.

Walking along the aisle to the motor pool, Louis pointed his face at the ground. He wanted no more Darwin sightings. Disturbing sounds emanated from behind canvas: retching, flesh splitting, toothless cries, weeping, hissing prayers, and so many varied unnatural screams.

Hofmann opened the door and stepped out of the barn, blocking Louis' way. As Louis moved to pass, the Nazi leaned over, until Louis could no longer avoid his gaze. Their eyes met and Louis backed away.

Hofmann stepped with Louis. The soldier's knees buckled. He gripped his stomach.

"What's wrong. General?" asked Louis, desperate for any of the afflicted to answer such a question.

Hofmann fell to the ground, arching his back and vomiting voluminously, a stream of earthworms. Down on all fours, the Nazi's head soon hung over a mound of stunned crawlers, covered in slime, stomach acid, and blood.

Louis muttered, "Oh, God," and covered his face. "What has happened?"

Hofmann looked up, displaying pain and confusion on his face. His ashen skin pulled taut as he spasmed again and bowed to throw up. He reached inside his mouth with muddy fingers and extracted squirming bits caught between his teeth.

Louis sensed eyes watching them, focusing his fear and anger. He thought the greatest danger had been the Nazis, but he had forgotten no German or American or anyone could expect to stand against time. Whatever this manifestation of Darwin might be, men must understand knowledge could not be valued like a commodity.

Pulling himself together, he crouched beside the Gruppenführer. "I thought you were the danger, but you're merely madmen thinking you've found a shortcut. And you would drag us all to a dead end."

The muscles in Hofmann's neck flexed as he strained to look at Louis one more time. A worm poked from the corner of his eye as the orb deflated, dripping fluid down the Nazi's cheek and onto the pile of writhing slime. The worm moved up the Nazi's forehead into his hair.

"Charles Darwin loved worms," said Louis. "I bet you didn't know."

Hofmann's arms gave out and his face landed in the heap of living mucus.

Louis watched as the dirt dwellers crawled in the Nazi's ears. He considered shifting the dying man. Louis shook the thought from his mind and rose to his feet. At the door to the motor pool, Louis leaned against the jamb and puked. He studied his dinner for any signs of adulteration and did not see anything untoward. He wiped his mouth on his sleeve and scanned the area for any sign of Darwin.

The camp had quieted slightly. Groans filled the air. The sounds of men shifting in pain came to his ears. He had never heard death on a grand scale, but he suspected this might be it. Did it always happen out of sight? Unwilling to go looking for the unimaginable, Louis chose to enter the garage.

No sound came from the direction of the radio equipment. Once the door shut behind him, all those noises from beyond the walls ceased. The air smelled of motor oil and gasoline and sweat- cars and fear. Ceiling fixtures created puddles of illumination. Louis staggered around a fender and walked into Walter's legs. His friend sat on the floor with his back against the jeep. Bending over, he saw blood on Cronkite's pants. "What did they do, Walter? You look terrible."

"We have to do the broadcast," Walter wrapped his hands around Louis' forearm and squeezed. "They won't let us leave if we fail again."

"You're bleeding. You need medical attention, Walter. I'm not going to do anything until you're looked after."

"I'm cold, Louis."

"You're probably going into shock."

"Unlikely," countered Walter. "The bullet grazed me. It hit Adolf Junior over there pretty much square in the middle."

Louis looked down the row of vehicles and saw Eichmann seated in pretty much the same position as Walter. "Why isn't he wearing any pants?"

Walter grabbed Louis' collar, "I said I'm cold. It's not shock, but it is winter. Can you find me a coat or a blanket?" He released Louis. "You ought to check on their little radio setup before you try anything else though."

Standing, Louis pulled a canvas tarp off the jeep and placed it over Walter. "Who shot you and Eichman?"

"Heydrich. He's around here. Follow the iguanas."

"What did you say?" asked Louis as Eichmann gurgled loudly. Irresistibly drawn in his direction, Louis found the Nazi in a pool of light. "Are you...?" Eichmann looked dead or close enough. His pants and undergarments had been dropped to his ankles. His shirt had been torn open. Ants crawled through the hairs on his chest. They must have been the biting kind because the skin bore ferocious red pimples. The tiny pests followed the trails of hair down the body's arms as well as below the waist into the pubic hair.

A lone ant dared to traverse Eichmann's forehead only to be caught by a bead of sweat from the oily hair. Encapsulated, the ant rode downhill, an out of control slalom skier making the terrifying discovery it rode the ski jump. The sweat plummeted onto the thigh far below, breaking apart and freeing the ant, which dashed for the safety of the hairy crotch.

Louis stared at Eichmann's penis. The opening at the tip had experienced a minor explosion, flaring, and torn. Ants poured in and out. They exited the phallus along the bottom and crawled along the top only to flip over and enter along the ceiling of the penis. They must have a nest within the swollen, enormous testicles which wriggled with miniature movements along the interior of the skin.

As Louis stood transfixed, the left testicle burst, dumping blood, mucus, inflammation, and a fistful of ants onto the floor. Eichmann finally stirred, apparently alive. His eyes moved within his head, shifting in Louis' direction. He mouthed words, but ants instead of sounds emerged from between his lips. Rasps escaped.

As Eichmann teetered on the edge of the final abyss, his left eyeball popped from the socket, releasing a wall of ants who tumbled onto Eichmann's chest only to initiate a war with the original abdominal residents.

Louis stumbled back to Walter, "He's dead."

"Ants in his pants? He screamed that they came out of his prick," said Walter. "I told him to calm down. You saw how Heydrich behaved at dinner. When you didn't walk in on time, Reinhard had already waved his gun around and it didn't take much for him to open fire. The funny thing is I could not guess at whom he fired, me or the Nazi used car salesman over there. Tell me again he's dead. It makes me warmer."

"If he isn't, then he will never stop wishing to be," said Louis.

A movement in the darkness.

"Did you hear?" Louis asked.

Walter's eyelids had drooped in the last few minutes. "I mainly hear the wind or rushing water. It has to do with this wound. Might be good to have it looked at."

Louis kept right on listening.

"I said... Never mind. Most of the damn Nazis ran out when Heydrich fired. More than one of them looked like he had his own sort of trouble, what with a skin thing or other terrible affliction. Louis, I don't want to die here."

An idea struck Louis, "I can find a working car."

"Heydrich is around here," said Walter. "Be careful."

Louis stood slowly. Small ovals of light gave him places to look. On the far side of the room, Darwin stood in the center of an illuminated circle. His head seethed with inhuman movements. Louis motioned to him, but the apparition shifted into the gray penumbra.

Louis headed toward the silhouette. He heard noises and paused to gain his bearings. The sounds came from the makeshift broadcast studio, hidden from view. Louis passed by his last sighting of Darwin and he slowed, carefully staying in the darkness. A hand switched on the radio equipment. They mumbled into the microphone.

Believing the perpetrator had to be armed, Louis hesitated.

A flash of light glowed in Darwin's hand- a match. His face rippled with anxious animals. Louis noticed Darwin's hands, shiny with reptilian skin, uneven with feathers. They had been plain human skin when the dead scientist first appeared to Louis. He lost sight of the dead scientist when the light extinguished.

Louis banged his shin on a fender and cursed.

Reinhard Heydrich turned on a lamp. He sat at the desk in the midst of the radio equipment. The light came at him from the side and Heydrich shifted the beam to blind Louis. "You're late."

"You shot Walter."

"A false equivalency," said Heydrich. Over the last two days, his appearance had deteriorated from the precision of a senior Gestapo officer to a dishevelment of a man in search of his cap. "I meant to reprimand Herr Cronkite, but it became necessary to shoot Adolf. Your man stood in the way." He extracted a final cigarette from a pack on the desk. After lighting it, he continued, "We treated Eichmann like a pet, but he did clever work. He never understood our aim but never stopped wanting to help. You could count on him to finish a job. Now I will have to find new men, perhaps English. Would any Americans be interested?"

Louis slowly moved closer. He shook his head.

"Stop!" shouted Heydrich. "Before you do anything which forces my hand," he placed his Luger on the table, "I have to tell you about Darwin's ghost. You might understand."

"I know all about the apparition," said Louis.

Heydrich tilted his head. The tips of his lips quivered. Straining like a puppet longing for a choice, his eyes wandered for a moment until he discarded Louis' comment. "Tell me, do you believe in things which man was not meant to know?" His fingernails scratched at the desk. "At times I tell myself national socialism isn't a political movement, but rather a religious tract to be passed from hand to hand. Our mistake proved to be giving it away for free. If we had been more like scientists who insist on college educations and laboratories and fancy jargon, then people everywhere would have lined up to share in our bounty."

Throwing his arms about, Heydrich continued, "We resort to begging, no better than Sunday morning priests passing around the hat. Even worse, we coerce proxies to relay our message." His attention changed and he stopped.

Louis followed the Nazi's gaze and saw Darwin off to the side. The old, dead manifestation stood engrossed in the pigeon perched on his arm. The bird had left a trench missing from the side of Darwin's head.

'So-called men of science are no better," declared Heydrich. "The master of Down House would never have published his theories if he hadn't been pushed into it by his friends. He would have kept it to himself, I imagine, because he felt afraid of what he would unleash."

Louis stepped forward, "Fear for his family and fear of what ignorant men would make of his ideas- men like you."

"Men of action!" Heydrich leapt to his feet and immediately staggered. Resuming his seat, he said, "Don't come any closer." He waved his gun.

"You see him, too," Louis pointed at Darwin. "If you won't stop what you're doing, then look at this terror haunting us both. Why is it here?"

Heydrich digested the realization he no longer faced the apparition alone. "Because I am right! From the moment I decided to repatriate Darwin's body to his dearest home, we walked the path of the special. His brilliance illuminated every aspect of life. People like Darwin pointed the way to the next step of human evolution without realizing they themselves embodied it."

Stepping around the desk, dragging a right leg apparently gone numb, Heydrich stepped toward the Darwin manifestation. "Du bist nicht er!"

Darwin turned but remained silent.

"Is this because I brought your body here?" Heydrich dared what Louis never could. He hobbled up to the reanimated man, the reconstituted man, the devolved man...

"What are you?" screamed Louis.

Heydrich and Darwin carefully tore themselves away from their moment and stared at Louis. In the darkness, Walter probably did the same.

"God help me, I thought you existed in my head.," said Louis. "You couldn't possibly be real, the product of illness, a fever; maybe wishful thinking or fear. All these damn Nazis had finally gotten to me. Even after all the... but the terrible things I've seen happen to men in the last few days... even with all this, I thought no one else could see you."

Heydrich laughed drily, "You and I both, Herr Stern, but here we are. Neither of us is special." He coughed and then studied his hand. When he held it out, blood glistened in the spotlight. "You're doing this," he accused Darwin.

Darwin finally spoke, "I am not a god to be invoked."

"Then how did you found a religion?" demanded Heydrich.

"Religions do not accept questioning," said the ghost in a baritone which sounded like the wind through a bellows. "My constitution is a mystery to me and I will not last. I am more Green Man and Albion and a few drops of scientist blood than I could ever be the personification of your desire for an obliteration of life's amazing variety."

Heydrich extracted a knife from his belt while Darwin and Louis watched. Then the Nazi raised it with a flourish and jabbed it into Darwin's chest.

The apparition instantly broke into its component parts, shedding nematodes, reptiles, birds, barnacles, and every other creature which had composed its being. They fell to the floor with squelches and squawks, thuds and thwacks, outcries, and anxious calls. The clothes dropped to the ground, covering Darwin's former denizens.

Louis held still and listened while the aisles of the motor pool came alive with scurrying critters. Even the birds remained ground bound. He feared crushing a part of the scientist's composition with a false step.

Heydrich had no such concerns. Knife in one hand and gun in the other, he moved like a broken toy, tugging his leg along, nearing Louis. He stopped within lunging distance. A trail of slime testified to his disregard for the fleeing animals. "As for this broadcast tonight, Louis, now we proceed."

Before any response, Heydrich's head jerked back as his face went toward the ceiling. His mouth opened to object, but his chin dropped to his chest, slamming his mouth shut with a clatter. In agony, he looked at Louis. A sliver of tongue protruded between his lips.

Heydrich dropped to the ground. A creature crawled under the back of his coat. The top of his spine bulged until the skin burst. A stream of sloppy curses fell from the Nazi's lips like a waterfall running dry.

The head of an iguana emerged from the hole in Heydrich's back. Its tongue scrabbled to wipe blood from its eyes. The reptile swiveled on its haunches and strutted longways across Heydrich's rear. Two pigeons jumped up beside the recently vacated hole and treated it like a bobbing bucket. Soon streaked with blood, their beaks came away with spinal cord and cartilage. With more than a hint of insanity in their eyes, the birds worked like slaughterhouse workers striving for the end of their shift.

The Obergruppenführer's body shook from the waist down, In response, tremors passed through Louis until he cried out, "You have got to be fucking kidding me! How is any of this real?"

Stepping around Heydrich, Louis ripped the pants down one leg of the body to reveal a dozen barnacles attached to the skin along the thigh and calf. As Louis watched, the leg flexed and spasmed like the corpse longed to invent a novel dance.

"Louis, I really need us to leave," Walter spoke from the shadows. Not receiving a response, he added, "They're all dead, Louis."

When Louis' mind returned, he saw his finger stroking a barnacle shell on the calf of Heydrich's corpse. "This is a good ending." He pulled his hand away. Heading to Cronkite, he selected a car.

They climbed inside the sedan closest to the exit. Walter explained to Louis how to wire the starter and then they pulled out of the motor pool.

To their right, the camp had grown quiet. German soldiers lay on the ground in a haphazard pattern. Their bodies had suffered numerous degradations. Faces exploded where bone forced its way through skin. Legs bent between joints. Numerous animals from the barely identifiable to the humanoid tormented the barely living.

Two prehistoric men disputed the division of a dead youth in a black uniform until they noticed the car. They dropped the body parts they carried with a thunk and ambled toward Louis and Walter.

Louis threw the gear shift as a loud bang hit the opposite door. Walter passed out. Louis stared at the terrified face looking into the cab. The frantic man yelled a long litany. Only when he slowed down did Louis recognize Andrew.

"Come around!" directed Louis, repeating multiple times, and adding hand gestures. Louis would not step out of the car while those two beasts waited nearby. "Run!"

Andrew finally nodded. He slipped at the corner of the bonnet but steadied his legs with a strong right arm. He took the final turn wide and passed Louis, who waited for the sound of the back door. He pulled forward.

When Louis turned to look, the two prehistoric creatures had Andrew on the ground.

Surrendering to self-preservation, Louis pushed down on the gas hard. In the rear view mirror, he saw Andrew swinging a determined arm at the nearest attacker. He threw the car into reverse. The tail plowed into one of Andrew's assailants.

Walter cried, "What are you doing?" as Louis stepped from the driver's seat.

Grabbing a likely looking weapon from the back seat, Louis caught Andrew's remaining opponent in the head with a baseball swing. The flat cricket bat smashed into the monster's head like a fresh melon.

Mud and muck covered Louis. He tasted sour and iron and salt from so many spattered fluids. A hand settled on his shoulder and he almost swung the bat again. Andrew gently tugged the bat free. Without another word, they climbed aboard the car and headed for a future frightening and unwritten.

***

For Suzanne, without whom this story and this collection
would not have come to fruition.
She is intensely missed.
*Jesse looked into Mildred's open, smiling face and knew that
in spite of danger, loss, and every other dark fact of life, he
would rather be here, now, than anywhere else in the world
or time.*
Territory
by Emma Bull

Craig Brownlie grew up surrounded by books and art. His contribution here is the natural byproduct of many youthful visits to art and natural history museums. Add in the occasional disturbing book like a pictorial history of World War II. This is the recipe for many lingering unanswered questions. Look for him at conventions and online. Buy his books. Feel free to engage. He's looking for answers, too.

Acknowledgements

Conversations in November of 2024 led to the creation of this anthology. I expressed a willingness to expand Koj Books into a functioning publisher by seeing our random ideas become a full-fledged work. Little did I know the harrowing year ahead of me. I am deeply grateful to all the contributors for their steadfast support. Wile, Judith, Mathew, Roxane, Chris, and Karella, your messages and kindnesses helped my walk through the valley.

Recognizing my ignorance, I reached out to those who had tread the publication road before and every single one had different advice, but they all offered their thoughts unstintingly. This book would be far, far worse without Christoph, John, Cassandra, Royal, Stephen, Kayleigh, Candace, Carrie, and Paul, as well as the many other authors, editors, and publishers have shared kind words and useful thoughts.

Go ahead and buy some books:

Cassandra Celia
https://cassandracelia.carrd.co/

Clash Books
https://www.clashbooks.com/

French Press Publishing
https://frenchpresspub.blogspot.com/

Grindhouse Press
https://grindhousepress.com/

House of Royal
https://www.houseofroyalproductions.com/shop/books

Madness Heart Press
https://madnessheart.press/?v=0b3b97fa6688

Thunderstorm Books
https://thunderstormbooks.com/thunderstorm/

Uncomfortably Dark
https://www.uncomfortablydark.com/

Also from Koj Books

Up until now (which is mid-year 2025), Koj Books has been a one author press with fluctuating support from its publisher/editor/author. The book you currently hold may or may not change that. All of this is prefatory to declaring that all the books below are by Craig Brownlie.

Read all the Little Books of Pain:
#1 Hammer Nail Foot
#2 Thick As A Brick
#3 A Book Of Practical Monsters

For YA, MG, and Young at Heart readers:
Comic Book Summer

www.ingramcontent.com/pod-product-compliance
Lightning Source LLC
Chambersburg PA
CBHW061014120726
47910CB00006B/1938